What Ian Wants

At The End Zone, Book II

by

Doreen Alsen

This is a work of fiction. Names, characters, places, and incidents either are the product of the author's imagination or are used fictitiously, and any resemblance to actual persons living or dead, business establishments, events, or locales, is entirely coincidental.

What Ian Wants

Cover Art by *Angela Anderson*

The Wild Rose Press
PO Box 708
Adams Basin, NY 14410-0706
Visit us at www.thewildrosepress.com

Publishing History
First Champagne Rose Edition, 2010
Print ISBN 1-60154-758-7

Published in the United States of America

He wore his eagerness to please like a cub scout wore his first merit badge. Her heart melted a little more. "Coffee sounds good, but don't worry about it." She reached in her purse. "I can get it."

"No, I'll get it. I insist." He came from around the table and glommed onto her elbow, then pushed her into a seat. "Your feet must be aching. Just rest a second, and I'll be right back."

Stunned, Gina had no choice but to do as he said. Curious about the array of blue books, she picked one up, one he had already graded. It was all in French. The questions, the answers, his red pen comments, all in French.

She couldn't understand a single word. She felt like a total doofus.

"Don't mind those. I'll gather them up and put them away." He placed the large coffee in front of her, then moved into the booth and started to pick up the blue books. "I feel like I'm constantly grading papers. If I don't keep up, they bury me." Stuffing the papers into the open briefcase at his side, Ian dropped the lid. It landed with a soft thud. He looked at her, his eyes hopeful. "I don't know how you take your coffee, so I brought both cream and sugar." Jamming his hands in his pockets, he pulled out enough packets of sugar to put her in a coma, as well as a handful of creamers.

She reached for a creamer. "Just cream, thanks." It made a hissing sound as she pulled the wrapper off the top. "What's up?"

Ian looked away for a moment, pulled the glasses off his face and cleaned them with a paper napkin. "There's no graceful way to ask this." He studied his glasses before slipping them back on his face.

"Why don't you just spit it out?"

"Right, then." He nodded. "I need you to marry me."

Dedication

To the Ithaca Fiction Writers' Group.
You guys are great.
As always, Eberhard, Emilia and Louisa.

Chapter One

Ian Ross stood in the front of the church and watched the love of his life walk down the aisle toward him. No. She didn't walk. She glided. Floated. His Andrea was beyond beautiful. His poet's soul took flight.

She glowed brighter than the fragrant white candles burning in the sanctuary. Her hair shone like the color of moonlight. She wore it up in an utterly feminine, utterly charming, classic style. A spill of lace cascaded down her back from a pearl-encrusted cap that looked like one Shakespeare's Juliet might have worn.

More pearls decorated her neck, in a single, matched strand. A perfect pearl clung to each of her perfect ears. Pearls were made *just* for her, warm and creamy like her skin.

If he really tried, Ian could hear the satin of her dress swoosh as she walked down the aisle. Those gorgeous blue eyes of hers danced, and her shy smile trembled, just a bit, with secrets she kept just for him.

She took his breath away.

Then she destroyed him.

She walked right past him, straight into the arms of the man she was marrying. The secrets in her eyes and her shy smile would never belong to him. They'd belong to the man she pledged her life to. Damn Mike Kelly.

Ian knew he was a masochist coming to watch

Andrea, *his* beloved Andrea, marry Mike Kelly, but he had to do it. If he didn't see her become Mike's wife, his poor, bruised, beaten heart would never heal. He needed healing quite desperately. He needed to get over Andrea and get on with his life.

So he watched. Every adoring smile, every tender touch, every vow, spoken and unspoken, cut through his heart like a knife. He wanted to keen out his grief at the top of his lungs.

But still he made himself watch.

When the priest pronounced them man and wife, when Mike Kelly gathered Andrea into his arms and passionately kissed her, Ian's heart shriveled up and died..

He would never fall in love again, he vowed as he watched the woman he loved marry another man. He wouldn't, *couldn't* afford to risk his heart again.

****

Gina Francisco stopped outside the ballroom doors at Addington Manor, the most elegant hotel in Addington, Massachusetts. The clink of glasses, the happy laughter and Jazz music inside filtered through the closed doors. It sounded like one hell of a good party.

Too bad she wasn't in a party mood. Watching Mikey marry Andi, the ice princess, pretty much ruined the warm, fuzzy feelings she normally felt at weddings. Going to the reception afterwards and making nice wasn't at the top of her list of things she wanted to do.

So why on earth was she here?

Good question.

Obviously, she'd turned into a glutton for punishment.

She sighed. Looking in the gilt-edged mirror next to the door, she checked her hair one last time before joining the party. She had pinned up her auburn curls in an attempt to look more sophisticated. "Curls" hardly did the job describing her hair. Corkscrews. Tons of squiggly red corkscrews covered her head. Frowning at her reflection, she pulled a couple more of those corkscrews out to frame her face. She puckered up her siren-red lips, the color lipstick she used when she needed some confidence. She looked pretty darn good, if she said so herself.

But she didn't feel so good. Her stomach churned, making her wish she'd remembered to pack a roll of antacids in her purse. She ran her hands down the extremely short skirt of her electric blue, velvet dress, squared her shoulders, and pushed open the ballroom door .

Someone had decorated the room to look like fairyland. Tiny white lights winked and twinkled all over, while yards of white and silver tulle draped everywhere. Long white tapers flickered in every available nook and cranny. Offering flutes of fizzy champagne, waiters in crisp, immaculate white jackets moved with practiced efficiency through the crowd. A Jazz trio warmed up in one corner of the room. In the opposite corner stood a small bar, and beside it, a gurgling fountain of chocolate and masses of strawberries waited to be dipped. Guests stood about in small clusters filling the room with the buzz of congenial conversations.

Then she saw Mikey, looking happier than she had ever seen him. He stood with Andi as they greeted guests. His arm wrapped around her waist, holding her close to his side, like he couldn't stand to let her get away from him. A glowing Andi leaned into his possessive embrace. Standing by the happy couple were Mike's mother and Andi's parents. A lump the size of a cannonball formed in Gina's throat. She had to work to swallow around it.

Life was unfair. The proof of it stood right in front of her. She summoned her most cheerful, congratulatory smile and pasted it all over her face. Ready to face the lions, she shook back her hair, lifted her chin, and walked into the arena.

Mike saw her first, and his grin broadened. Even though she recognized it as his *Hey, Buddy!* grin, the smallest hint of a smile from Mike Kelly could make her weak all over.

Man! She hated that.

She smiled back anyway. Quite simply, she couldn't help it. It was just how she rolled.

She walked over to him, and he let go of his bride long enough to give Gina a big hug and a sound kiss on the cheek. Inhaling deeply, because he always smelled really, really fantastic, she hugged him back. "Congratulations, Mikey," she whispered against his chest, and then she pulled back to sneak a peek at Andi, certain she would see a sour lemon look on the bride's face.

Andi's eyes and smile were as welcoming as Mike's were. Didn't that figure? Just when Gina got all set to hate Andi Nelson Kelly, Andi acted nice.

Reluctantly disentangling herself from Mike, Gina held out her hand to Andi. "Congratulations. I hope you'll be really happy. Mike's a great guy."

"Thanks!" Andi ignored Gina's hand and gave her a friendly hug instead. "Let me introduce you to our parents. Sheila? Mom? Dad?" Andi took Gina's arm while she got hers and Mike's parents' attention. "This is Gina Francisco, a good friend of Mike's. Gina, meet Pamela and Deke Nelson, my mom and dad. I'm sure you know Mike's mom, Sheila Kelly."

"Actually, I've never had the pleasure." Sheila smiled as she reached out her hand for Gina's. "Mike is always so close-mouthed about his friends. He never tells me anything about anybody!"

All the greetings Gina had practiced in front of her bathroom mirror flew away and deserted her as she returned Mike's mother's handshake. How many times had she imagined meeting Sheila Kelly? How many times had she imagined being presented to Sheila as Mike's intended bride? Man. She'd practically tried on the dress and ordered the china. What a fool. She managed to babble out what she hoped was a charming response before turning to greet Andi's parents.

Pamela Nelson's smile was gracious. Deke grabbed hold of Gina's hand and pumped with gusto. "Good to see you again, Gina," he blared, then glanced at Pamela. "I met her at The End Zone when I went there with Mike."

Pamela rescued Gina's hand from Deke's, then pressed it between her two palms. "Deke says the food is good at The End Zone."

"Great onion rings," Mike offered.

Gina rolled her eyes. Bobby's onion rings were an obsession with Mike.

"Gina is the one who got Hope Monahan's shrimp recipe for you." Andi had a sheepish look on her face as she imparted this information to her mother, probably due to the fact that Andi should have gotten that recipe for Pamela herself. Gina had done it as a favor to Mike, and in doing so, had beaten Andi to the punch.

It had been a very sweet moment.

Pamela's eyebrows rose. "Really. Thank you." She turned an accusing eye toward her brand new son-in-law. "Here I thought you'd done that on your own." She looked back at Gina, her smile full of a joke just shared. "I've been trying to con that recipe out of Hope for years. What's your secret?"

"She owed me a few favors." Suddenly uncomfortable in her come-get-me stilettos, Gina shifted her weight. She once again cursed herself for being so short. Height was just another thing to hold against Andi Nelson. Kelly. Andi Kelly.

How could she have forgotten?

Don't go there, girlfriend. She focused again on Pamela Nelson. "The room looks lovely. You did a wonderful job."

"Thank you." Pamela looked around the room. "Talk about calling in favors. When Mike and Andi decided on a Valentine's Day wedding, I was sure we'd never get everything done in just six weeks."

"Once I got this woman to say yes, I wasn't going to waste any time and let her get away." Mike smiled at Andi with such a goofy, in-love look in his eyes that Gina felt another chunk of her heart break off. It fell to her feet with a *thunk*. Watching Mike with Andi was killing her, piece by excruciating piece. She had to get out of Dodge.

The faster the better.

A cool hand touched her arm, and she looked up to find Pamela's kind eyes on her. "We're being rather informal with the food," she said. "Please. Go get a plate and try everything." Pamela scrunched her nose conspiratorially. "Let me know if there's anything wrong."

Gina wasn't fooled. Pamela knew the score. She handed Gina a way to make a graceful exit. Unable to decide if she was grateful or mortified, Gina felt her cheeks flame bright red.

Wasn't that just fine and dandy?

She managed to thank Pamela. Toddling off with most of her dignity intact, she made a hasty get-away. Why had she thought coming to Mike's wedding was a good idea? She should leave. She *would* leave as soon as she could. Until then, she'd find a friendly face and keep a low profile.

Dave. She'd find Dave Mason and hang out with him. Dave could always be counted on for a laugh. She scanned the room.

Oops. She'd forgotten. Dave was Mike's best man. No way could she keep a low profile if she hung with Dave. She'd have to act all smiley, all happy.

Yuck.

Some idiot pinged on his glass with a fork. Gina looked over to see Mike give Andi an incredibly hot look, right before he proceeded to give her an incredibly hot kiss.

Double Yuck.

A waiter hustled by with a tray full of champagne flutes. Gina snagged one on the fly, almost making the guy lose his tray. He stopped to give her a dirty look until he realized who she was. "Hey, Gina! How's it going?"

"It goes." It was her friend, 'Softball Nemesis' Eric, from Zack's Bar at the Addington Hotel.

"That it does." He cast an eye out over the crowd. "Gotta go. The natives are thirsty. Catch you later."

"Catch you later," she echoed. She watched him disappear into the crowd. Then, privately toasting the happy couple, she tossed back the champagne in three big gulps.

The bubbles burned as they went down her throat, making her eyes water. Another waiter traded her empty glass for a full one. She wheezed her thanks. What a guy!

Her new best friend.

The second glass went the way of the first, and she started to feel a bit better. She tapped her foot, keeping time with the Jazz trio.

With a sinking feeling, she realized the time had come for the happy couple to dance the first dance. Only Mike didn't dance as much as he swayed.

She remembered that from their one and only date, a gala ball he'd taken her to in order to make Andi jealous. Gina had stood on the sidelines then and watched Mike sway with Andi.

Come to think of it, the same song had played that night—Duke Ellington's *Prélude To A Kiss*.

Mike drew Andi to the middle of the floor and pulled her into his arms. He held her close while they did this tiny little back and forth motion to the music. He pushed the lace of her headpiece out of the way so he could nuzzle her hair.

Gina liberated another glass of champagne from another harried waiter's overloaded tray. She tossed back the contents. No stinging bubbles this time. The champagne went down smooth and easy.

A very British voice caressed her ear. "Haven't we done this before?"

She looked up to find Rupert Giles from *Buffy the Vampire Slayer* whispering juicily in her ear. No wait. Not Giles.

She knew this vision in tweed. He was Andi's ex-boyfriend, what's-his-name. The Anti-Mike. Whatever.

She giggled. His breath tickled the back of her neck, and a chill shivered down her spine. She sucked in a quick breath.

What's-his-name, the Anti-Mike, smelled good. She inhaled again.

He smelled hot-diggity-*damn* good, a mixture of sandalwood, citrus and musk.

Shoot, maybe the Anti-Mike would be a handy antidote for the black funk threatening to engulf her. As he came around to look at her, she glanced up at him. "What?" She flashed him her brightest smile.

"I said, I do think we've been in this situation before."

Gina stumbled. He caught her elbow and held her steady.

"Not me holding you, I mean, nice as it is. I mean..." He gestured with his head to the dance floor where Andi and Mike were wrapped around each other. "Us on the sidelines, them in the clench of the century."

She looked at him, focused and really looked at

him, and her heart broke all over again. Here stood a soul mate, a kindred spirit.

She remembered standing next to him, watching Mike and Andi practically making love on the dance floor. It had been horrible for them both.

Horrible as it had been, though, it hadn't stopped her from noticing what an absolute hottie the Anti-Mike was.

After all, she wasn't dead, was she?

She took a big sniff of the Anti-Mike standing oh so close to her. Yum. It was absolutely true.

She was not a dead woman.

She struggled to remember his name. Evan? No. Stephen? She fixed an over-bright smile at him in a pitiful attempt to disguise the fact she couldn't remember his name. He blinked at her, but then looked beyond her to watch Mike and Andi. Whatever his name, watching the happy couple was killing him if the pained look on his face meant anything.

His name wasn't Stephen, either. Wait. Wait just a minute. It was coming to her. Eureka! Silently congratulating herself on how slick she'd become, she upped the voltage on her smile. "You know what you need, Ethan?"

He turned his attention back to her and squinted. "What do I need, Gina?"

She blinked. He'd had no trouble remembering her name. What a cutie-pie. "Ethan, my friend, I think you need to come with me to the bar and let me buy you a drink."

He braved another tortured look at the dance floor. "Maybe you're right." He looked back at her. "On two conditions."

"Name 'em."

He took her elbow and steered her in the direction of the bar. "Number one, you let me return the favor and buy you a drink."

"I am *so* down with that. What's number two?" She wobbled a little on her three-inch spikes.

"That you stop calling me Ethan." His self-deprecating smile was touched with mischief. "My name's Ian."

Chapter Two

Ian swallowed a chuckle as Gina babbled an apology. "Don't worry about it." He kept a good grip on her elbow to keep her from stepping on his toes. Those shoes of hers were killers, in more ways than one. "You can buy me two drinks to make up for it." Behind them, the music stopped. People started clapping. Ian could only hope the bride and groom had stopped 'dancing' and had decided to go get a room.

He forced his attention back to the woman toddling along next to him. She was short. Even in those outrageously sexy heels she wore, she only came up to his shoulder. Her dress was inspired, he thought, just the thing to wear to her ex-boyfriend's wedding—bright, short and curve-hugging.

It especially showcased her exemplary chest. Even though he felt madly in love with Andrea, he could still appreciate Gina's extremely noteworthy pair of breasts. They proved to be very distracting.

Which, he decided as he heard glasses pinging again, was a very good thing. He glanced down at Gina and immediately wished he hadn't.

Her head turned, she watched Mike and Andi give each other tonsillectomies. Her face held a look of such longing, such pain, it hurt Ian to look at her. If she lost it and broke into tears, he'd be sunk. He gave her a gentle nudge with his elbow. "Hey."

She looked at him.

With what he hoped was a consoling smile, he

11

said, "Breathe."

A ghost of a smile trembled on her lips. She shook her head as if to clear it and took a breath, but wouldn't meet his eyes.

Ian caught her elbow. "C'mon. I owe you a drink."

The silence between them throbbed. It provided a buffer against the sounds of the Jazz music, the unintelligible conversations, and the underscore of laughter. They made it to the bar where Ian helped Gina on to a stool. She smiled, but again wouldn't meet his eyes. He sat next to her and signaled the bartender.

The bartender was a perky woman with long blond hair, expertly pulled back into a ponytail that curled artfully at the end. Her nametag proclaimed her name to be Amber. Amber had a big, bright smile that showed more teeth than Ian knew human beings to have. It broadened when she saw them. "Hey, Gina!"

As if someone had just thrown a switch, Gina immediately transformed. Her smile grew just as bright and nearly as toothy as Amber's. "Hey! I didn't think you'd be working tonight."

"Couldn't pass on the money." Amber tilted her head toward the dance floor. "Or the chance to see the woman who finally brought Mike Kelly to his knees."

There was something amiss with Amber's tone. Ian stared at her. Could that be a malicious gleam he saw in her eyes? He narrowed his gaze to study her. Yes, indeed. He did think the toothy Miss Amber was trying to give Gina a hard time. There wasn't much he could do about Andrea and Mike Kelly, but he could help Gina out with Amber. He slipped his arm around Gina's waist and pulled her as close to his body as the bar stools would allow. "I don't know how anybody could see anyone else but this gorgeous woman sitting next to me."

Gina stiffened against him while Amber hiked her eyebrows up. Looking between Gina and him, she said, "Nice accent." She refocused on Gina, baring those teeth one more time. "I don't think I know your friend, Gina. Care to introduce me?"

Gina's gaze slunk up to Ian's, then, without missing a beat, she smiled back at Amber. "Amber, this is Ian, a new friend of mine. Ian," she looked back at him, "this is Amber Brock, one of the best bartenders in Addington." She leaned toward him and whispered in his ear, "You don't have to do this, you know. She's not that big a deal."

"What was that?" Amber asked with curiosity.

Gina tossed her head back. "I asked Ian what he wanted to drink. Why don't you tell Amber?" She batted her lashes, then like an afterthought, added, "Darling."

Ooooo-kay. "I think champagne is just the thing for a celebration of this magnitude."

"Gotcha." Amber winked at him and turned to Gina. "And for you?"

Gina shook her head and raised her chin. "Absolutely. Ian's right. This is a party." Her barracuda smile reappeared.

"Sure thing." Amber drifted off to get their drinks.

Gina's lips thinned, and the epithet she muttered at Amber's retreating back didn't bear repeating.

Ian chuckled. He figured he could afford to. Gina could possibly be the one person in the world who felt worse than he did at the moment. "Friend of yours?"

"Oh, yeah." She held up her hand and crossed her fingers. Sarcasm oozed from her voice. "We're tight."

They sat in silence until Amber brought their

drinks. "Do you want to run a tab?" She popped open their champagne.

"Sounds like a good idea," Ian decided. "Why don't you leave the bottle?"

Amber grinned. "You got it." Reaching underneath the bar, she produced a small bowl of Goldfish party mix. "Enjoy!" She went away to talk to other customers.

Again, the glasses pinged, and Ian downed his champagne in a single swallow. "Damned barbaric custom you Yanks have." He poured himself another glass of champagne. "That banging on glasses to make the bride and groom swallow each other whole." He shook his head sorrowfully.

Gina slammed her empty glass down on the bar. "You said it."

"Are you still in love with Mike Kelly?" Ian asked as he poured her another hit of champagne.

She sighed. "Much as I hate to admit it, I am. Is it that obvious?"

"Only to a fellow sufferer."

"What? You're in love with Mike Kelly too?"

"Hardly." He savored the burn of the bubbles in his mouth.

"That leaves the ice princess." She shook her head and took a healthy sip. "What is it about her?"

"Who?"

"Andi, you idiot."

He might not be the world's foremost expert on women, but he suspected he needed to be careful with what he said next. He downed the rest of his champagne in a gulp, felt the alcohol take hold, and he suddenly didn't care about cautious answers. "Andrea is..." he waved his empty glass in the air, catching Amber's attention.

She came over. "Want a new bottle?"

Ian gazed at the oh-so-helpful Miss Amber. "Indeed." He looked at her and said with great earnestness, "There seems to be too much air in this bottle."

Gina giggled.

Amber looked at her. "You okay?"

"I'm fabulous."

Amber gave them each a knowing smile. "You two are going to hate yourselves in the morning."

Gina shook her head and braced her hands against the bar to steady herself. "She's wrong," she said. "I hate myself now, never mind in the morning."

Astonishment conked Ian over the head. "Why? Because that Neanderthal cretin Mike Kelly married Andrea?"

Gina bristled. "He's not a," she imitated a bad British accent as she repeated "*Neanderthal cretin.* Mike's the best." She looked down at her hands that were still braced against the bar. "I've never loved anybody the way I love Mikey."

Amber brought the new bottle of champagne. She looked at them, chuckled, then left again.

Ian didn't miss a beat. "He's not fit to tie her shoes." Ian had never been more serious in all his life.

"Whose shoes? Amber's?"

He blew out an exasperated breath. "Andrea's. My beautiful, wonderful, lovely Andrea."

Gina snorted and poured herself another glass of champagne. "Yeah, right. Whatever." She hiccupped then took a very ladylike sip. "She's not good enough for him, y'know."

He filled his glass. "I beg to differ, he's nowhere near good enough for her." He cursed, then chugged his drink.

Gina sighed and up-ended the first bottle into her glass. Some champagne spilled onto her fingers, and she put them into her mouth, sucking it off. The sight of the gesture enthralled him. He didn't think that he would ever be able to put two coherent words together again. Gina was a very sexy woman. His mouth went suddenly dry, so he licked his lips.

She looked at him and blinked. "What? What's wrong?"

He opened his mouth to tell her... what? What could he possibly say to this gorgeous woman who loved Mike Kelly?

The glass-pinging idiot started up again. There had to be a ring reserved in hell just for him. Ian would check Dante's *Inferno* first thing tomorrow morning. Ian saw Gina flinch, then look past him to the reception.

The sound of Hoagy Carmichael's *Stardust* filtered into the bar from the ballroom. Ian looked back at Gina. She was clearly miserable. That was so sad, because the music sounded beautiful. She was absolutely entrancing. Tears welled in her eyes, but she blinked them back. He reached out a clumsy finger, gave in to temptation and touched one of those fetching curls surrounding her face.

She jolted, as if his touch was electric. "I don't think..."

"Dance with me."

"Ian, you're a nice guy and all, but..."

"One little dance. What could it hurt?"

She chewed her lower lip. The red lipstick she wore had smeared on her teeth. Rather than being put off by that, it made him smile. He cupped her cheek in his hand. "Be a sport. Dance with me."

He slid off his bar stool and stood in front of her, holding his hand out in expectation.

She looked behind her toward the dance floor, then back at him. "I don't think so."

"We don't have to dance in there. We can dance right here."

Like a puppet dragged along on shaky strings, Gina slid off the barstool. She stumbled when her heels hit the floor. He put his arms out to steady her.

"Oops," she breathed. "Didn't expect to hit the floor so fast."

Ian didn't feel too secure on his pins either, but he held onto her. They swayed a couple of times until he got his balance, then looked at each other and laughed. Not breaking contact, he attempted a few dance moves, but her feet wouldn't cooperate.

She pulled away. "Sorry. It's the shoes. They're not made for dancing."

He thought about it. "How about this? Take them off and stand on my feet."

"What?"

"Take them off."

She waited a beat, cocked her head and considered. Then she kicked the shoes off her feet. They landed with a resounding *thunk* near a potted plant. She looked up at him for approval.

"Good shot." He held his arms open and with both hands made a *c'mere* motion.

She gifted him with a flirty little smile and took a deep breath that made her incredible breasts strain the skimpy neckline of her bright blue dress.

He went a little weak at the knees and got a tad woozy in the head. He hoped it wasn't too much champagne and not enough food. Closing his eyes, he inhaled long and deep. When he opened them, Gina still stood in front of him, uncertain, but so very, very desirable.

It had been so long since he'd held a desirable woman. Too damn long. All he had to do was glance into the ballroom to realize that. Again, pain shafted through him as he watched Andrea cuddle up to Mike.

Taking Gina's hand, he pulled her to him. Her palm was cold and small in his. "Dance with me." He helped her onto his feet and looped her arms around his neck. The move didn't gain her too much height, but did press all her interesting body parts against him. He wrapped himself around her with exquisite gentleness and rested his cheek against the top of her head. Her wild curls tickled his nose, making him smile.

For a moment, she held herself rigid in his arms, but then she shuddered. "Don't cry. Please, don't cry." His hands made small circles against the small of her back.

She let out a tiny, snarfling noise. "I wish I hadn't come here. I just didn't expect it to hurt so much."

"Yeah. I know. Don't think about it."

"It's so hard."

"Shhhhh, now. Just let me hold you."

****

As Ian began to shuffle and sway with the music, Gina lurched, almost falling off his feet. She curled her toes against the top of his shoes in an effort to keep her balance.

"Easy." She felt him breathe against the top of her head. "Just relax. It'll be all right."

She swallowed a sob. "It'll never be all right again."

He started to say something, but a cheer from the ballroom drowned it out. His chin left the top of her head and she guessed he was trying to see what was going on.

"Bloody hell." His sharply exhaled oath crackled in her hair.

She twisted from her waist to see what he saw and nearly fell off his shoes.

He tightened his hold on her, keeping her firmly in place.

"I want to see."

"No, you don't. Listen." He looked at her, his eyes earnest and full of an emotion she knew all about. He hurt just as much as she did. "Let's grab a bottle of champagne and get out of here. This charade is doing neither of us any good."

Maybe leaving was an idea whose time had come.

"Where do you want to go?"

He thought for a second. "Here. We'll rent a room here."

"I don't know, Ian. I'm not sure..."

"*I* am sure. Come with me. Please." His eyes pleaded with her. "I don't want to be alone right now."

Well, for sure, neither did she. She glanced around and caught sight of Amber watching them. That made up her mind in a hurry. "Why not?" She raised her voice so Amber would be sure to hear. "This party is getting pretty dull anyway."

His smile was beautiful. "Right, then." He lifted her up and off his feet, setting her down as if she were made of spun glass. "Amber, can we get a couple bottles of bubbly to take with us?"

Amber stopped mid-pour, her eyes narrowed. "I can't give it to you if you're going to take it out of the hotel."

"Not a problem, my dear. We're just going to take it to another part of the hotel." He looked at Gina. "Get the bottles from our friend Amber, and meet me in the lobby." He winked at her, then at Amber. "The front desk will tell you where to charge them." With that, he was gone.

Gina moved to where Amber put the bottles on the bar.

"Here you go." Amber grinned.

"Thanks." Gina rooted around in her purse for a tip, found a ten, and after two tries, managed to slip it into the jar on the bar.

"Thank *you*." Amber's smile had become a smirk. She nodded to the potted plant. "Don't forget your shoes."

Gina blushed bright red, grabbed the bottles and wrestled with them while she tried to slip her shoes back on.

She made it to the lobby without mishap.

Chapter Three

Ian waited for her at the front desk, just like he said he would. He relieved her of the champagne bottles and motioned with his head toward the elevator. "We're in room 428."

They didn't talk on the way up in the elevator. Nor did they talk when they got to the beautifully-decorated room with its two, big, comfy-looking beds. She plopped her butt down with a couple of bounces on the bed closest to the door while Ian unwrapped the plastic glasses on the bureau. He popped the cork, and champagne blasted out of the bottle with a juicy fizz. He managed to get some of it into the flimsy little glasses and brought them to the bed. He sat down beside her with nary a bounce, handing her a glass. "To us."

She accepted the cup, then toasting him, knocked it against his, disappointed when the plastic clicked rather than clinked. She wanted the brittle sound of glass against glass.

Well. Life sucked. Didn't she already know that?

They sat in silence, two companions drowning their sorrows. Somewhere around the end of the first bottle, Ian shook his head. "I still can't believe she married him."

"Yeah." Gina felt she had to say something but didn't know what to say. If she started talking about Mike, she would cry, like she almost had in the bar, and that wouldn't cut it.

A girl had to have some pride.

21

Instead, she kicked off her shoes again, launching them across the room. They hit the opposite wall with a satisfying *thump*. Seemingly understanding she didn't want to talk, he got up to open the second bottle of champagne.

****

Though they hadn't said very much, midway through their second bottle, Ian noticed Gina had started to cry. Not big, heaving sobs, just poor little sniffles that snuck behind his defenses and struck his heart. He put his arm around her and pulled her close. She wove her arms around his neck, accepting his embrace. Head swimming, he clung to her like a drowning man to a life vest. If he kissed her, it was only to soothe their poor, battered souls.

Once their lips met, there was no going back. Electricity jolted through him as her mouth moved against his. She pulled away and turned bleary eyes to his.

He mentally begged her not to have second thoughts, not to think better of this, not to stop. He needed to be with her more than he needed to breathe.

He struggled with her clothes, desperate for the taste and the warmth of her skin. He freed her breasts, and she cried out when he kissed them. Her heart pounded against his lips. She threaded her fingers through his hair.

Ian's world tilted. He had to cling to Gina as an anchor. He kept his eyes closed so she could not see his despair.

He flexed his fingers into her arms, then slipped his hands on either side of her head. He tried to capture her lips while he levered himself over her. He conked her nose on the way.

"Ow," she mewed.

"Sorry," he murmured. He didn't want to hurt her, but his hands felt five times their normal size.

Finally finding her mouth, he planted a kiss on it. Hers seemed to have lost all firmness and had gained juiciness.

A lot of juiciness, which an unkind person might call *drool*.

He was, he hoped, a kind person.

Her breath huffed raggedly, and she tasted of champagne as she tangled her tongue around his. She moaned.

He shifted so he could kiss her breasts. It took him a couple of tries to find her nipple.

She hiccupped as he attempted to join their bodies. Triumph washed over him when he made it on the first attempt. Though it had been a long time for him, his body was hungry and by-passed his brain. They moved together until pleasure exploded from his body.

He hoped like crazy she had come as well, because he couldn't go on, but he would, if it turned out she needed more. He guessed she didn't, because she went limp underneath him.

Curled together as partners in heartbreak, the alcohol overcame them. Ian passed out cold.

****

"You look terrible," Gina said to the reflection in her bathroom mirror. She leaned in close, opened her mouth wide and stuck out her tongue. It wasn't a pretty sight. Shaking her head, she closed her mouth with a snap. "Let's face it, cookie. Last night isn't going into the annals as the best night of your life."

Huh. That surely had to be an understatement. She never should have gone to the wedding, never mind the reception. It had seemed like an okay idea at the time. She shook her head. "When are you going to learn?" Her reflection didn't have an answer for that one, so Gina settled for brushing her teeth for the fifth time since getting home.

She'd had sex with Andi's ex-boyfriend. "That was a bad thing to do," she admonished the woman in the mirror around a mouthful of toothpaste. Gina still didn't know how it had happened. One minute she'd been slurping up champagne, the next she was doing the wild thing with the Anti-Mike.

"Ian," she said to the mirror. "His name is Ian."

He seemed like a nice guy and all, but... He wasn't Mike. "Still, he didn't deserve the way I left him."

Her reflection didn't have a comeback for that one, but then again, Gina was used to these one-sided conversations. "What else should I have done?"

That's right, Gina thought. And she had lain there for several long moments, listening to him breathe, when the contents of her stomach had decided they needed a change of venue. She had barely made it to the bathroom before she had violently thrown up.

Leaving had been easy after that. She had pulled her clothes on, called a cab and mamboed on home just as fast as the cab driver could drive.

Do not pass go, do not collect two hundred dollars.

"The thing is," she rationalized to her reflection, "I like the poor guy. I not only feel crappy about losing Mike, I feel crappy about running out on Ian."

After all, she had known the score when it came to Mike. He had never misled her. They were buddies, that's all they had ever been. He would never know how much she loved him.

"Am I pitiful or what?" The woman in the mirror remained mute, a grim reminder that Gina had quite possibly lost her mind.

Guilt made her stomach roll. For a brief moment, Gina thought that she had to upchuck again. She pressed a hand to her midriff. "I hate this."

Okay, Ian was a nice guy. He also had a lot more to gripe about than Gina did. While Gina had totally hidden her feelings for Mike, Ian had worn his like a banner. The whole world knew he loved Andi Nelson.

A stabbing pain in her jaw made Gina realize that she was gritting her teeth. She *so* didn't need this.

With a little bit of luck, she would never see Ian again. For some reason, that thought didn't bring her any comfort. Instead, her stomach lurched. She bolted across the tiny room to throw up.

Long, horrendous moments later, she leaned her clammy forehead into her equally clammy hand. The corkscrews of her hair lay matted against the back of her neck, hot, heavy and clumped. She lifted them to cool off. The effort cost almost too much.

Defeated and alone, Gina closed the toilet seat, slumped over it and wept.

****

Ian's head throbbed as he signed his credit card slip. It continued to throb as he negotiated his car home. It throbbed the entire five minutes it took to fit his house key into the lock on his front door.

Bloody hell.

His beard stubble itched like crazy, so he shaved. Because he didn't believe in wallowing in self-pity, he made a mental list of all the things he had to do.

Calling Gina would have been at the top of the list, but he didn't know her last name and couldn't look up her number in the phone book. Ouch.

Besides, if she wanted to talk to him, she wouldn't have run off like she had. She very clearly regretted what had passed between them. Well, so did he. Perhaps leaving it alone would be best for now.

But he couldn't leave it alone. Gina dominated

his thoughts while he dressed, made coffee, booted up his computer and stared at the blank screen.

It wasn't very well done of him, having sex with Gina while pining after Andrea. He still couldn't figure out *how* they had gotten around to having sex. After all, it wasn't like he planned it. It had just happened.

Bloody hell. Bloody, everlasting hell.

He bolted up from his office chair and began to pace. The sudden motion made his head pound again. He brought both hands up to massage his temples. Making his way back to the kitchen, he poured himself another cup of coffee. It burnt his tongue as he took a slug. He didn't care. He welcomed the pain. It was a wake up call.

The true irony of the thing was Ian had only ever made love to Andrea in his dreams. They had dated, enjoyed each other's company, but had never crossed the line into intimacy.

Which totally sucked, as his college freshmen would say.

He doubted, with every fiber of his being, Gina had not slept with Mike Kelly. Of course, the two had been together. Mike would have to be the biggest fool in the entire universe not to have slept with Gina.

She was a very beautiful, sexy woman, who happened to be in love with Mike. Yeah, Mike had slept with Gina.

If Ian owned a family farm, he'd bet it.

He meandered back to his office, not really ready to sit down to prepare tomorrow's lessons on Pierre de Ronsard and the *Pleïade*. But his lectures weren't going to write themselves.

The leather creaked as he settled into his desk chair. He took his glasses off and polished them with his shirttail. Getting down to business, he focused his concentration on the computer screen.

The phone rang, and for one brief, giddy moment, he thought it might be Gina. Trying not to appear too pitiful, he let the answering machine pick it up.

Buzz, click, beep. "Ian, this is Vivian. If you're there, please pick up. You know how I detest talking to these machines."

Ian shook his head. Great. What he really needed right now was a call from his mother.

"Anyway, you need to ring me back at once. You'll never believe this, but your father has gotten married once again." Vivian's enormous sigh caused an explosion of static on Ian's machine. "He's really gone and done it this time. He's married a *stripper* of all things, with an IQ considerably smaller than her bosom, if you know what I mean."

Ian groaned. Dear old mum was on a roll.

"You need to call him and talk some sense into him. I mean the girl is thirty years younger than he is. She is *five years* younger than you are. I don't believe it. I mean, what can he possibly be thinking? It boggles the mind. One would not believe him to be the respected surgeon that he is. Well. He certainly won't continue to be respected if he continues to go along like this. The bride is an infant. A veritable child. Honestly, I can't begin to imagine..."

Mercifully, the machine stopped recording with a loud beep, thanked her for her message and shut down. The red light indicating he had a message started to flash on and off. He held his breath and waited for her to call back and continue her diatribe, but she didn't.

His parents' divorce had been horrific, especially for a lonely, bookish boy. Frequently demanding and unreasonable, they both stretched his patience to its limits. They didn't need a son as much as they needed a referee. He just wasn't going to play that game with them anymore. They were grown-ups, no matter how childish they sometimes acted. He was well served to stay as far out of it as he could.

His chair creaked again as he pushed out of it. The wood floor was cold against his bare feet, but that barely registered as he walked over to stare out his study window. A winter afternoon, it was grey as well as cloudy. It spit snow out of the sky in fits and starts. He sighed as he leaned against the window frame. The only other sound in the room was the whirr of his computer. Afternoon bled into night while he stared out that window, trying to make sense of his life.

No matter which way he tossed it, his personal life sucked. He was a good scholar and an even better teacher. The scads of articles and the three books he had published, as well as the student evaluations of his teaching, were proof of that. His book of poetry had gotten good reviews.

There. He would concentrate on his career. Books had been his salvation as a child, and they would serve him well now that he was an adult.

****

Gina hid in her apartment for as long as she could, right until her shift at The End Zone on Monday night. She pulled her car into the employee's lot, parked crooked in the only space left and turned the car off. She sat there, gathering up her courage to go and face the music.

Maybe Dave wouldn't be here. After all, it was a school night. He probably had lots of Vice-Principal things to do.

He was most likely sitting at the bar, waiting for her to come in so he could pounce on her to lecture her about the advisability of a relationship with the Anti-Mike.

Huh. Relationship. That was a laugh.

If Dave wasn't waiting to pounce on her, her best friend Sandy would be. She had to be the most well-informed person on the planet. Give her five minutes—she'd be able to find out where each and every Al Qaeda member hid and what they had eaten for dinner. Gina had no doubt Sandy had known all about her thing with Ian in about, oh, five minutes after it happened.

She went through the kitchen. "Hey, Bobby."

Bobby was her boss, and was currently up to his elbows in coleslaw. He smiled, revealing a line of white teeth broken by one shiny gold cap. He wore a hot pink and orange Hawaiian shirt covered by an apron liberally spattered with today's special. "Gina. Heard you had quite a time at Mikey's wedding."

She groaned. "What did you hear?" She dumped her bag in her locker, grabbed an apron, then punched in.

"Just that you were seen sucking down the joy juice with some English dude and that the two of you left together." His grin grew, almost engulfing his face. "Come on, Gina. Spill. Enquiring minds want to know." Bobby did love his tabloids.

"There's nothing to know." She moved over to the steam table, lifted a lid and stood on tiptoe to sniff. "What's this? Gumbo?"

"Shrimp and sausage. The other soup's minestrone. Come on, Gina. Confess." He gleefully mixed coleslaw with latex covered hands.

"I've got nothing to confess, Bobby." Brazen is as brazen does, she decided. She wasn't going to admit a thing to Bobby, if she could help it. Tying her apron around her waist, she ignored him and went into the dining room.

The End Zone was a neighborhood sports bar, a fun and comfortable place. It attracted lots of regulars, which really helped her pay the bills. More than a few of them were there tonight.

More to the point, Dave sat at table 24, nursing a beer and waiting, most likely, for a burger and fries and the chance to grill her mercilessly.

She checked the station assignments and breathed a sigh of relief when she found out that Dave wasn't in her station. That would make him easier to avoid.

Thank God for small favors. They were the only ones he seemed to be granting her these days. She put the station chart back in its place and grabbed an order pad. Looking around, she noted with considerable relief that Sandy was busy with a big party of fourteen volleyball players who all looked really thirsty.

"Hey, Gina. What's up?"

Gina looked back to see Spike wiping down the bar. Six feet tall, with bright pink hair and a series of tattoos down her right arm, Spike could be the best bartender Gina had ever worked with. She had an unlikely Betty Boop-type voice and a right hook Gina hoped she never met face to face.

Or would that be face to fist? Gina shrugged. The best thing about Spike was she pretty much lived and let live. She had no interest in trading gossip. Gina was pretty sure Spike hadn't paid attention to any stories floating around about Mike's wedding and Gina's subsequent misdeeds. "Spike! Not much. Been busy?"

"Nah. Just the volleyball team over there. Other than that, it's pretty quiet." She motioned with her head over to where Dave sat. "Dave wants to talk to you."

"Fabulous." Gina stole a pen from the top of Spike's cash register and stuck it in her ponytail. "Better go and take some orders."

She conferred with Becky, the waitress whose section she was taking over. It didn't appear anywhere near full, but she had enough tables to keep her busy. She felt Dave watching her, but she ignored him.

It was harder to ignore Sandy. "You're holding out on me, girlfriend," Sandy said as she cornered Gina when she poured a draft Bud Light. "I hear you had quite the time at Mike's wedding."

Gina went for nonchalant. "I don't know what you're talking about."

Sandy laughed. "Give it up, Gina. While I don't like Amber, she is a very reliable source of information. She's been a fount of wisdom these past days."

"She doesn't know half as much as she thinks she does."

Sandy was unconcerned as she garnished the drinks Spike put in front of her. "And then there's our good friend Dave. He's more than a little bit anxious to have a word or two with you." She loaded the drinks on her tray.

"I bet." Gina sighed. "He probably thinks I'm an idiot."

Thoughts of one brilliant, gorgeous, college professor who was certainly *not* an idiot threatened to surface. She refused to let them.

Sandy gave Gina a very amused look. "Sweetie, we're all your friends here. You can give us the 411."

Gina studied the foam overflowing the glass. It was cold and sticky against her fingers. She let go of the glass and rinsed off her hand in the sink. "Nothing to tell. No matter what Dave thinks, he's not my mother."

Sandy looked at Gina across the top of her tray and laughed. "That's true. The man's too gorgeous by half."

Gina smiled. This was most certainly the truth. "He's got that Rob Lowe thing going on."

"Oh, yeah." Sandy trotted off to take some drinks to table 12.

"Got a minute?"

Gina looked across the bar only to see Dave

standing there, his gray eyes full of mirth. Great! The first time she'd had sex in ages, and it's a big joke to everyone.

She really didn't want to talk to him. "Only just. The duo at 23 wants their Bud Lights."

"I just want to know if you're okay."

"Of course I'm okay. Why wouldn't I be?"

"Then Amber was making things up when she passed the story around about you and Andi's ex being very up close and personal."

Gina tossed her head back, aiming her chin at him. "Ian is a very nice guy."

"I've got no doubt about that." He shrugged. "It's not like you, that's all."

"It just kind of happened." She wagged her finger in his face. "And that's the end of it."

He opened his mouth to say something, but his cell phone chirped. He flicked it open with a frown. "Sorry, Gina. I've got to take this."

"Believe me, that's not a problem right now," she tossed to his retreating back. Literally saved by the cell.

As she schlepped the Bud Lights to table 23, thoughts of Ian dogged her footsteps.

She sighed. It was going to be a long night.

****

"Ian! Can I have a word with you?"

Ian turned at the sound of his name. His Department Chairman and mentor, Ralph Jameson, lumbered down the French Department hallway. Though a tall man, he was at least fifty pounds overweight, so he huffed and puffed as he walked down the hall. His usually florid complexion was an even brighter red, in large part due to his exertion. Concern stabbed at Ian's gut. "Slow down, Ralph. I'm not going anywhere."

"Yes, well. This is important." Ralph drew a worn, white handkerchief out of his jacket pocket and mopped his damp forehead with it. He followed that up by taking his glasses off and using the handkerchief to clean them. The streaks were less apparent when he put them back on. "It's not public yet, but I'm retiring at the end of the semester. Margaret and I want to buy an RV and go off to see the world."

"That's fantastic! Congratulations, Ralph. I know you've wanted to do this for a long time."

"Yes, I have. Let me get to the point, Ian. There's going to be a committee to screen applicants for the chairmanship of the department. I want you to..."

"I'd be honored to serve on the committee, Ralph. Thank you for thinking of me."

Ralph let out an exasperated snort. "I don't want you on the committee, Ian. I want you to apply for the chair."

Ian blinked. That was something he hadn't considered. In spite of the fact that he was young, he deserved it, certainly. His scholarship and teaching were top notch. His ambition flattered, he realized he wanted the honor.

Badly.

"I don't know what to say. This is certainly a surprise."

Jameson harrumphed. "I don't know why you should be surprised." He looked down at his feet, then up at Ian. "This is between you and me. Donald Unger is also in the running for the chair. Things could get..." He paused while he searched for the word. "Well, difficult, to say the least."

Ian wouldn't play it coy. Donald Unger was the dead last person he wanted running the department. "I'll get my paperwork in order and submit it."

Jameson nodded curtly. "Good." He turned and started back to his office, but then stopped and looked over his shoulder, which reminded Ian of the old Columbo TV mysteries. He half expected Ralph to say, *Oh, by the way...*

"Margaret and I are throwing a reception for our retirees. She's concerned you won't have a date for the evening."

Ian felt his stomach drop. Oh, blessed holy hell. "Yes, well, I'm sure..."

"We were very sorry things didn't work out with Andrea. She is a lovely woman. She would have made the perfect wife."

For some reason, that got Ian's hackles up. But he had been brought up to be diplomatic. It had been a necessary skill in mediating between his parents. "It wasn't to be. I've accepted that and moved on."

"Good. As well you should. As they say, lots of other fish to fry."

Ian really didn't want to discuss his failed attempt to win Andrea's heart with Ralph. "Quite."

"Still. You'll need a hostess if you want to get the position. You will have so many social events to organize." Jameson stroked his jaw. "Margaret has a niece she'd like you to meet."

Oh, boy. Ian couldn't think of a single thing to say. A phone rang in an office down the hall. Sun streamed through a window high above the hallway, and he watched the dust motes dance in the light. His mouth suddenly dry, he licked his lips. The last thing he needed in his life was to be fixed up by Margaret Jameson. "Really."

A little devil lit on his left shoulder and poked him with his little red pitchfork. Ian spoke before he thought. "Actually, I'm seeing a woman, a wonderful woman. I'm keen for you to meet her."

Ralph raised his eyebrows. "Great news. I'd love to meet her, as will Margaret."

"I'm anxious for her to meet the whole crowd." And as soon as he figured out who *she* was, he'd be happy to introduce her to the whole damn department.

Gina's smiling face immediately jumped to mind. He didn't have to use his Ph.D. to figure out why that happened. He'd been thinking about her a lot after Andrea's wedding.

A vision of Gina and Jameson sucking down beers flashed across his eyes. He smiled. It was a comical image, Bohemian fairy princess meets Professor Santa Claus. "Yes," he answered before he had a chance to think twice. "That sounds great."

Jameson beamed. "Fantastic. I'll tell Margaret to set something up. I'm so glad you've moved on. Andrea is a lovely woman, but she's not the only one in the world, now, is she?"

Ian nodded. Jameson turned away and bustled back down to his office. Ian's stomach sank with each step Jameson took.

Somehow, he had to find a way to get Gina to pretend to be his girlfriend.

Not his girlfriend. Someone who keenly interested him. Someone he thought of marrying.

Hadn't he had enough of that the first time around with Andrea? Where had his pride gone?

The answer to that one was painfully apparent. He had *no* pride.

And he had no choice. If Ian wanted his boss' wife out of his love life, he needed to get a fiancée. Not just someone he casually dated. That wouldn't stop Margaret.

Some days it didn't pay to get out of bed.

Chapter Four

The place was only sparsely filled when Ian pushed open the The End Zone's door. He would have preferred to call and ask Gina to meet him on neutral turf, but he didn't know her last name. Besides, he was desperate, and desperation made a man do lots of things he ordinarily wouldn't even consider.

Like, say, going to Mike Kelly's hangout to ask the woman who still loved Mike to go to a few parties and pretend to be in love with him instead. Hopefully, he could even talk her into pretending she was dating, maybe even engaged to him.

That must rate one million on the sad-o-meter.

He shook his head. He liked Margaret Jameson, his chairman's wife. She was a generous person and had opened her heart and home to him many times. He quite simply didn't want to date her niece and didn't know how to say no gracefully. Gina was a decent sort. She'd understand. Surely it wouldn't be a hardship for her to attend a few social functions with him, right?

Bugger it. How did he get into these situations?

His eyes flicked over the room as he walked to the bar. The TV above the bar blared out a hockey game. A couple of old guys sat at one end of the bar, their heads close together as they conferred about the game. The air was fragrant with the aroma of grilled meat. His stomach grumbled, reminding him of the fact that he hadn't eaten. In spite of that, he didn't know if he could handle food until after he'd talked to Gina.

Gina was nowhere in sight.

"Hey. What can I get you?"

Ian swiveled to see the person talking to him. He shook his head, then blinked. The woman working behind the bar had pink hair, an armload of tattoos and was clearly formidable. He cleared his throat. He really didn't want anything alcoholic in light of the weekend's debauchery. "A ginger ale, please."

Pinkie the bartender reached under the bar, pulled out a bowl of pretzels and put it in front of him. "Do you want to see a menu?"

"No thank you. I'm fine for now."

She cocked a brow. "You sure? I've got a happy hour special goin' on—a dozen Buffalo wings for $3.50."

His stomach did a slow, sour roll. "Sounds great," he lied. He just didn't get the whole chicken wing thing. They were greasy and messy. "But just the ginger ale for now, please."

"Okey-doke." She sauntered off to fetch his drink.

Ian rolled his shoulders in an attempt to look around for Gina. All he managed to do was get a crick in his neck. Awkward didn't even begin to describe how he felt.

"Here's your ginger ale." The pink-haired bartender dropped his drink on the bar with a sturdy *thonk*. "You lookin' for someone?"

Obviously, *his* middle name wasn't sly. He should just come out and ask.

He opened his mouth. Words stuck in his throat, a very odd occurrence. He was good with words. He was a published poet, for goodness' sake.

His mother had raised a coward as well as a fool.

Might as well alert the world to those facts. "Is Gina working tonight?"

"Francisco?"

Bollocks. What if there were two Ginas working tonight? He must certainly look like a damn fool. "Is she short, with red, curly hair?"

"Yeah, that's her. I don't know if she's working. Let me ask. Hey, Sandy," she boomed across the room to another waitress. "Gina on tonight?"

"What?" Sandy must not have understood Pinkie.

Pinkie jacked up the volume. "Gina working tonight?"

"I think so. Why?" Sandy bellowed back.

"This guy's askin' for her." Pinkie jerked her head in Ian's direction.

"Oh, yeah?" Sandy's eyes snapped with interest as she made her way across the room. She sidled up to the stool Ian was perched on and leaned against the bar. "What do you want with Gina?"

Her tone sounded friendly, but her body language spoke of mistrust. He measured his words before he spoke. "I need to speak with her about something."

Sandy stared at him, then her eyes narrowed. "I know who you are. You're the English dude from the wedding."

"Gina told you about me?" The question popped out before Ian could stop it. He wouldn't think about the slight hitch his heart made at the thought that Gina had mentioned him to her friends.

"No, Gina hasn't said word one about you. I heard all about you from Amber. Remember her? The bartender?"

Ian did remember Amber, though for the life of him, he couldn't bring her face to mind. "Unpleasant woman? Gina doesn't like her."

"Omigawd! You totally rock that accent." Sandy

danced around the bar stool to get a better look at him. "Pierce Brosnan has nothing on you. You are just way too cute."

Ian had been called many things in his life. Cute was not one of them. He felt his face color. This was going worse than he'd imagined it would.

****

"Some guy's out front looking for you." Bobby looked up from chopping onions and motioned with his machete-sized knife.

Gina turned around. "Who, me?"

"Yeah. Been there a while, getting his drink on with ginger ale."

Gina scrunched her brows together. Frowning, she asked, "I wonder who it is?"

"Don't know, but if you don't mind, get him out of here. Sandy is flirting with him big time and isn't getting any work done." He scooped up onions with the knife and sniffed as he slid them into a big aluminum mixing bowl. Their pungent odor cut through the thick scent of grease to make her eyes water. While she carefully swabbed at the corners of her eyes, she thanked her Maker for the invention of waterproof mascara.

Opening her locker, Gina jammed her stuff inside it while she muttered, "My luck, this guy is a bill collector." She ran her fingers through her hair and then took her time getting out to the bar.

And just look at who sat there, nursing a ginger ale while he watched a hockey game. She'd have felt better about a bill collector.

What the hell was Ian doing here?

Sandy inched up to her. "Honey, you really have been holding out on me. He is gorgeous."

"Oh for Pete's sake. Do you want me to go get the smelling salts before or after you swoon?"

"Don't bother with the smelling salts. Let *him* give me mouth to mouth."

39

Gina shook her head. "Did he say why he's here?"

"He's looking for you, girlfriend."

"I was afraid of that."

A group at a table in Sandy's section gave her a holler. Sandy smiled in their direction and started to move over to them. Gina hoped she would go without a parting shot, but she really did know better.

Sandy stopped. Looking back at Gina, she said, "This guy is great, Gina. Give him a chance."

"Sandy, I know you mean well, but you're being a pain in the butt. Go see what your table wants."

Sandy laughed, then resumed her mission to the group plagued by thirst. Gina had two choices. Door number one, she could get a sudden stomach bug and spend the rest of the night hiding in the bathroom. Door number two, she could deal with Ian and get rid of him as soon as possible.

Since he had noticed her and now watched her with adorably uncertain eyes, she chose door number two.

****

Ian watched Gina walk toward the bar. He knew she'd seen him. What he couldn't tell was whether she was happy to see him or not. That baby doll face of hers gave nothing away.

He didn't remember many details about their night together. The one thing he did remember—she had never looked directly at him. Her eyes were shut the entire time.

He took a big sip of ginger ale. It did nothing to assuage the sudden ache in his heart.

She looked fabulous. His breath hitched at the sight of her walking toward him, eyes shining, her gorgeous curls escaping right and left from the pony tail she tried to confine them in. She had a body that made his hands itch to touch her.

All over.

40

Her fire engine red *The End Zone* tee shirt fit snugly across her breasts. It was a splendid sight. Ian shifted his position on the bar stool, trying to give the boys some breathing room.

It didn't work. All battle systems were at alert.

So he watched Gina saunter toward him. He desperately tried to look casual. This would not work. She was never going to agree to date him.

Why had he come here? What had he been thinking?

Oh, yeah. Margaret Jameson's niece. He needed Gina and the illusion of a committed relationship to help him get out of being set up.

Guilt nipped at him with little sharp teeth. He had no right to ask this of her, considering what she had just lost. But he had no choice. He didn't have the time, nor the inclination, to date.

"Ian. Hi. How are you?" Her big brown eyes were guarded.

He swallowed. "Fine. You okay?"

She wiggled as she wrapped her apron around her waist. The motion made her breasts lift and jut forward. Her nipples were erect and pushing against the fabric of her shirt.

Ian took a hefty sip of his ginger ale. It didn't help that he suddenly remembered very clearly the way those nipples tasted and felt against his tongue.

From the wide-eyed look on her face, Ian could tell she knew what he was thinking. Chagrined, he felt himself blush nearly at the same time she did.

She crossed her arms in a protective move across her breasts. "I'm fine," she said. Then she tossed her head back. "Why are you here, Ian?"

"I've come to see how you are, if you're okay. You were gone when I woke up and... "

"Shhhhh." Moving fast, Gina put her hand across his mouth. "Not so loud! The whole bar doesn't need the details."

He took her hand away from his mouth and held it between both of his. As before, it felt small, cold and fragile. "True. But I can't help being concerned."

She snatched her hand back. "Well, I'm fine. I'm great. Never better. You don't have to worry about me."

"Good. I'm glad."

They stared at each other as an awkward silence stretched between them. All around them were the sounds of the busy bar—the clatter of silverware scraping across plates, the ping of glasses, the laughter of the patrons, the muffled commentary about the hockey game from the television. But in that one moment, the palpable silence suspended between their two aching hearts was all he heard.

"Hey, Gina. There's a new party on twelve. That's your table."

Gina broke eye contact with Ian to look at Pinkie behind the bar. "Thanks, Spike. I'm on it." She smiled at Ian, a tiny, trembling curve of her lips. "Bye, Ian. See you around."

Panic that she was getting away made him blurt, "Gina, wait. Do you think we could go someplace and talk for a bit after your shift here, or during your break? Maybe get a coffee or something?"

"I just got back from my break. I'm working a split today, and I'll be really tired later."

"I promise I won't take up too much of your time."

Gina looked at him then sighed. "I guess. I get off around ten. Where can I meet you?"

He thought about Esmeralda's, but decided he couldn't take the risk. Too many of his colleagues went there after hours. If she refused to go along with him, then he was out of a plan. "You name it, I'll be there."

"How about the Mickey D's on Chestnut Ave.?

It's on my way home."

He cringed a bit at the thought of the golden arches, hoping he didn't show it. "Sounds fine. I'll see you there at ten, then."

"More like ten-thirty. It'll take me a few minutes to get out of here and get there."

"No problem." He watched her turn and negotiate her way through the customers to get to her table. Her cute little backside was just as much a treat to watch move as her chest. No doubt about it, she was one hell of a sexy female.

As he sat there watching her smile and laugh with the people ordering drinks, an all too familiar feeling crept through him. He wanted her to smile for him, really smile, not those tentative smiles he'd received during their conversation.

Saddened, he swore as he pulled out his wallet, plucked out a ten and threw it down onto the bar. Then he hightailed it out the door, wondering how to fill the time between now and ten o'clock P.M.

He had papers to grade. It was a fact of his life in the same league as death and taxes. He'd take them to McDonald's with him.

****

"I'm tired, my feet hurt and I smell like greasy French fries." Gina jammed the key into her car's ignition. "I want to go home, take a really hot bath then go to bed." She backed out of her parking space and maneuvered her car into the sparse traffic.

"I know he's going to want to talk about what happened after the wedding. I *really* don't want to talk about it. I want to forget it ever happened." A horrible little thought danced across her brain. She slapped her palm against the steering wheel, then winced as she shook out her hand.

"He's realized we didn't use a condom. He's going to want to talk about consequences."

Not that there were any. She'd gotten her period

just that morning. It reminded her they hadn't used protection. The cramps were just a bonus on an otherwise rotten day.

Of course, if she had gotten pregnant, it would have been a true disaster. All in all, cramps were a better deal.

When she got to MacDonald's, it didn't take her long to find Ian. He sat in a booth for six and had spread out all over the table what had to be about fifty blue books. Red pen poised in his left hand, he cupped his forehead in his right as he read. He shook his head as he brought the pen down to notate something on the open pages.

Since he was totally immersed in what he was doing and didn't have a clue she had arrived, Gina took a moment to gather her courage and to study him. For a college professor, he was a pretty studly guy, especially now, all rumpled and with the shadow of an evening beard.

Something passed in the air between them, something that made him look up and smile. That smile...

It was the stuff dreams were made of, sexy, sweet and kind of shy. Intimate, like he could read her mind.

Which, of course, was ridiculous. He was a college professor, not a psychic. She steeled herself up before she embarrassed herself by melting in a puddle at his feet.

He stood. "Oh, good. You made it. Can I get you something? A coffee? Tea?"

He wore his eagerness to please like a cub scout wore his first merit badge. Her heart melted a little more. "Coffee sounds good, but don't worry about it." She reached in her purse. "I can get it."

"No, I'll get it. I insist." He came from around the table and glommed onto her elbow, then pushed her into a seat. "Your feet must be aching. Just rest a second, and I'll be right back."

Stunned, Gina had no choice but to do as he said. Curious about the array of blue books, she picked one up, one he had already graded. It was all in French. The questions, the answers, his red pen comments, all in French.

She couldn't understand a single word. She felt like a total doofus.

"Don't mind those. I'll gather them up and put them away." He placed the large coffee in front of her, then moved into the booth and started to pick up the blue books. "I feel like I'm constantly grading papers. If I don't keep up, they bury me." Stuffing the papers into the open briefcase at his side, Ian dropped the lid. It landed with a soft thud. He looked at her, his eyes hopeful. "I don't know how you take your coffee, so I brought both cream and sugar." Jamming his hands in his pockets, he pulled out enough packets of sugar to put her in a coma, as well as a handful of creamers.

She reached for a creamer. "Just cream, thanks." It made a hissing sound as she pulled the wrapper off the top. "What's up?"

Ian looked away for a moment, pulled the glasses off his face and cleaned them with a paper napkin. "There's no graceful way to ask this." He studied his glasses before slipping them back on his face.

"Why don't you just spit it out?"

"Right, then." He nodded. "I need you to marry me."

Chapter Five

Gina looked straight at Ian, blinked twice and shook her head. "Come again?"

Ian would rather talk to his mother about his father's stripper wife than have this conversation with Gina. But quite simply, he had no choice. "I didn't mean that the way it sounded. I'm not really asking you to marry me."

"Well, maybe I should get a Miracle Ear. I could have sworn you just asked me to marry you."

Ian took a sip from her coffee cup. He put it back down very carefully. "I didn't mean it the way it sounded."

"Oh really? How did you mean it?"

"That wasn't well done of me. Let's backtrack." He cleared his throat a couple of times and then took another hit of her coffee. "I am in the running for the chairmanship of the French Department. It's an incredible opportunity for a scholar of my age." He hazarded a look toward her. Her eyes were big and round and filled with trepidation.

She looked so pretty. Those red curls of hers shone, her eyes flashed bright and intelligent while her kewpie doll mouth begged to be kissed.

She also looked suspicious and oh, so silent. He soldiered onward. "Unfortunately, getting this job means going to a lot of social functions." His smile defined rueful. "I'm going to need a companion."

Gina smiled and liberated her coffee from his grasp. "Do tell." She took a sip.

"The competition is keen. My student evaluations are very good. My scholarship is competitive and can stand on its own against anyone else's work. I'm on the trail of something big, something so big it will set the academic community on its ear. If I can get all my facts together and in place by the time the search committee meets, I've got an excellent chance." He flashed her a smile again. "Or at least, that's the plan." He sighed. "It's a good job. It's an honor to be considered, never mind to get on the short list."

"Are you on the short list?"

"Yes, I am."

Gina's smile exploded. "Ian, that's great! You must be so thrilled."

"Here's the thing. I need a date for several social engagements. That's where you come in."

Those eyes of hers went wary again. "Okay."

"I need you to pretend to be my fiancée until I get the chairmanship." He frowned. "There's some competition, and I don't trust at least one of them to play fair."

She protectively wrapped her fingers around her coffee and drank deep. "You've got to be kidding me."

"I'm deadly serious, unfortunately. Academia can be cut throat. And then, Margaret Jameson, my boss' wife, has the tenacity of a Rottweiler and a niece she's dying to fix me up with."

Gina just stared at him. "Even if I were willing to pretend to date you, I'm the last person you want to do this. I didn't go to college. I didn't even graduate from high school." She lifted her chin a little as she said the last bit.

He didn't know anyone who hadn't finished school. He couldn't wrap his brain around it. "Why didn't you finish school?"

"My mother was dying. I had to quit to take care of her and work to pay the bills."

"Where was your father during all this?"

"Not around. He left when I was six. We never saw him again."

"Surely there were other family members who could have helped out?"

"There weren't, okay? Can we just drop it? You just have to see that I'm the least likely person for your little game of pretend. You need someone like, well, Andi."

His face clouded. "Since she's married, I think we can cross her off the list."

Gina clicked her fingernails on the Formica table. She looked directly at him. "You must know other women who could pull this off better than me."

"Uh, not really. It has to be someone no one at the college knows."

She pursed her lips. "No one is going to believe for a second that you and I are together."

Ian took off his glasses and began to clean them with the bottom hem of his sweater vest. With elaborate care, he put them back on and then folded his hands on the table. "Of course they will. We just pretend to be together, go to a few parties, a few functions. After Margaret backs off, or I get the chairmanship, we can break up."

"The niece is that bad?"

"The niece really isn't the issue. I just don't want the department chair's wife meddling in my love life, or lack thereof."

"What's going to stop her from trying again once we break up?"

"I don't care once I get the chair, because, quite simply, it won't matter. Ever." He flushed red and looked away. "Unless I sleep with a student or rob a bank."

Gina wished he would look at her. She wanted to know what he was feeling. "Sounds like a real bad idea."

He looked back at her. "Which one?"

"Take your pick."

He laughed. "You're right. Both sound dreadful." Then he turned serious. "Please, Gina. You have to realize how difficult this is for me. I wouldn't ask you if this weren't so important. I really need your help."

****

Gina looked across the table at Ian. She was such a sap. If she decided to do this, which she hadn't yet, she had to get a little control over the situation.

So... She had conditions.

Gina brought her hand up and ticked off the items on her list as she said them. "If I do this, then there's no physical stuff. No mouth to mouth, no groping, absolutely no sex."

He raised both hands up in a *Who-me?* gesture. "Goes without saying."

"We put the cart before the horse. I'm uncomfortable about this, because I don't sleep with guys casually. I'm not proud of getting drunk and sleeping with you. But I did, and so I'll deal with it." In for a penny, in for a pound. "I actually thought maybe you wanted to talk to me because you realized we didn't, you know, when we were at the hotel, that we didn't use... Well, you know."

His eyebrows scrunched together. "Uh, actually I don't know."

Damn. He was going to make her say it. She leaned forward, so she didn't have to talk loudly. "We didn't use a condom."

Those eyebrows nearly shot straight off his forehead. "Well, I don't... That is, my word, this is embarrassing. No, we didn't. You don't have to worry about anything from me. I mean I don't have any diseases. But, could you be pregnant?"

She sighed. "No."

49

"You're sure."

Man, this all just kept getting more and more embarrassing. "I'm about as sure as a woman can be."

"Ah, well. Good then." Ian looked about as embarrassed as Gina felt.

"So, the upshot is, if, and I do mean *if*, I decide to do this for you, there'll be no sex."

"I don't expect there to be. I just need you to play along until Margaret backs off."

"I still don't get why you want me. It's not like I'm really educated and stuff. I won't know what to say to your friends. They'll think you're marrying a mime."

He gave her that incredible grin again. Mike had an entire repertoire of smiles, but the whole bunch of them didn't add up to one of Ian's genuine grins. "Just ask them about their latest projects, then nod while they talk."

"And what if they ask me about what I do?"

He stared at her. "Tell them the truth."

"I suppose." Her brows knit across her forehead. "Won't it hurt you that I'm a waitress?"

"I'm stunned. Why would it?"

"Think about it now. Would my being a waitress hold you back? Stop you from getting this chair?"

"This is America, land of the free, home of the brave, all that good stuff. What you do for a living has nothing to do with me getting the job."

She clacked her red polished fingernails against the table. "I don't know, Ian. You're a nice guy and all, and I'd like to help you out, but... I don't know. I'm really not the right person for this."

"You're the perfect person. The rest of the faculty will know everyone else I know." He put his warm hand over hers. "You're my only hope."

She shook her head. "I'm sure we have nothing in common. I don't know a single thing about you, except that you have lousy taste in women."

That took him aback. "What do you mean?"

She felt a smile ghost past her lips. "I meant Andi, the ice princess." The look that came across his face made her feel like she had kicked a puppy. "I'm teasing you."

"Oh." He took off his glasses and threw them on the table. "I suppose then that I can tease you about your deplorable taste in men."

"Absolutely not." She felt her smile widen, until she saw the very intense look on his face. It made her feel all squirmy inside.

Ian took her hand. "How about this? Why don't we go on a few dates to see if we can stand each other's company when we're not under the influence, and then you can decide if you'll do this."

Well, that sounded reasonable. There was no harm in going on a couple of friendly dates with Ian Ross.

Besides, did she have anything better to do?

Sadly, no. "That sounds like a good idea."

"Great! What kinds of things do you like to do?"

"Sports. I love to watch sports. I *live* to play softball in the local restaurant league, but it's a coupla months 'til that starts up again. I don't suppose you play softball?"

"That would be a safe bet." He frowned. "Sports, that's it? No movies, concerts, that kind of thing."

"A movie might be fun." Not to mention safe.

He opened his brief case and pulled out his date book. "I've got a ballet board meeting tomorrow night, but the evening after that, I'm free."

She shook her head. "I have to work."

He seemed genuinely disappointed. "That's too bad. There's a film I've been wanting to see, and it's only in the theater at the college that one night. That is, if you were interested in seeing it. I promise it's an amazing film."

51

"Well, maybe. Let me see if I can get someone to work for me."

"Could you? That would be fantastic. Here's my card, it has my numbers on it." He handed her a pristine white rectangle. The way his name and number were printed looked classy and expensive. "You can call me when you know."

"Yeah, sure."

They sat there in silence for a few long moments, and then the silence began to feel awkward. She yawned until her jaw popped. Time to go home. "I'm really tired."

"Yes, you must be after being on your feet all night." He began to pack up all his things. "Let me walk you to your car."

"No," Gina said, a little sharper than she meant to. She needed some space to process what she had just agreed to. "You just stay here, and I'll get myself home." She stood. "I'll call you tomorrow afternoon, either way."

"Great." He stood while he offered her his hand. "I'll talk to you tomorrow then."

She grabbed his hand, gave it a shake, then pulled back and fished her gloves out of her coat pocket. "Okay. G'night."

"Good night." His voice scraped over her ears, kind of raspy and low. It was amazingly sexy, making all her nerve endings jump up and take notice. If she didn't leave right then and there, she was going to give in to temptation and kiss him.

On the ride home, she wondered if that would have been such a bad thing.

****

"So, wait, let me get this straight. You got Linda to work for you so you could go out on a date with Andi Nelson's ex?" Sandy ran a wet rag over the table she was bussing to clean up a ketchup spill.

Gina briefly considered poking Sandy in the eye.

"It's not like it sounds. He needs someone to take to a bunch of work things he's got coming up, and we're seeing if we get along well enough to, you know, go to them together."

"Well, he's pretty cute. You could do worse. Come to think of it..." Sandy threw the rag into the bus bucket. "You have done worse. I say go for it."

"Go for what?"

Gina wanted to groan, hearing Dave Mason's voice over her shoulder. She turned to face him. "Hey, Dave. You here for lunch?"

"Yeah. Go for what?"

Most of the time Gina could appreciate Dave's ability to stick to a point and ferret out information. Now was not one of those times.

"She's going on a date with that English guy who used to go out with Mike's wife."

"Ian Ross?" Dave looked befuddled.

Sandy the helpful said, "She's getting to know him better, since they hit it off so well at the reception."

"At the reception? When did you..."

Gina saw the precise moment when Dave remembered the reception.

"I'm not sure this is such a good idea for you, Gina."

Well, now he was trying to make her mad. "Why not? He's a great guy. And it's not like I have any better offers."

"I just don't want to see you get hurt, that's all."

"We're going to the movies, Dave. That's all." Gina figured God would forgive her that lie. There was no way she would tell Dave the whole truth.

"Look, it's got to be a rebound thing, right? That can't end well for you."

Gina decided then and there Dave could stuff his concern where the sun didn't shine. "It's okay Dave. I know what I'm doing." She pulled a menu out of the station by the bar and handed it to him. "The special's good today. Bobby made chili. Let Sandy know when you're ready to order."

She turned on her heel and walked to the kitchen.

Ian Ross was handsome, intelligent and sweet. She thought for sure she could stand to go on a few dates with him. After all, he had been right. Their hearts weren't involved; they both knew that, so neither of them would get hurt. He'd get his promotion, whatever that was, avoid the niece from hell. Big bonus, she'd dress up and get to go to a few parties.

Besides, it didn't matter that he still loved Andi. After all, wasn't she still pitifully in love with Mike?

She was, right?

She definitely needed to get a life and this was a step in the right direction. Ian Ross was a handsome, sexy man. She could do much worse.

Chapter Six

"And don't forget the essay due Friday on Guillaume de Lorris' contributions to *Roman de la Rose*." Backpack zippers buzzed and chairs scraped across the mottled, cracked linoleum floor. "It's due at the beginning of the class period, not the end."

Ian watched the students tug on their backpacks and shuffle out of his 3:00 class on Medieval French poetry. They worked hard for him, but they didn't seem to be getting the point of the assigned work. Yes, it was difficult, but this was university. Difficult challenges ruled all their lives. They needed to get used to it.

He knew why he was so frustrated. It had nothing to do with the students and everything to do with the fact that Gina hadn't called about the movie. Somehow, it had become more vital than breathing that she go with him.

He gathered his lecture notes into his briefcase and started the trek to his office. The more he thought about Gina, the more he realized asking her to pose as his fiancée was a bad idea. What had he been thinking?

Well, quite obviously, he hadn't been thinking. She still loved Mike. Why would she want to go out with him? He would stop by The End Zone on his way home and tell her she was off the hook. He'd find another way to avoid Margaret's niece.

Okay, his decision had been made. Why did his stomach still feel so queasy?

At the main office he checked his mailbox. Sorting through the envelopes and memos he had picked up, he rounded the turn in the corridor leading to his office. Balancing papers and his briefcase, he rummaged in his pocket for his keys, until he realized with a jolt his office door stood open.

Someone had unlocked the door to his office and had left it open.

Well, then. It appeared that someone had to die.

Gathering his dignity and his righteous indignation around him like a superhero's cape, he stormed into his office, prepared to do battle with the hapless person who had invaded his sanctuary.

Donald Unger sat at his desk. While Ralph Jameson might think Unger to be a good man, Ian had profound doubts about Unger's character. He just didn't trust him. "What are you doing in my office?"

Donald offered him a toothy smile. "Don't get feisty, Ian. I came down here to run a few things by you. Your office door was open, so I came inside to wait." Unger got out of Ian's desk chair and out of Ian's way. "If you're so fussy about people being in your office, you really should lock up when you leave."

"I did." He *had* locked his office. He *always* locked his office when he wasn't in it. He couldn't take the chance someone would come across his research and pirate it. He put his briefcase and mail on his desk. Facing Unger across the desk he said, "What do you want?"

"I came to find out if you want one or two places at Jameson's retirement dinner." Unger looked at Ian with a trace of amused disdain. "Especially in light of the fact that Andrea won't be coming with you this year." Evil sparked in Unger's eyes. "Unless her new husband doesn't mind sharing."

Arrogant bastard. That had to be, quite possibly, the flimsiest excuse to be caught snooping that Ian had ever heard. And the Andrea remark—there were no words. "I'm quite sure that Mike Kelly doesn't share. Nor do I, for that matter. But, please, do put me down for two places at the table. Someone will be joining me as my guest." The stakes most definitely had changed. He'd beg Gina if he had to. He'd pay her.

"Well, it's wonderful to hear you're back in the game again. Mary Louise will be delighted to hear that, of course. She had several friends she wanted you to meet."

Ian had no more desire to meet Mary Louise Unger's friends than he had to date Margaret Jameson's niece. "Yes, well, thank you, but that won't be necessary. Is there anything else you wanted?" *Get the hell out of my damn office.*

"No, that's it. Congratulations on the new lady friend." That said, Unger left.

Obnoxious, stupid git. Ian very quickly checked his desk drawers to make sure they hadn't been opened. Call him paranoid, but he had devised a system for detecting if anyone had been messing around inside his desk, especially the drawer that held the drive with his research.

He breathed a sigh of relief when he ascertained Unger hadn't touched it. He may have tried, but he hadn't gotten into the drawers.

That done, Ian closed his office door. Sitting down, he checked his voice mail for a message from Gina. He hated the way his heart pounded as he listened.

He hated the feeling of utter relief that flooded him when he heard her say she could meet him for the movies, and could he call The End Zone before five o'clock to tell her where. She insisted she take her own car.

He phoned with a pounding heart and an aching head. A lot was riding on tonight being a total success. He couldn't afford to blow it.

****

Gina maneuvered her car through the Byzantine tangle of streets that ran through Barrett University. She knew her way around because she had worked at a couple of events at B.U., but that was the only reason. The campus movie theater usually showed movies she'd never heard of, films with artsy foreign names.

She should have taken Sandy's bet that Hugh Jackman wouldn't be starring in tonight's movie.

Wasn't that just a damn shame. Hugh was beyond hot.

She circled the block five times before she gave up on finding a parking spot. With a heavy sigh, she drove about six blocks away, finally tucking her ancient little Volkswagen into a space she found on a side street. She didn't lock it because she was afraid that the lock would freeze.

The weather felt cold and nasty. It had snowed the day before then rained that morning. Toward midday, the temperature dropped, putting an icy crust on all the slush. She tugged her hat down over her ears, not caring that it squished her hair down

Frigid, moist wind blew into her face making her eyes water and her nose run. She was *so* going to make a charming impression on Ian.

That made her snort, which hurt her nose, which made her wince. She shouldn't be worried about making a good impression on Ian. After all, he wanted the favor. He should be worried about making a good impression on her.

So there.

She slipped on the ice. Helpless, she grabbed wildly at the air, somehow regaining her balance just before she fell on her butt. As she put her full weight on her left foot, a throbbing pain shot up her ankle. She swore as she ploughed onward. It was sheer vanity to always wear the highest heels she could get away with, but she hated being short. Limping, she made it to the cinema.

Ian was not where he told her he would be. She sighed as she unwrapped her scarf and took off her gloves. This night just kept getting better and better.

She looked around and an unexpected pang of jealousy pierced her heart. All these young kids milling about—did they know how lucky they were to be there? There had been a time she would have killed to go to college, a time when she had longed to be free to pursue her dreams.

But that was all done now. She tried to never look back or dwell on lost opportunity. What was the point? She couldn't have turned her back on her mother, end of story.

"Sorry I'm late." Ian appeared next to her. "I got hung up with a student who was having a problem with an essay that's due tomorrow. Have you been waiting long?"

"Nope. Just got here."

"Great. Let me just get our tickets and some popcorn if you want it, and we can go find our seats." With his face flushed from the cold, his nose a bit red, and sporting that heartbreaking grin, he looked too darn good.

If you went for the professorial, egghead type, which she didn't. Well, she didn't until maybe five minutes ago.

Aw, crud. "What are we seeing?"

He rubbed his hands together. "You're in for a treat. We're seeing a special showing of Renais' *L'Anèe dernière à Marienbad*." He flashed that killer smile of his, and her heart beat a little bit faster. It almost made up for the fact that her buddy Hugh was in no way likely to be in Marien-whoozits-face.

Almost. Not quite.

He came back laden with tickets and popcorn and a couple of sodas. "Here we go." He motioned with his head to where a bored Goth wannabe took tickets. "Have you seen this film before?"

"Uh, no. Can't say that I have."

"Well, it's fantastic. The director sets out to challenge every preconceived notion we have about storytelling, particularly in film. It's a spectacular example of modernist film and the fracturing of narrative."

"Can't wait."

He steered them to seats smack dab in the middle of the theater. To Gina's amazement, the place was packed. A couple of kids greeted Ian and showed him great respect. She could tell they liked him. His genuine responses said he liked them equally as much. He was a nice man.

The lights dimmed, and the curtains opened. Music started, the credits rolled by in French, and as far as she could tell, it was totally in black and white. Ick. She amended her previous thought. He might be a nice guy and a caring teacher, but he had terrible taste in movies.

She practically had to pinch herself to stay awake. First off, the whole thing, not just the credits, was in French. Yes, it had subtitles, but if she had wanted to read, she wouldn't have fought the elements to go to a movie to do it. She would have run herself a nice hot bath and read in the tub.

Second, nothing happened. The whole thing started out with people acting practically like statues. They all just talked real fast in French, trying to convince this woman she'd known them all before in Marienbad. Gina wasn't stupid, but man, when she went to a movie, she wanted something to happen. She wanted a story.

Then, even if she could have understood the

words she wouldn't have been able to hear them. The sound quality was so bad, the words weren't in sync with the actors' movements.

Not that the actors moved very much. It was one good ol' bore-fest.

She yawned. She didn't care if Ian noticed it. Frankly, if pretending to be his fiancée meant watching another movie like this one, she'd pass, thank you very much.

****

Ian had been stunningly aware of Gina over the course of the entire film. She smelled fantastic, a magical combination of raspberries and almonds.

Apparently raspberries and almonds were an aphrodisiac because he had the erection to end all erections.

Since he had promised her there would be no sex involved in their deal, he was pretty sure she wouldn't appreciate him ogling her breasts. He forced himself to focus on the film, which had to be a first. This was one of his favorite films. It had never been a problem for him to lose himself in it before.

The house lights came up, and he blinked until his eyes adjusted to the light. It had been a satisfactory evening in almost every way, with a beautiful and desirable woman beside him while he watched one of his favorite films. He stood and offered her his hand so that he could help her up.

She looked at his proffered hand as if it were made of worms. She took it, once she realized what he meant.

He very much wanted to go to Esmeralda's Café and get her impressions of the film. He had so much he wanted to share with her about it. "Would you like to go to Esmeralda's for a drink?"

"Uh, no thanks. I appreciate the offer, but I think I'll just head on home, if it's all the same to you."

"Are you sure? I'd love to talk to you about the film, find out what you think of it and all that."

"Trust me, you don't want to know."

Ian hadn't just fallen off the turnip truck. He could tell when a woman was peeved about something, and Gina's body language screamed *peeved* in flashing neon. "You didn't like the film?"

Gina exhaled a huge sigh. "It just wasn't my thing, okay? I'm sure it's probably a great monument in the history of movies, and I'm a dunce for not getting it, but there you go." She raised her chin, shrugging while she looked at him.

"Please let me make it up to you!" He hoped he didn't sound as desperate as he felt. "What kind of movies do you like? What's your favorite movie?"

"*Kate and Leopold.* Look, it's getting late. I've gotta go."

His heart started racing when she talked. Suddenly, it became vital that she go with him someplace to talk this out. "Let me buy you a drink."

"Really, Ian, thanks for the offer, but I'm tired. I want to go home." She pushed past him to get into the aisle out of the theater.

"Are you sure?"

"Yeah, I'm sure." She shoved her arms into her coat as she began walking away.

Disappointment swamped him. He followed her, determined she wasn't going to get away so fast. "Let me walk you to your car, at least."

She stopped in the aisle. "This isn't going to work, Ian. I'm sorry, but I'm just not going to be able to help you out with this pretend engagement thing."

"You can't know this on the basis of one date. I'll do better next time."

She bit her lip. "I don't know..."

"You decide what we're going to do next." He'd go anywhere, do anything, to make it up to her, anything to get her to help him avoid Margaret's matchmaking attempts.

After all, that's what this was all about.

They stood in the lobby. She looked at him, a frown drawing down the corners of her totally kissable mouth. Finally, she sighed and said, "You like hockey?"

"I don't know. I've never followed the sport."

"Well, it's about time you learned. Deke gave me a pair of tickets for the Bruins home game next Thursday."

"Deke. As in Deke Nelson, Andrea's father." A.k.a. Lucifer, as far as Ian was concerned. The man disliked Ian, and Ian returned the feeling in spades.

"Yeah. He's a good guy, actually. He can't use 'em, and he knows I like hockey. Do you want to go with me?"

Hockey; men beating each other with sticks. It sounded like misery, but he wanted a second chance to convince Gina to help. "Sure. Why not? It sounds like fun." He was starting to think any time spent with Gina would be fun.

Chapter Seven

"Tell me about tonight's hockey game?" Ian asked Gina as they found their way to their seats in the On-Center. "There'll be some skating, I assume."

"Oh, yeah." Gina looked around the arena, her excitement palpable. She was practically jumping up and down in her seat like a child on Christmas Eve. Her eyes glittered; her grin spread from ear to ear.

Adorable. Absolutely adorable. "So, tell me about hockey."

"Guys with sticks skate around the ice and try to knock a little round rubber thing into the goal."

Ian snorted out a laugh. "Quite succinct, but that much I knew already. About tonight, are the Bruins a good team?"

"They're getting there. They had some bad years, but they're second in their division. They've got some good players, like Joe Thornton and Sergei Samsonov." She frowned. "'Course, Samsonov had surgery on his wrist. He's out for a while."

"So, how come you know so much about hockey?" He looked at her and caught her frowning. He was having none of that. He loved to see her smile.

She shrugged. "I had a boyfriend in high school who was a hockey player. He ate, slept and drank hockey. Not a minute of a day went by that he didn't devote to hockey. If I wanted to be with him, then I had to put up with a lot of hockey."

He should have known. Of course she'd dated a hockey player. He knew she went for the macho, jock-type of guy. Didn't her devotion to Mike Kelly prove that? "Well. I've never been to a game before. What should I expect?"

Gina smiled. "Expect a *lot* of yelling. And it'll be cold."

"Loud and cold." He snuck another look at her. "Gotcha." He gestured to the row right behind the penalty box. "Looks like these are our seats." He guided her to their places.

Loud and cold was an understatement, he decided as he tried to follow the breakneck action on the ice. He'd given up on catching more than a passing glance at the puck about ten minutes into the first period. Right now, mid-way through the third, and blessedly final, period, the score was tied. The players, as well as the crowd, were wild and out for blood.

There had been several instances of players dropping their sticks and stopping play so they could push each other around. Two players were particularly out to get each other.

Seated directly behind him were two louts who managed to plant their bony knees and boot clad feet in his kidneys with just about every move they made. They were swilling prodigious amounts of beer. The insults they hurled out onto the ice were as crude as they were creative.

Of course, Gina screamed just as loud and got just as upset over the game as the boys behind them. She had undergone a slight transformation when they arrived at the rink, pulling her hair into a ponytail then stuffing it under a Boston Bruins baseball cap, taking her coat off to reveal a huge Boston Bruins jersey emblazoned on the back with the number 77 and the name Bourque. Apparently Bourque was a Bruins legend and Gina's all-time favorite player.

And unbelievably, Ian felt jealous of him. It

made him fidget in discomfort.

So fast Ian never saw it coming, the two players who had been antagonizing each other all night went for each other's throats. They dropped their gloves so they could punch the living daylights out of each other. Blood gushed from the Bruin's players nose. He leapt onto his opponent's chest, all the better to choke him. They both fell and started rolling around on the ice.

The other players and referee went to break it up, and both players were sent to the penalty box, which sat right below Ian and Gina's seats.

The guys sitting behind them had some special words for the non-Bruin in the box. Ottawa fans took exception to the boys' insults about the player's masculinity, his intelligence and his mother. Before anyone could blink, the Ottawa fans leapt over their seats in an attempt to punch the lights out of Dumb and Dumber.

The stands erupted, the result being one giant mêlée of flying fists and insults. Ian immediately moved to cover Gina to protect her, but not before ice-cold beer sloshed down his back.

Pain exploded as a fist crunched his nose. His mouth filled with blood and beer. His glasses broke, then flew off his nose. He dropped to his knees to find them.

Someone shoved Gina against him. She tripped over him onto the concrete steps of the aisle.

He scrambled to try to cushion her fall, managing only to sprawl on top of her. She gasped and pushed against his chest.

Of course, it could have been because his nose started to drip blood all over her. He averted his head while he tried to sit up to put his broken glasses back on.

She rolled to sit up, her breath came in hard, sharp little pants. By now the party had, for the most part, moved out onto the ice. Ian stood. He held his glasses with one hand, using the other to help Gina. She grabbed it, and he hauled her up.

"Omigod, you're bleeding like a stuck pig. Let me get you a tissue." Gina dove into her bag and came up with a pack of tissues. She ripped the package open with zero finesse, stood on tiptoes to press the tissue to his nose.

"Aaarrrgh!" He winced as shards of pain lanced through his face.

"Sorry," she said. She looked about ready to burst into tears. "I'm really, really sorry." She put the tissue pack in his hand. "Maybe you better do this."

"Thanks," he mumbled as he took the tissues.

"Do you think it's broken? Do you want to go to the emergency room?" She seemed truly distraught. He couldn't have that.

"No, I'm okay. The bleeding is already going away." He looked around at the ensuing chaos. "Is it safe to say the game is over?"

"Probably. Want to get out of here?"

"Oh, yeah. I most definitely want to get out of here."

****

"Are you sure you don't want me to drive?" Gina asked for what might have been the fiftieth time.

"Quite sure."

This was not what she'd planned when she had invited Ian to the hockey game. She had only wanted to prove to him that she was the wrong person to do this date thing with him. It had been a great game, though. She suppressed a grin and checked out Ian from under her eyelashes, then grimaced.

He looked like hell. Even though he'd stopped to clean up in the men's room before they hit the road, he looked bad. His broken glasses were held together with a band-aid she fished out of her purse. Plus he smelled like a brewery from having beer dumped on him. In fact, she didn't quite trust his vision, since his glasses didn't sit on his poor, bloody nose like they should. "Just let me know if you want me to drive, because I'd be happy to."

"I don't want you to drive, okay? I'm fine."

And if his jaw clenched any more, it would shatter. She shut up and let him drive.

The trip from Boston back to Addington took about an hour, and they'd been on the road for about twenty minutes. He had the radio turned on to a public radio station, which had some Jazz playing with horns wailing plaintive tunes, soft, slow and sweet. Not her usual choice in tunes, but she had to admit it sounded pretty.

Then she heard him sigh. "So, you do that kind of thing often?"

"What kind of thing?"

"Drag unsuspecting French professors to violent sporting events and get them beaten up."

She laughed in spite of feeling guilty. "No. You're the first."

He smiled and winced. "Lucky me." Squinting as he looked out onto the road, he leaned over and adjusted the car's heater. "Let me know if you get too hot."

"I won't. It always takes me days to get warm after I've been to a game."

The silence felt a bit more comfortable after that, but she still worried he had trouble seeing. While there was hardly any traffic, she didn't miss the fact the oncoming lights made him grimace and squint.

If her own car hadn't been ready to die, she would have insisted on taking it and driving. After all, going to Boston had been her suggestion.

"Whatever happened to the boyfriend who introduced you to the wonders of ice hockey?"

His change of topic made her blink. She didn't like to talk about that time in her life. "It's a long story."

One she really didn't want to tell.

"We've got a bit of time. Come on. Share."

Might as well get the whole thing out now and let him see she was the last person he wanted for a fake fiancée. "It's not pretty. When I was fifteen, my big brother got arrested for grand theft auto." She shrugged. "It wasn't his first offense and he was over 18. He's been in and out of jail for years, mostly in. That's where he is right now."

"Dear Lord." He jerked his head to look at her so fast and so hard that in spite of the Band-aid, his glasses slid down his nose. He sniffed, gingerly pushed them back on, then turned his face to look back at the road.

She heard the pity in his voice and hated it. "Anyway, Jared, the hockey player, broke up with me on account of I always had to work. Plus, his parents really didn't want him to date a convicted felon's sister."

"That's so unfeeling! I can't begin to imagine how terrible that must have been for you."

Gina shook her head. "No, I don't think..." Something pricked at the back of her neck, and she sat up straight, swiveling to look out the back window. "Is that a cop?"

Almost immediately, the air filled with the loud *wee-ooh* of a siren along with the red and blue flashing lights of a cop car.

The cop pulled them over.

"Bloody hell," Ian muttered as he stopped the car. "Just what this night needed." He reached over Gina to open the glove compartment and dragged out a plastic envelope with his registration in it.

The cop knocked on the window and shined a flashlight in. Rolling down the window, Ian smiled a tad too brightly at the officer.

"Do you know why I pulled you over?" The Statie was all business.

"Actually," Ian said. "I don't know. Why did you pull me over?"

Frowning, the cop took a deep breath and got a whiff of the eau de Budweiser Ian had been doused with, courtesy of the guys at the hockey game. "I'm going to need you to step outside, Sir."

"Why? What did I do?"

"It smells like you've been drinking. You need to step outside your car now."

Ian closed his eyes and briefly rested his head on the steering wheel, winced at the contact, then sighed. Lifting his head, he murmured, "Bloody hell. Bloody, everlasting hell."

"Sir," the cop thumped on the window again. "Please step out of the car now."

"Right." Ian did what the cop wanted.

Gina didn't know Ian very well, but the rock-like set of his jaw told her he was either extremely ticked off or extremely embarrassed. Probably both. She would be.

The cop put Ian through the whole routine, from walking along the white line to touching his nose to making him take a Breathalyzer test. With each new hoop the officer made him jump through, Ian's jaw ratcheted another degree tighter.

Finally when the cop was satisfied that Ian wasn't drunk, he wrote him a ticket for having a taillight out and sent them on their merry way. Only, merry wouldn't be the word Gina would choose to describe it.

It was more tense than merry.

When they reached the Addington city limits, Ian cleared his throat. "Sorry about the scene back there. You know..." He cleared his throat again as he gestured to the window with his head. "With the state police."

"It's not your fault." Gina felt the blood rush to her face. Nothing about this night had gone the way she planned it. "It's my fault for dragging you to the hockey game in the first place."

Ian frowned. "You couldn't have predicted that those two Neanderthals would start a brawl." His lips quirked up in a slight smile. "It was quite enlightening, actually. Interesting."

Gina snorted. "Right. Interesting." She drew in a deep breath. "You've probably had better evenings."

"I've had worse."

"I don't know about that, but I'm sorry for dragging you all the way to Boston so you could get punched in the nose, doused with beer and harassed by a cop who was determined to get you for DWI."

"Yes, well, none of that is your fault."

"That's very generous of you, but I still feel really bad about it. It just goes to prove I'm not the best choice to help you with this chairmanship thing."

"Don't be so hasty." Ian maneuvered the car into the parking lot alongside Gina's apartment building. "I still think this could work." He parked the car. Turning, he put his hand over her hands, which she had clenched in her lap. "Please, don't give up yet."

Gina studied his face. His bottom lip was cracked and bloody, his left eye drooped to half-mast, which had to hurt. Streaks of blood decorated his collar.

He smiled at her in that earnest way of his.

She wanted to reach out, touch his cheek then kiss his poor, cracked lip with a soothing, gentle kiss, but she didn't because underneath it all, she was a chicken. She could really fall head over heels for Ian Ross, which scared her half to death.

She was even more afraid that he was still in love with Andi Kelly.

Ian's little smile wilted. "I can see you still have some reservations about this. How about I give you a little bit more time so you can think about it?"

She dragged her bag onto her shoulder before reaching for the door handle. Suddenly shy, she demurred when all she really wanted to say *yes*. "I guess I can do that." She pushed the door open.

"I'll call you in about a week, okay? You can give me your answer then."

Gina stepped out of the car and peered back in at him. She really had to work to stop herself from reaching in to smooth his blood matted hair off his forehead. This was not the way the evening was supposed to end. He should want nothing more to do with her. "I can do that." She smiled. "Thanks for the ride and all to the game. I had fun until the last part of it."

Ian nodded. "Thank you for my first hockey game. It was interesting."

Yeah, right. And she was the Queen of England. "Sure." Her bag slipped off her shoulder. She jerked it back up. "Well, thanks for driving. Good night."

"Sweet dreams."

Gina turned and walked to her apartment, opened her door, reached in and hit the inside light. Looking back, Gina saw him waiting for her. She waved, and he drove off into the night.

The next week was going to be a long one.

What the heck was she going to do about Ian?

Chapter Eight

"No! And then what happened?" Sandy's eyes were like big golf balls, set to bounce right out of her face. Naturally, she had to know all the gory details of the hockey game and its aftermath.

Gina shook her head with a smile, before drinking another hit of the coffee she was mainlining by the gallon. After the night she'd had, the dead last thing she wanted was to get up and prep for the Friday lunch crowd. However, a girl needed to eat and pay the rent.

Taking advantage of the before-lunch calm environment, Gina leaned back in her seat at the bar and tried not to cringe. "Then, we got stopped on the way home because he had a taillight out. The cop smelled the beer and suspected Ian was drunk."

"Holy crud." Sandy ran her finger around the edge of the plate that had held her lemon-filled, powdered sugar donut, then sucked it into her mouth. "What'd the cop do?" Sandy asked around her finger.

"If you're hungry, go have another donut."

Sandy made her fingers into a cross and held them in front of her face. "Get thee behind me, Satan!" She put her hands down while shaking her head. "I can't have another donut. You *know* I have to lose ten pounds." She glanced askance at the empty plate. "I probably shouldn't have eaten *that* donut. But don't change the subject. What happened after the cop stopped you?"

Gina sighed. "The same stuff that always happens when they stop you and think you're drunk driving, I guess. I wouldn't know."

"Yeah, okay, but you were there. What did he do? Hey, Spike." Sandy smiled as Spike came on for her shift. "Is that today's paper?"

Spike slid a glance over to Gina as she jammed the newspaper up under her arm, as if she were trying to hide or protect it. It was a little weird. Spike always put the paper out on the bar for everyone to read when they got a chance.

Stowing the paper and her purse under the bar, Spike smiled really, really huge. "Hi," she said. "What's up?"

Sandy looked at Gina, her eyebrows raised in question.

Gina shrugged.

Frowning, Sandy looked back at Spike. "Anything good in the paper?"

"Nope," Spike said a little too quickly. "Nothing good at all."

Hmmm, curiouser and curiouser. Spike followed the Bruins with a fervor that bordered on the religious. "You mean there's nothing about last night's Bruins' game?"

Spike turned her back to check the liquor inventory. She counted the same bottle of whiskey five times. Something was up. She moved onto the vodka bottles as she said, "You mean when they cleared the bench?"

"Yeah."

Spike stopped and stood dead still.

Gina could hear Bobby slamming around pans in the kitchen. The coffee machine gurgled as it finished brewing the latest pot.

Sandy clicked her fingernails on the top of the bar, an impatient gesture that said she was dying to discover the reason for Spike's unusual behavior.

"You know, Spike," she said, "You can't hold a secret for crap. What's going on?"

Spike turned to face Gina and Sandy, looked at them for one long, slow moment, then pulled the paper out from under the bar and laid it on top. "I guess it's only a matter of time until you see this," she said to Gina. "I just hate to be the one to show it to you." Misery written all over her face, she pushed the paper Gina's way.

Sandy intercepted it and opened it with a snap. "Enquiring minds want to know," she murmured as she flipped through the pages, then stopped. "Whoa," she breathed. "Would you look at that?"

Gina leaned in for a better look. In black and white, the announcement of Mike and Andi's wedding along with a lovely portrait of the happy bride and groom, stared back.

How sucky was it that the wedding announcements usually came out so much later than the actual event?

She could feel Sandy and Spike staring at her, waiting for some sort of reaction. But to tell the truth, she didn't know how she felt. Not so long ago, like, say, yesterday, she knew she would have felt sorrow, jealousy, anger, envy, probably all at the same time in a sort of nasty emotional stew.

But she *didn't* feel that way. She looked at that picture and yeah, she felt a little jealous of Mike and Andi's happiness, but no more than that. She certainly didn't feel like her world was ending.

She wondered if Ian had seen the picture, and if he had, how he felt about it. Probably pretty damn bad, like she should be feeling. The first distinct pang of sadness bubbled in her gut. Poor Ian.

Wow. Knowing that this picture was going to bother Ian, now *that* gave her more than a pang or two of jealousy. Thinking about Ian pining away as he looked at Andi and Mike's wedding picture made her so jealous, the ugly emotion sang whole operas through her system. She snatched at the pen stuck in her ponytail, then tapped it on top of Andi's gorgeous, happy, smiling, so-in-love face. "She isn't very photogenic, is she?" Gina blacked out one of the bride's teeth. "There. That's more like it, don't you think?"

Sandy grabbed Gina's pen, blacking out another.. "I don't know. I think it needs more." She added a pair of devil's horns to the top of Andi's head. "That's better. What do *you* think, Spike?" She handed the pen over to Spike, who then drew a scar across Andi's forehead, a tongue hanging out of Andi's mouth and a noose around her neck. "Whaddaya think?"

"Hello, girls. How's it going?"

Gina froze as she heard the gruff, rumbly tones of the man behind her. Only one man owned this force of nature voice. Deke Nelson. The father of the bride whose picture they were gleefully defacing. She turned to look at him.

Spike slammed the paper closed. Smiling a huge, cheesy smile at Deke, she chirped, "Hey, Deke. What can I do for you today?"

"A table would be nice. I'm meeting Dave Mason to talk about a mentoring program. We're trying to match up kids in need of motivation with some of the Rangers' guys." He shrugged. "Maybe it'll work."

"That's great, really great." Gina directed Deke by inclining her head. "I'm sure that will make Mike real happy."

Deke wasn't budging. "Yeah, but it's more Andi I'm worried about. She's got a list of kids who need mentoring that's about as long as my arm."

Uh-oh, Deke dropped the A-bomb. Time to get him to a table, STAT. "Well, I've got a real nice table for you. I'll set you up with a beer while you wait."

"Sure. But first," Deke reached over and opened

the closed newspaper back up to the social page. "Give me a pen." He grinned as he took the pen out of Spike's hand. "Thanks." He drew a Groucho nose, mustache and glasses on the picture of Mike's happy, smiling face, then handed the pen back to Spike. "Now it's perfect." He turned that grin to Gina. "Where's that table?"

****

"Ian, may I have a word with you?" Donald Unger's voice echoed down the French Department's empty corridor .

Ian stopped dead in his tracks, then closed his eyes to mentally curse Donald Unger. His nose ached, his head pounded. He had hoped to sneak in and out of the department without anyone seeing him.

It was a freaking Sunday. The halls of the University were supposed to be deserted.

Wasn't it just his damned luck to get caught by the one man he wished would vanish off the face of the earth? He turned to face him. "Unger." He nodded. "What do you want?"

Unger's rubber-soled shoes squeegeed as he trundled down the hall. When he caught up to Ian, his eyebrows lifted as he took in Ian's face. "Well, it looks like you had quite the weekend."

"You could say that." Ian looked at his watch. "I'm pressed for time right now, so..." He left the question hanging in the air.

Still smiling the ugly, oily little smile that Ian hated, Unger looked at his own watch. "I won't take much of your time. As you know, I'm helping the chairman of the personnel committee compile the credentials for the candidates for merit pay increases. I've got some questions about your publication list."

Ian hadn't known that little fact, but it didn't surprise him Unger had questions about his publication list. If God were up for merit pay, Unger would have problems with *His* publication list. "The information I turned in is complete and up to date. I can't imagine what questions you could have." He knew exactly what was going on. If Unger could discredit him, he'd have a clearer shot at the chairmanship.

Hmmpff. That would happen when pigs flew.

"You know how these things go. Sometimes a second pair of eyes can pick up discrepancies we don't see when we're too close to the project."

Discrepancies? Not a chance. "What discrepancies?"

"Nothing that can't be easily explained, I'm sure." Unger rooted around in the pile of files and very quickly found the item he sought. "We simply need more outside verification of the items I've circled in red." He offered the paper to Ian. "I'm sure you can clear this up *post haste*."

Ian took the list. Fourteen of the fifteen articles he had published in the past academic year were circled. "What kind of outside verification? Everything you need to know is right there on the list."

"Nothing much. Just attach a copy of the journal's table of contents for each article on the list. For verification purposes when we process the merit pay raises." There was that slimy grin again.

Ian suppressed a sigh. This had to be some Mickey Mouse stunt designed to annoy him. He would bet his last dollar he was the only one applying for merit pay who'd been asked to provide such documentation. Ah, well. Though most of his articles had been published in French journals, as well as being written in French, he owned copies of all the journals. Documenting his work would be easy. "Fine. I'll have your documentation ready for you by the end of the day tomorrow."

"Splendid." Unger looked at his own watch. "Well, I know you're in a hurry. Don't let me keep you."

"Right." Ian turned and walked the rest of the way down the hall to his office. He got there, let himself in, then shut the door. After dropping his things on his desk, he went to the shelf where he kept the journals that contained his published articles.

The ones he needed were missing.

Immediately, he remembered finding Unger in his office that day last week. That rat bastard had nicked his journals! Ian had been so worried about his current research it hadn't occurred to him Unger might be undermining him in other ways.

Furious, but powerless to do anything more than fling out accusations he couldn't substantiate, Ian fumed all the way to the library. Wouldn't you know it—all the journals Ian needed were checked out to a graduate student.

A graduate student Ian knew was in Paris for the semester.

A graduate student who just happened to be Donald Unger's teaching assistant last semester.

Being a Sunday, none of the librarians were there. All the work-study students could do was to leave a note for them. But really, there was nothing they could do. Those journals weren't there, and it would take longer to find them than it would to call France and request faxed copies from the publishing houses.

Damned inconvenient.

He made it back to his office, forced himself to calm down by breathing deeply twenty-five times, then began to make his calls. The phone rang once, twice, all the way to nine times before Ian realized that not only was it Sunday in France, it was also 9:00 in the evening, given the time difference.

He clenched his hand around the receiver and started to shake. Swamped by frustration, he jerked on the phone cord so hard he pulled it out of the wall. Without a second thought, he flung it across the room where it hit a wall with such force it shattered.

Calmer, he made a few decisions, the first and most important of which had to be making sure Donald Unger's dirty tricks didn't work. Ian would be the department chair , if it was the last thing he did. Then he would rub Unger's nose in it and make the man's life a living hell.

Yeah, that sounded like a good plan.

****

As far as Gina was concerned, there was nothing better than having a free Sunday night. It ranked right up there with the scent of roses, chocolate truffles and world peace. She had taken a bath in too-hot, rose-scented water and brought a piece of the restaurant's most calorific and irresistible cheesecake home with her.

She'd figure out world peace later.

But right now, she was ready to indulge in her most guilty pleasure—any and all movies by the most bodacious Hugh Jackman.

An hour into X-Men, she desperately wished for another piece of that chocolate cheesecake. About to rummage through her kitchen cabinets for anything that would be a comparable substitute, she swore when she heard her doorbell ring. She put the DVD player on pause while she went to the door, so she didn't miss any second of too-luscious-for-words Hugh.

She went to her apartment door and peeked through the peephole. "Damn," she whispered. Just what she needed, Ian Ross on the other side. Against her better judgment, she opened the door.

"I need your decision now," he said without

preamble, without observing any of the social niceties the British were so famous for. He took off his coat and tossed it on her sofa. Grim and rigid, he oozed anger.

"My decision?" Boy howdy, he looked mad.

"Yes. Some things have happened, and the stakes have been upped." He fixed a very intense stare on her. "I need to know right away if you are going to help me get this chairmanship."

Gina stopped breathing for a second. The energy pouring off of him made her squirm. "I don't..."

Without any warning, he took her in his arms and pulled her close. "Maybe this will help you decide."

He crashed his mouth down onto hers and swept her into a stunning, mind-blowing, sanity-stealing kiss.

Chapter Nine

Ian swallowed Gina's initial *hummmpf* of surprise, and then coaxed her lips open. He teased her tongue out to play with his. His nerve endings sizzled as she kissed him back and rubbed up against him. She climbed up on tiptoe and twined her arms around his neck.

He hadn't meant to kiss her, but now that he was actually doing just that, well, might as well be damned for a lion instead of a lamb.

Something inside him loosened and shifted, making some of the desperation driving him dissipate. Oh, Lord, she wasn't wearing a bra. Those centerfold breasts of hers pillowed soft against his body. He slid his hands down to her hips to yank her closer. She hummed again while she twined her arms around his neck.

Well. Happy Christmas to him. He deepened the kiss. He slid his hands under her shirt and reveled in the soft skin he found there.

Sweet, she tasted so sweet, of chocolate, of coffee, of every seductive hunger he'd ever had. And he wanted more.

He steered them to Gina's couch and fell on it, bringing Gina down to straddle his lap. Pulling her tee shirt off over her head, he bared her breasts, cupped them and brought his mouth to suckle first one nipple, then the other.

She threaded her hands in his hair as she pulled herself closer to him, giving him easier access to her breasts. Her response thrilled him and sent all the blood in his body to pool below his waist, as she undulated on his lap.

****

Ian's mouth was so hot and just felt so *damn* good, Gina's head fell back as she let him suckle her nipples. Her breathing hitched as he nibbled on her stiffened little nubs.

She grew impossibly wet. He grew impossibly hard against her stomach. She rubbed herself against him, center to center. Gina felt the ends of her hair whisper softly over her spine. Ian murmured something as he moved his mouth from one breast to the other, but she couldn't make out what he said. "What?"

He lifted his extremely unfocused gaze to look at her, for all intents and purposes stopping his magic mouth. "What?"

Suddenly it was as if a strong, cold wind had blown through the room, breaking the spell between them. Gina became extremely aware of the fact that she was naked from the waist up as goosebumps the size of moon rocks popped up on her skin. "Where's my shirt?" She pushed herself off his lap and covered her breasts with her hands.

Ian pushed his glasses up his nose and looked to either side of him. Locating the shirt wedged between the seat and the back of the sofa, he liberated it and handed it to her. Then, adjusting himself, he levered himself off the couch to pace. "I'm sorry. I swear I didn't come here to attack you."

Gina scrambled into her shirt. Her face flushed hot. "I think you need to go now."

"No!" Ian winced. "Please, just hear me out." He gentled his voice. "It's been an extremely bad day, and you looked so... I can't justify my actions. I know you should just toss me out the door, but please, I beg you." He blinked. "Don't. Just let me make my case."

Gina put her thumb in her mouth to gnaw at her nail." You promised..."

He turned to face her. God, his eyes were on fire. "I know I did, but some things have happened in the department to raise the stakes. I have to know now."

"What will you do if I say no?" Never mind that the point of the whole hockey game exercise was to make him give up the engagement of convenience idea.

He rubbed a hand over his face. "God. I don't know. I hadn't counted on you saying no."

"Well, that's *so* flattering. Poor Gina's got nothing else going on in her life; she can pretend to be in love with me."

He shook his head. "No, it's not like that at all. I know you've got a life. I'm not saying this well." He took off his glasses, pulled a handkerchief out of his pocket and began to clean them. It looked like he was contemplating breaking them then swallowing the glass. Then, he nodded. "You are a wonderful, beautiful, vibrant woman. A woman any man would be crazy to resist." His self-deprecating smile looked a little bit shy. "Lord knows, I can't."

He gave a small, cute little exhale as he tilted his head to one side. "Look, Donald Unger has started to undermine my position in earnest. If I want that chair, I have to gather my defenses and rally my troops. There's a really big reception coming up. I told Unger I have a date for it." He looked around for his coat. "Never mind, it's not your problem. I'll go now. Sorry I bothered you."

Damn. "When's our next date?"

Ian stopped in the middle of shrugging into his coat. "What?"

"I'll do it. I'll help you kick some academic, French Department chairmanship butt and save you from your boss' wife's niece."

"Do you mean it?"

"I wouldn't say it if I didn't. Besides, what the hell? What do I have to lose? You're an attractive guy and a good sport. A girl could do worse."

"Yes, well." Ian looked embarrassed. His smile was so sweet. "I can't thank you enough. I'll ring you tomorrow with the details, if that's okay?" He reached for the door handle then stopped and looked at the floor. His throat opened and closed at random, like he didn't know what to say. "Uh, you really think I'm attractive?"

She gave him her best *get real* look. "Given what just happened on my couch not fifteen minutes ago, I'd say yeah, you're attractive. Totally sexy."

He blushed like a schoolgirl. Totally enchanted, Gina reached up to caress his cheek.

He caught her hand and pressed a kiss into her palm. "Well, then, I'll say good night." He opened her door, then looked back at her. "You're an amazing woman, Gina. Don't let anyone tell you you're not."

****

Donnie wiped his greasy hands on an equally greasy rag. "I don't know what else to tell you, Gina. The clutch is shot. Nothing else to do except pull out the engine and put a new one in."

As garages went, Donnie's was typical. There were only two lifts which both had cars up on them. The light was diffused, due to the amount of grime on the window. The air was redolent with the smells of tire rubber, motor oil, and then layered with heavy-duty hand soap. The radio blared, while Clint Black sang about seeing nothing but the taillights. His competition was some sort of electric tool that made a loud, rhythmic *whizzzz-thwap* noise.

Gina's car had finally given up the ghost and she'd had it towed to Donnie's for him to fix it.

"A new clutch? That's pretty expensive."

Donnie nodded his head. "I could find you a

rebuilt one. It wouldn't be as expensive. The problem isn't the part, it's the labor. The whole engine has to come out."

Gina sighed while she did the math in her head. "I guess I better go talk to Bobby about pulling some double shifts."

Donnie grimaced. "I'm sorry, Gina. I wish I could cut you a little slack." He gave her a crooked little smile. "Business has been down, what with the price of gas and all. I gotta pay attention to the bottom line."

"Yeah, sure." *Whatever.* "Thanks." Donnie had been one of her brother's drinking buddies back in high school. In spite of that fact, he was an okay guy.

"Come on in the office. I'll write you up an estimate." Donnie stuck the grease-laden rag in his coveralls' back pocket.

Gina followed him into the office, still counting the money she currently had in her checking and savings accounts. She had nowhere near enough to cover even a part of this bill. She was in for a few long weeks of double shifts.

She wouldn't mind working. It was just that she'd agreed to do this date thing with Ian. How could she explain this to him?

"Hey, Gina. What are you doing here?"

Gina's head turned with a snap as she heard Mike Kelly's voice. Yep, there he was, in all his hunky glory. "Mikey! I thought you were on your honeymoon?"

Mike grinned. He looked so happy it had to be nearly obscene. He looked so gorgeous, all tanned and windblown. "I was. We just got back yesterday."

"Oh." She totally lost her ability for small talk. "Well, did you have a good time?"

Mike's eyes kind of glazed over for a moment. "Oh, yeah."

"Here ya go, Mike." Pete, Donnie's assistant,

handed Mike a set of keys and a credit card slip.

Mike took the keys and pocketed the slip of paper. "Thanks, Pete." He looked back to Gina. "You need a ride somewhere?" He tilted his head toward the garage. "I saw your car up on the lift."

Well, wasn't that an interesting offer. While she'd rather not walk to work, she didn't think she wanted to spend any time enclosed in a small space with a delirious, so-in-love-with-his-wife, just-back-from-his-honeymoon, Mike. "Uh, I..."

"It's pretty nasty out there. Are you going to work? I've got to go by The End Zone anyway to catch up with Dave."

She glanced down at her boots. With their high, funky heels and brown suede uppers, they were not made for negotiating through slush. She *so* didn't want to ruin them.

That's right. She'd take the ride for the sake of her shoes. What girl wouldn't? "Sure. Thanks." She looked away from Mike and focused on Donnie, who came out of his office with her estimate. "You've got my number?"

He nodded. "Yep."

"Any idea when you'll have it finished?"

"Coupla days at the earliest. Call me on Thursday morning."

Oh, goody. A week of having to mooch rides off of Sandy. Her mood turned a little blacker. "Will do. Thanks, Donnie."

Donnie grinned, then nodded again, like an eager but not too bright puppy.

Mike held the door for her and motioned her through it. She looked but didn't see his car. He noticed. "I've got Andi's car. We got it inspected while we were away." He steered her toward a classy, dark green, late-model BMW.

Of course, Princess Andi would have a BMW. The training wheels on her first bike had probably been precision engineered in Germany.

Mike held the door open for Gina so she could slide in.

Sliding into the driver's seat, he turned the key. The car purred to life. The radio came on, and some lovely classical music filled the plush space. "I don't think so," he murmured, while he punched some buttons. Country music pumped out of the speakers. He grinned at Gina. "I love my wife, but *damn*, she has terrible taste in music."

Gina looked at him. "I don't know. It must be nice to know about all that music and art stuff." She thought of Ian. She would need to take some crash courses in the arts if she intended to fool or impress anyone on the French faculty.

Mike laughed. "If you say so. I'll leave all that to Andi. You got time for me to run an errand before I get you to work?"

"Depends on the errand." Man, she was in a bad mood if she got grumpy with Mike.

"I want to run through the drive-thru at the photo place. The pictures from our trip should be ready."

"Why not? Go for it." Gina looked out the passenger side window.

The detour to Photo Express took only a couple of minutes. Mike was annoyingly cheerful, whistling along with the radio. They went through the booth, got the photos, and then Mike pulled over to park. "Do you mind? I just want to flip through them."

"Go ahead. I'm good."

He smiled as he looked through the photos, his eyes bright and avid. He spent an inordinate amount of time on one photo. "I knew this one would turn out great." He handed it to Gina.

The picture showed Andi, dressed in a romantic, floral print, floaty dress. She stood on a beach at the water's edge, the brilliance of a glorious sunset rising behind her. She was laughing and lovely.

Gina handed it back to Mike. "It's a good picture of Andi," she said. "Looks like you had a great time."

Mike looked at the picture with a goofy, sappy grin, and then put it in the photo envelope. He slipped the car into gear, navigating out of the parking lot towards The End Zone.

They got there none too soon.

Sandy grabbed her the minute she walked in the door. "Look what just came for you." She pointed to the biggest flower arrangement Gina had ever seen outside of the winner's circle of the Kentucky Derby. Sandy practically salivated as she handed Gina the card. "Who are they from?"

Gina raised an eyebrow as she waved the card at Sandy. "You mean you didn't already look?"

"'Course not. I respect your privacy."

"It was touch and go, though," Dave added from his perch at the bar. "Hey, Mike."

Mike nodded. "Nice flowers. Who're they from, Gina?"

Gina took a deep breath while she opened the card.

My eternal thanks. Yours, Ian.

Well, well...

"What's the card say, Gina?" Sandy plucked the card out of Gina's numb fingers, then read it. "You've been holdin' out on me, girlfriend." She ran the card against the fingers of one hand, so that it made a muffled *thwip* against each finger. "That must have been some hockey game the other night."

Dave's brows knitted across his forehead. "Hockey game? You went to the hockey game with Ian Ross. Those flowers are from him?"

"Ian Ross as in Ian, the Haiku Guy?" Mike leaned against the bar. "How do you know him?"

Gina rolled her eyes. Someone needed to give the man a clue. "We met at that ballet gala thing.

Remember?" She sighed. "You took me to it."

"Oh, yeah." Mike scratched his left temple. "You've been seeing him?"

"He took her to the hockey game the other night," said the ever-helpful Dave.

"Oh, really." Mike had a funny look on his face. "Did he send you a poem, too?"

"Poem?" Gina stared at the flowers, like they might jump up and bite her.

"Yeah. He used to send Andi flowers all the time, usually with a poem or something like that. Haikus." Mike suddenly didn't look so content. "He wrote a whole book of poems and dedicated it to her."

Dave slapped Mike on the back. "Looks like you need to brush up on your poetry skills."

"I managed one poem in my life, and that's my quota." Mike looked around. "Want to get a table?"

Sandy took the hint. She took Dave and Mike to a table while Gina brooded over the card.

No poem. Only freakin' Andi Kelly inspired poetry. Gina inspired thank you notes. Well, she should be happy with the flowers and the note. She shook her head at herself then took the bouquet and buried her face it. They smelled lovely. Really, when was the last one anyone had sent her flowers?

But she needed to face facts. Ian could never love anyone the way he had loved Andi. She should stop herself from falling for him before it was too late.

Except, maybe it already was too late which totally sucked.

Chapter Ten

As a general rule of thumb, Ian hated department parties. One would think since everybody in the department was interested in French as well as literature, he would have a good time talking to like-minded people about their similar passions.

Uh-unh.

Every party he had ever attended turned into a dog and pony show, littered with fake joviality.

Truth be told, he didn't have a single friend among his colleagues, save the department chair, Ralph Jameson, and his wife. Not a single one of them had ever invited him out for a beer.

Of course, that could be his fault. He was not incredibly interested in socializing with any of them.

He saved what he had been writing, then rose from his desk chair and started to pace. He had been beyond ready to make love to Gina the other night. She had been very nearly naked, and oh so willing in his arms, until something had made her stop.

Most likely, she realized his arms held her, not Mike's.

Bugger it.

He went to the liquor cabinet and poured himself a brandy. While he poured, his phone rang. He let the machine answer it.

"Ian, if you are there, you must pick up."

His mother.

He took a healthy swig of brandy as she rattled

on.

"Your father has really done it this time. Not only has he married this... this... this stripper, but now she is with child. Are you there, Ian? Are you hearing this? In a few months, you are going to have a baby brother or sister. My God, Ian, I could positively retch, that's how sick this whole situation makes me. It is absolutely, positively humiliating. Why, if I didn't know better, I'd think your father is doing this just to embarrass me. It's galling, that's what it is. Simply..."

"Thank you for your message," beeped the answering machine.

"Bloody hell." Ian took another huge swallow of his brandy.

The phone rang again. Since Ian knew it to be his mother on a rampage, he left the room.

****

Gina looked into her closet while she prayed for a clue as to what to wear to a French Department party. She doubted her Ray Bourque jersey would suffice.

More's the pity.

She rubbed her eyes. Damn, she felt tired. All she wanted was a bath, followed by a bed. She could probably sleep for a thousand years, if she got the chance.

Instead, she was going to be Ian Ross's fiancée for the night. She caught a glimpse of herself in the mirror and shuddered. "You look terrible," she pointed out to her reflection. "You should run a bath and soak for a good long time. Until you feel human again." Problem was, she'd most likely fall asleep in the tub.

Okay, so it was the shower for her. She ran the water a little cooler than she liked, more a cold, needle-like spray rather than the hot mist she usually preferred. At least she could feel some blood pumping to her heart, giving her a new lease on life.

As for the rest of her, she tried for dignified with her hair and make up. She did all right with the make up, but her hair...

There was no way her hair would ever do dignified. She managed a really lumpy looking French twist.

Of course, Andi Kelly wore her hair in a perfect looking French twist every day. She probably wore a perfect French twist to bed only to wake up with every hair still in place. Gina knew for sure every person at the party would have met perfect Andi. Andi probably fit in like Flynn with Ian's colleagues.

The reasons to hate Andi Kelly just kept coming.

In the end, Gina settled on a black suit with a kicky flared skirt and a tight, peplum jacket she had bought with the idea of going to visit her brother in prison. In the end, she hadn't gone. Nick hadn't wanted her to visit, so she hadn't. She'd never worn the suit.

With some cubic zirconias in her ears and some fake pearls around her throat, she was ready to rock and roll. Shoes were the only thing she would not compromise on, so she had some killer patent leather stilettos that pulled everything together.

Her stomach churned while she waited for Ian. No way, was she going to fit in with a group of card-carrying academics.

No doubt about it, she was toast.

Her doorbell startled her. Ian was here. Grabbing her coat, she plastered a smile on her face and opened the door.

Ian was there all right. He looked adorable. His hair was attractively rumpled; his glasses a little foggy from coming in from the cold, and his hands were jammed into his pants pockets. "Hello." He smiled. "Are you ready?"

She shoved her arms into her coat sleeves.

"About as ready as I'll ever be." Grabbing her bag, she slung it over her shoulder.

"Well, you look incredible." Could that be admiration she saw shining in his eyes? A girl could hope.

"Let's go." She closed the door behind her and pretended to be a whole lot more confident than she really felt.

****

"You should try these escargots. They're really great." A very rotund, very enthusiastic older man shoved a plate of garlicky, buttery, snail-filled puff pastries under Gina's nose.

I think not. While she considered herself a foodie, she was not particularly fond of snails. The ones being waved around in front of her looked none too appetizing. "No thank you." She looked around for a glimpse of Ian. He still waded through the crowds around the bar, trying to get some drinks.

Pudgy pulled the plate out of Gina's space and shrugged. "You sure? You don't know what you're missing." He picked one up and popped it in his mouth. "They're scrumptious," he said around the mouthful of food. "I don't think we've met." He pulled a balled-up napkin from his pants and wiped his buttery fingers on it before holding out his hand. "Marshall Jenkins. I teach Balzac."

Wow, did this guy have a cushy gig, if all he did was teach this one Balzac kid. Sheesh! She shook the hand he offered. "Gina Francisco. It's nice to meet you." She gave him an enthusiastic smile. "What subjects do you teach him?"

Marshall opened his mouth and blinked a couple of times. Gina noticed he had butter stains on his tie.

"Here we are, Gina." Ian sidled up to her to press a plastic glass filled with white wine and a cocktail napkin into her hand.

"Thanks." She smiled at him. "Marshall was just telling me about his student."

"His student." Ian looked from Gina to Marshall. "Which one?"

Realizing she had made a mistake, Gina took a big sip of wine.

Marshall took the opportunity to mutter an excuse to get away and took off toward the buffet table.

Ian shrugged his shoulders. "Must have been something I said."

"No, I think I just made a fool of myself." She took another sip of wine. It tasted pretty awful, nearly as bad as the house white at The End Zone. "He told me that he taught Balzac, so I assumed said Balzac was Marshall's only student." She rolled her eyes as Ian choked on a mouthful of scotch. "I'm sorry. I'll keep my mouth shut from now on."

He barked out a laugh. "You're joking."

"Like I could make that up," she muttered.

"Actually," Ian's eyes twinkled. "We don't want it to get around that old Marshall only teaches the one student." Ian sighed. "His name is Porky Balzac. He is the ne'er do well scion of the Philadelphia Balzac's Sausage fortune." He cleared his throat. "Hence the name Porky. Porky is none too bright, so his parents are paying Marshall a small fortune to get him through school. It's sinful, really. Disgusting." He shook his head.

Gina nudged him in the side with her elbow. He gave a satisfying oomph sound. "Stop teasing me, Ian. I know I screwed up. Just tell me who Balzac really is and let me die of embarrassment in peace."

"Balzac was a famous French novelist, sort of the French equivalent of Charles Dickens." He took a sip of his scotch. "But it is a little known secret in academia that his mother called him Porky." He reached out to touch a curl that was escaping from her French twist. "Pretty. I'd much rather look at you than talk about poor old Porky."

When he said things like that, her insides melted. Her knees turned wobbly, which, given the height of her heels, was *not* a good thing. She flicked her eyes up to his. Glory, hallelujah, the look in his eyes was hot, hot, hot. It absolutely thrilled her. It totally should be illegal since they were in a public place. She blushed, and pulled away from him.

"Ian, hello. Are you going to introduce us to your companion?"

Gina blushed while she watched all the heat leave Ian's eyes. He set his jaw, then turned his head to greet the new arrivals. "Unger." He then nodded to the woman. "Mary Louise. How lovely to see you again."

"Hello, Ian." A well-kept, fifty-something woman gave Ian a brief hug. Dressed like a walking advertisement for Talbots, Mary Louise Unger exuded confidence and class. She turned her gaze to Gina, smiling as she held out her hand. "Mary Louise Unger."

Gina smiled back and shook hands. "Gina Francisco."

Mary Louise looked at her husband. "Donald, I think you've been keeping secrets. You didn't tell me Ian has a new girlfriend."

Unger slapped Ian on the back, earning himself a dark look from Ian. "Our Ian is quite the man of mystery these days." He extended a hand to Gina. "Donald Unger." He grabbed her hand and pumped it. "Pleased to meet you, Gina."

"Hi." Gina had a second sense about difficult people. It was necessary in her business to anticipate the tough customers. Even if she hadn't already known about how Donald Unger tried to undermine Ian, she would have been able to tell just by the looks of him that he was not Ian's best buddy.

She snuck a glance at Ian. He downed what looked to be a healthy dose of single malt. She really wished she knew what he was thinking.

"Ian, darling! Is that you, dear boy?" Gina looked beyond Ian to see a mountain of a woman, resplendent in a peacock-tail print, silk muumuu, move in to greet Ian.

A look of genuine pleasure lit up his face. "Margaret." He turned to greet her. "Good to see you."

Margaret huffed a little as she stood on tiptoe to kiss Ian's cheek. "You devil. Where have you been keeping yourself these days?"

"I would have thought he was up to his ears in his new project, but I think I would be wrong," Donald Unger piped up. "Have you met Ian's new friend?"

Margaret's gaze zoomed in on Gina with the speed and accuracy of a laser guided missile. "No, I haven't had the pleasure." She extended her hand. "Margaret Jameson. Ever since my husband told me Ian was seeing someone new, I've been dying to meet you. Of course, my niece is *très desolé.*"

"Gina Francisco." Gina shook Margaret's hand. "Ian's mentioned me?" She glanced up at him.

"Well, yes," Ian said, very clearly discomfited with the direction of the conversation. He juggled his glass of scotch to his left hand then took off his glasses. "I, uh, I did mention you in passing to Ralph. I hope you don't mind."

Gina held back a sigh. Flustered Ian was really cute.

She took the scotch from him and looped her arm in his. "Guess our secret's out, right, sweetie?"

Ian put his glasses back on then reclaimed possession of his drink. "Indeed."

Margaret beamed at them with unashamed and rapt attention. "Secret? I love secrets." She linked her arm with Gina's to pull her away from the group. "You'll have to tell me everything, young lady. Absolutely all of the scintillating details."

Gina felt a momentary moment of panic, but then looked at Margaret. Kindness and a touch of mischief lingered in her expression, relaxing Gina. Maybe she'd get some big clues on how to proceed from here with Ian.

****

Ian felt a guilty twinge as he watched Margaret pull Gina away. He knew Margaret meant well, but he also knew she was a veritable steamroller when on a fact-finding mission.

Right. He might as well hope that the sun wouldn't rise while he was at it. Margaret Jameson was a force to be reckoned with.

Rather like a hurricane or an erupting volcano.

With a short, silent, heartfelt prayer that Gina would be okay, Ian turned his attention to Donald and his wife. The pair stood there with matched sharky smiles, clearly out for blood. He cast another glance Gina's way, wishing he had gone with her.

"She's a lovely girl, Ian. Not at all your usual type. Where did you find her?" Unger toasted him with his own cocktail then took a fussy little sip.

Ian felt his hackles rise. "Not my type? What makes you say that?"

"Of course, she's a beautiful woman, Ian," Mary Louise simpered. "But she's very different from Andrea, that's all. I'm looking forward to getting to know her." She swished the ice in her glass around. The melting cubes made a clunky knock against the inside of the plastic glass. "What does she do?"

Ah. He'd been waiting for this question. Trust Mary Louisa Unger to bring it up. "Do?"

Unger chuckled. "Yes. What's her field?"

Unger was a pompous blowhard. "She's a waitress at The End Zone." *Go choke on that, idiot.*

He craned his neck to see over Unger's shoulder.

Gina stood at the buffet table with Margaret and Ralph Jameson. The Jamesons were laughing at something she said. As for Gina herself, she was rearranging the food set out on the buffet table. Fortunately, the Jamesons didn't seem to notice.

Still, the strong urge to go to the buffet and make sure all was going well pulled at Ian's gut. He nodded to Unger and his wife. "If you'll excuse me."

"Of course. We'll see you later, Ian."

But Ian hardly heard her. He took off to forestall disaster.

****

"Now that is interesting." Mary Louise Unger pursed her lips.

Donald Unger concurred, as if he had a choice. "One would surmise our Ian doesn't trust his new lady friend with the department chairman."

Mary Louise sniffed. "She doesn't seem particularly bright."

"One doesn't need to be a rocket scientist to figure out why he's attracted to her."

If looks could kill, he'd be six feet under. "Much like you and that graduate teaching assistant I caught you with?"

Donald couldn't win. He opened his mouth to apologize—again—but Mary Louise would never forgive or forget. "I've heard it all. Save it for someone who cares." She cocked her head to the side. "I wonder how much our Ian has told her about his research?"

Donald shrugged. "Why would that matter? My sources tell me he's on the verge of something big. The girlfriend doesn't look the type to understand much, if any, of it."

"Still, pillow talk and all. He might have let a few things slip. She looks like she's just dim enough not to know what to say and what to keep to herself." She put her glass up to her mouth and downed the melted ice cubes. "We had to spend an enormous chunk of my inheritance making sure that graduate assistant keeps her mouth shut about your extra-curricular activities, all so you could get that chairmanship. I will not lose it now because Ian Ross has some brilliant project that makes your work look like moronic scribblings."

Donald hated her most of all for her disdain for his scholarship. "My work is hardly moronic. Some find it brilliant…" He motioned with his head toward Ian. "*More* brilliant than wonder boy's."

"No matter." Mary Louise waved her hand in dismissal. "We need every last bit of ammunition we can get so you're the one to win the chair, not Ian Ross." She looked him right in the eyes, direct enough to make him squirm. "We can't let Ian Ross get that chair, Donald. I simply will not let that happen."

Chapter Eleven

"Why did you tell everyone I'm a waitress?" Gina shook her head as she looked out the passenger's window of Ian's car. The night flew by.

"Because you are." Ian kept his eyes on the road. "Why are you ashamed of it?"

"I'm not." At least she didn't *think* so. "I don't see how dating a waitress is going to help you get the chairmanship."

Ian looked at her. "What you do or don't do has no bearing on the quality of my work or my ability to lead the department." He looked back to the road. "That's the final yardstick, when all is said and done."

"Then why do you want me to go to all of these things with you?" The question flew out of her mouth before she could stop it.

"Hmm. Let me see." He flipped on the directional to make a left. The *blinka-blinka* noise filled the car until he made the turn. "I enjoy spending time with a fascinating and beautiful woman."

"Come again? I thought you wanted the chairmanship." Surely he'd had too much to drink.

"I do. I also very much enjoy your company." He chuckled then frowned. "Why is it so impossible to believe you are fascinating and beautiful?"

Gina sighed. Time to change the subject. "About this opera Margaret invited us to. I know less about opera than I do about artsy-fartsy French movies."

He snorted. "I appreciate your willingness to try it out."

"Yeah, well, Margaret didn't give me much choice. She practically invited herself over to my house to pick out my outfit."

"It's a big deal for her to invite us. Thank you for saying yes."

"Don't thank me yet. I still have to get the night off from Bobby."

Ian frowned. "Do you think you'll have a problem?"

Gina bit her bottom lip. The real problem was she needed to be working all the shifts she could in order to pay for her clutch. A night at the opera was the last thing she needed. "No. I'm pretty sure I can get the night off."

Ian looked very relieved. "Great. I promise I'll make it worth your while." He chuckled, no doubt at the grimace of doubt she couldn't conceal. "Really. The piece being performed is truly beautiful."

"Oh, really."

"One of the most beautiful operas ever written."

Like that told her much. She hadn't forgotten ancient black and white movies were his idea of rockin' entertainment. "If you say so." A thought occurred. "Don't they sing operas in other languages? As in *not* English?"

He cleared his throat. "Well, uh, yes. The one we'll see, *Tosca*, is in Italian."

"Oh, boy! I'm trembling with excitement now."

"The story is easy to follow. There's lots of action."

"Like what?"

"Oh, the usual things. People getting stabbed, shot, murdered, throwing themselves off of parapets to a horrible, gory death."

"Gee, sounds like a normal day at The End Zone."

"More like a day in the French Department, if you ask me."

That made Gina smile. "There were a lot of undercurrents going on at that party."

"To say the least." He let out a breath. "You made a very good impression. Ralph was quite taken with you. Of course, Margaret loved you. There wasn't a single mention of her niece all night long."

She bit her lip. "So this opera thing is a big deal then."

"Oh, yes. Very much so."

"That's what I figured."

Ian drove the car into a parking space next to Gina's apartment building and shut it off. She grasped the door handle, intending to get out, but he put his hand on her arm and stopped her.

"Wait right there," he said. The next thing Gina knew, Ian got out of the car to open her door for her. Smiling that shy, sweet smile that always turned her to mush, he extended his hand. "I'll walk you in."

It was a sad commentary on the state of her love life, on the state of her life in general, that a man offering a simple courtesy had the power to make her knees turn to Jell-O, not to mention how her heart got all soggy. She placed her hand in his and let him help her out of the car. The look on his face made her heart beat so heavily it was all she could hear. *Ka-thunk, ka-thunk.*

Careful of her high-heels, he helped guide her to her door. A patch of ice loomed up, and he grasped her elbow a little bit tighter.

No one in her life, in her memory, had ever cared about whether she made it past a patch of ice without hurting herself. His casual thoughtfulness made her insides hum with pleasure.

They went into her building, then up to her apartment. She started to dig into her purse for her keys and couldn't find them. Her fingers felt fat, stupid and clumsy.

He put his hand over hers and held it tight. "Stop," he said.

She looked up into his face. His smile was crooked. He wore a look in his eyes she didn't recognize. Not lust. That she would recognize. Not a just friends look either. That she had too much practice recognizing.

He brought his right hand under her chin and lifted her face to meet his gaze. Her lips parted as she took in a small gasp of breath. He didn't give her a chance to say no, he just brushed her lips with his once, twice, then settled in for a sweet and giving kiss.

He still treated her so carefully, so gently. While she would have been okay with him turning up the heat, he didn't.

Ian ended the kiss, but kept his hand on her chin as he looked into her eyes. "Thank you for tonight. I'll ring you about the opera."

Her power of speech deserting her, Gina nodded.

He smiled and kissed her again. "Good night, then." After she found her keys in her mess of a bag, he took them, opened her front door for her, then handed the keys back. "Don't forget to lock up." That said, he left.

Everything about that incredible man sang to her. Her skin prickled up when he was around. Her first thought in the morning was of him. She dreamed about him every night.

She went into her apartment, closed and locked the door, then stood there in the dark, wondering when she had fallen in love with Ian Ross. What the hell could she do about it?

The way she figured it, there wasn't much she *could* do. Ian's heart was already taken. It didn't matter that he loved another man's wife.

Or did he? Those kisses made her feel like she

was the only woman in the world. A guy had to have feelings for a woman to kiss her like that.

Well, she could only hope.

****

"Certifiably daft, that's what I am." Ian grimaced at himself in the bathroom mirror while he lathered up his face. He stared into his sleep-deprived eyes.

He had spent the better part of the wee hours of the morning on his sofa, watching his beloved video of Jean Renoir's classic film *The Grand Illusion*. It usually relaxed him. This morning, it had only filled him with questions.

Everyone at the party the night before had commented on how different Gina was from Andrea, but not everyone had had a friendly smile when they'd said it.

Well, Unger and his harpie wife didn't count. If Ian were really being honest, he'd admit he'd panicked because of the damn fool he'd made of himself when he took Gina home. What had possessed him to bare his soul like that?

Ian prided himself on his ability to gather and analyze facts. When all the gathering and analyzing was said and done, one very salient fact remained.

Gina Francisco loved Mike Kelly, not him.

He shook his head before swabbing down his face with a towel. It was scratchy because he had forgotten to add the dryer sheets again. The hardwood floors were cold as he padded down the hall to his study. He hated wearing house shoes. His mother was a maniac about them and it was a small rebellion to go barefoot.

How ridiculous for a man of nearly thirty to have cold feet just to defy his mother.

He plopped down on his desk chair and booted up his computer.

Ian had every intention of clicking on the file

that would bring up his research. Instead, he clicked on his work-in-progress poetry file. He surveyed the contents and cringed.

He hadn't been able to write a word since Andrea had married Mike Kelly. That was probably a good thing, since every single poem he had written from the last book he'd published to the blessed event was crap.

He closed his eyes and prayed for inspiration. The image of sparkling eyes, bright red curls and a gorgeous smile filled his mind. He concentrated further, conjuring the smell of Gina's perfume. Now peaceful, he smiled, cracked his knuckles, and got down to work.

****

Gina yawned and propped her chin on one hand while she stirred her coffee with the other. A week of double shifts was catching up with her. It would have been one thing if the bar had been slow, but play-offs had The End Zone hopping. She thanked the saint responsible for waitresses for the brief lull in business that allowed her to get off her feet.

Just one more week, and she'd have her clutch paid for. She hoped she lived long enough to enjoy it. She put her coffee mug to her lips and drained it. It tasted too cold and too sweet from the tons sugar she had added to give herself a sugar rush as well as a caffeine boost.

"Hey, Gina." Jeff Myers moved behind the bar, carrying a tray of clean glasses.

"Hey, Jeff. How's the new job going?"

Jeff shrugged. "It's okay, I guess." He deposited the tray of clean glasses and picked up a rack of dirty ones. Grinning at Gina, he balanced the glass rack on his shoulder. "It's not the most exciting thing I've ever done, but I need the money."

"I know what you mean." Gina shook her head. "At least you're saving up for college. That's a *lot* more exciting than paying off a new clutch."

Jeff's eyes sparked with a male's interest in all things automotive. "I don't know about that."

"Well, I do. Believe me, saving up for college beats car repairs any day."

Spike came up behind Jeff and gave him a hip check. "You two are so depressing, talking about all this saving up stuff." She tossed a bar towel over her left arm and leaned against the bar. Giving Jeff a pointed look, she said, "You should be spending your money on romancing the ladies."

Jeff blushed while he looked at his feet. "I wish," he muttered then high-tailed it out of there with his rack of dirty glasses.

Spike crushed her eyebrows together. The silver bar pierced through the corner of the left one glinted briefly. "What'd I say?"

Gina sighed. She didn't want to gossip, but... "Jeff's got a girlfriend."

"Cute guy like him> 'Course he does."

"Yeah, well, she got pregnant, then her parents just up and took her out of town. The whole family just vanished without a trace. He's taking it pretty hard." She shook her head. "He really loves her."

"What does a kid know about love?" Spike started to wipe down the bar. "For that matter, what do any of us know about love?"

Good question. Gina sure as hell didn't have an answer for it.

****

Hours later, as Gina schlepped her duffel bag into one of The End Zone's employee bathrooms, she still didn't have any answers. What she did have were sore feet, a mild case of exhaustion and about ten minutes to get herself together for a night at the opera.

Both bathrooms had showers, allowing Gina to take a quick one and get rid of the *eau de greasy*

Doreen Alsen

French fry that clung to her skin, courtesy of a double shift. She slapped some fresh makeup on her face, fluffed up her hair and slid her tired tootsies into a pair of too-tight heels. Surveying herself in the mirror, she hoped the dress she had on was all right. Since she'd never been to the opera, and she didn't know anyone who had, she was flying blind with regard to what to wear. Squaring her shoulders, she moseyed on back to the bar to wait for Ian to pick her up.

Just her luck, she ran smack dab into Mike and Andi. Mike looked like his usual gorgeous self, in jeans that were worn in all the right places and a weathered, brown leather, bomber jacket. Andi, on the other hand, though perfectly matched and coordinated, looked extremely pale. "Hey, Mike!" Gina nodded in Andi's general direction. "Andi. How's it going?"

"Hey, Gina." Mike turned on his million-watt grin. "Lookin' good. Got a hot date?"

"She's goin' to the opera," said Sandy as she passed by them with a tray of drinks.

"You're going to *Tosca*?" Andi sighed. "I'm so jealous. Mike was supposed to get us tickets, but he didn't get to the box office in time."

Mike cleared his throat. "Now, spud, you know you're going to enjoy the monster truck show just as much as the opera." He ooomphed as Andi's elbow connected with his ribs.

"It's a once in a lifetime experience. Miles and Miranda Maxwell are amazing artists." Andi's eyes sparkled with enthusiasm. "I heard that Sir Roger Cook is stepping in as the conductor tonight. He's the greatest interpreter of Puccini since Toscanini."

"Guess who she's going with," said Sandy as she passed by on her way back to the bar.

Mike frowned. "Don't tell me you're going to the opera with the Haiku Guy."

His facial expression would have been comical if Gina hadn't been annoyed by Mike's nickname for Ian. "Okay. I won't tell you."

"Mike, behave." Andi put her hand on Gina's arm. "I think it's great that you're spending time with Ian. He's a wonderful man who deserves to be happy."

Gina opened her mouth to say something, but was saved because Andi suddenly put her hand over her mouth and bolted away in the direction of the restrooms. Gina flicked her eyes up to Mike's face, stunned by the depth of emotion she saw there.

He caught her looking at him. Flashing her an embarrassed smile, he said, "Andi's pregnant. You're the first to know."

"Mike, that's great. Congratulations." Gina was surprised to discover she meant that.

"Thanks. Listen." He looked over her head to the restrooms. "Don't tell anyone yet. We want to tell our parents first."

Gina shrugged. "Sure." Like she'd run to Ian with *this* little tidbit.

Watching Andi come out of the ladies' room, Mike skirted around Gina to go to her. "Have a good time at the opera." He shuddered. "Better you than me."

Gina watched Mike give Andi a little hug, kiss the top of her head and then gently lead her to a table. His love for her was a palpable thing, at once a beautiful and difficult thing to behold. She had to turn away.

When she did, she ran smack dab into Ian, who watched Mike and Andi from behind her. The look on his face broke her heart. "Hi."

He flicked her a glance, but his gaze bounced back to Mike and Andi. He cleared his throat, then with great care and deliberation looked back at Gina. "Hello. Are you ready to go?" He managed an almost convincing smile, but he didn't fool Gina. Ian was in all kinds of misery watching Mike with Andi.

"Yeah." Gina was *so* ready to get out of there. "Let's go."

Chapter Twelve

"Gina, it's lovely to see you again." Exuding a cloud of Chanel No. 5, Margaret Jameson settled her considerable bulk into the seat next to Gina's. "We are in for such a treat tonight. What a stroke of luck that we have tickets for the night Roger Cook is filling in for the regular conductor. It's quite a coup."

Gina didn't know what to say, so she nodded. Going to the opera had turned out to be something of an event. The inside of the concert hall was very elaborate. Gold dripped from the statues on the walls, the floor was covered with a rich carpet that made her heels sink as she walked with Ian to their seats. The chairs were well upholstered in a soft, gold, velvety fabric. She drifted into her seat.

Margaret chattered on. "Cook hasn't graced the same concert hall with the Maxwells since Miranda broke her engagement to him to elope with Maxwell. Rumor has it she broke his heart and he's never recovered." She sighed. "Isn't that romantic?"

Gina wouldn't have used the word romantic, especially with Ian sitting right next to her. Sappy summed it up best. She looked at Ian out of the corner of her eye. He read his program with great concentration.

Still holding onto the subject of the Maxwells, Margaret rhapsodized, "*Scarpia* is one of Miles Maxwell's best roles. Really, no one sings it better, don't you think so, Ralph?" She didn't wait for her husband to answer. "He's so wonderfully evil."

Gina was saved from answering by the lights turning down and the orchestra tuning up. A distinguished man in a tuxedo stepped out on stage and bowed. The crowd went wild.

The great Roger Cook had entered the building.

He looked younger than Gina expected. He waited patiently for the applause to subside, then descended into the orchestra pit.

Music, absolutely incredible, beautiful music filled the concert hall. Margaret sucked in a sharp breath. Gina wondered if the woman was still breathing. She was glad she had taken those CPR classes at the Y. One never knew when something like that would come in handy.

They singing started. It was pretty, to be sure. The woman personified perfection. Her face was a classic oval, her hair a rich blond, her voice high, agile and sweet. The man, a dumpy little Italian tenor named Dante Toscano, as Margaret informed her, looked like a troll but sang like an angel.

Gina had a little trouble believing the woman was madly in love with troll boy. Ah, well. Love was supposed to be blind.

And deaf. The noises pumping out from both singers were only meant for dogs to hear.

As the opera progressed, Gina felt her eyes getting heavy. She made it through the first act and chugged a glass of wine at intermission. Having made it through the second act with a bit more good cheer, she managed to choke down another glass of wine during the second intermission before she settled into her seat for the final act.

Her eyelids continued to droop midway through the first song. The weeks of double shifts, along with two glasses of wine on an empty stomach, caught up with her. Her head fell against Ian's shoulder as she fell sound asleep.

****

Ian hardly heard a note of music all night, thanks to the incredibly sexy, desirable woman in the seat next to him. Extremely aroused, he blamed it all on Gina.

When she dropped her head on his shoulder, he fantasized briefly about what would happen when the opera ended, if he took her to his house. That is, until he realized she was sound asleep and starting to snore.

They weren't loud, choking snores. They were more like delicate, ladylike little snarfles.

He absolutely knew Gina would be mortified to the depths of her soul about them.

He did his best to wake her up without alerting the Jamesons to the fact his date had passed out. He didn't think Margaret would appreciate Gina's falling asleep during the operatic event of the century.

So, he nudged her. She murmured something unintelligible, then snuggled in closer to him. He whispered in her ear. She batted at his face. He pinched her nose closed. She gasped for air but remained asleep.

He gave up, put his arm over her shoulders and pulled her as close as he could get her. The trusting way she melted into him filled his heart with so much joy it hurt.

He figured he could pinch her when the time came to wake up, but he hadn't bargained on the audience going so crazy at the final curtain.

The lights came up, and one very sleepy waitress blinked as she came to. Ian knew the minute she figured out where she was, along with what happened. She stared at him with big, round eyes filled with horror. He smiled at her, then pulled her to her feet to join in the standing ovation.

She clapped enthusiastically. In fact, he wondered if her hands were going to fall off, that's how hard she slapped them together. He almost expected her to stick her fingers in her mouth and whistle, but she didn't. More's the pity. In fact, she stood ramrod straight with nothing in her demeanor that communicated she had fallen asleep and snored during the entire third act of *Tosca*.

He chuckled. He couldn't help it. She was too cute.

She shot him a dirty look.

He wanted to kiss her.

He would, too, when he got her alone. He'd kiss the daylights out of her. He'd show her he was every inch the man Mike Kelly was. Maybe more.

In spades.

Margaret turned to Gina and said something to her. Gina smiled and nodded. He knew she was just humoring Margaret and felt such a jolt of love for her because of it. He hadn't felt such emotion for a woman since... since...

Well, since never. What he had felt for Andrea was nothing compared to what he felt right that minute for Gina. He couldn't describe it. He was a poet, spoke several languages fluently, and he *still* didn't have the words to tell her what he felt for her.

He'd just have to show her.

She caught him staring. He could tell she still felt embarrassed because she blushed bright red. "I'm sorry," she mouthed.

He longed to take her in his arms and show her she had nothing to be sorry for, but he couldn't, not with the Jamesons there. So he smiled and took her hand. Her brows smashed together in confusion. On her, it looked cute.

He refocused his attention on the stage, where Miranda Maxwell took her bow while being fêted with flowers. She was a beautiful woman, certainly not even close to anyone's clichéd image of an opera singer. No indeed. Miranda was a tall, cool, elegant blond, much like Andrea, actually.

Again he glanced at the short, curvy redhead standing next to him. Neither Miranda Maxwell nor Andrea Kelly held a candle to Gina's beauty.

They stood through the seven curtain calls then finally got a break when the Maxwells wouldn't come out again. Ian puffed out a breath. He itched to get Gina alone, preferably naked, in a bed.

"That was wonderful, simply marvelous." Margaret sounded ready to swoon. "I can't remember the last time I enjoyed the opera so much." She laid a hand on top of her chest. "Wasn't it wonderful, Ralph?"

Ralph rolled his eyes, but gave his wife an indulgent grin. "A superlative performance."

Margaret slapped at her husband's arm, then looked at Gina and Ian. "He loves to tease. How did you like it?"

Gina folded her hands in front of her, as prim and proper as a novice nun. "It was very beautiful. Thank you for inviting me."

Ian choked on a laugh, but when Gina's pointy little heel connected with his big toe, he grimaced. Of course Margaret noticed, skewering Ian with eyebrows raised in question. He gave her the smile he usually saved for his mother, while he took off his glasses to gesture in the air with them. "It *was* lovely. The Maxwells *and* Roger Cook all on one stage." He nodded. "Historic. It was historic."

Margaret, feathers smoothed, beamed at him. "It was, wasn't it?"

Ralph grabbed Margaret's arm to pull her out of the row of seats, into the aisle. "Come along, Margaret." Over her shoulder, he said, "We're going to Esmeralda's for coffee and dessert. Would you like to join us?"

Gina sucked in a breath, but Ian spoke before she got to very politely decline. "Thanks, but we need to get going. Gina's got an early morning."

"You're sure? We'd love to get to know Gina better." Ralph took Margaret's elbow and lead her up the aisle.

"Unfortunately, yes." Ian crossed his fingers behind his back. "Another time, perhaps."

As much as it could be a bad move politically to blow off the Jamesons, Ian couldn't summon the effort to care. He was too focused on Gina and how he would go about bringing his own plans for the end of the evening to fruition.

****

"Omigawd, I am *so* sorry!" Gina still had a stomachache from the embarrassment of falling asleep. She felt simply, absolutely, deeply mortified right down to the soles of her feet. "You know if you just want to drop me off at home and join the Jamesons at Esmeralda's, go right ahead. Don't feel bad."

Ian smiled, but kept his attention on the road. "Don't worry about it."

They were on their way home. Well, at least Gina thought Ian was taking her home. The night felt mild, moist and unusually balmy for late March in New England. The sky was pretty clear. There were millions of stars. It might have been romantic, if she hadn't just made a major fool of herself.

"I hope I didn't ruin your chances..." She bit her lip. "Look, you can probably salvage this thing by telling them you broke up with me."

He huffed out a breath. "I don't want to tell them that. I don't need to. Everything is just fine."

"How can you say that? I fell asleep at the biggest operatic event of the century!" She wanted to die.

"I think you snored a little, too."

Gina moaned. Never mind just die. She wanted to die painfully, right there on the spot. "Just shoot me, okay? Both barrels, no paces, right between the eyes." She put two fingers in front of her eyes as she crossed them.

He laughed. "I'm sorry. I shouldn't tease you. The fact of the matter is that Margaret didn't notice. She was too engrossed in what happened on the stage. As for Ralph," Ian chuckled and shook his head. "He hates the opera. He only goes to indulge Margaret."

"I don't believe you."

"It's true! He's hard of hearing and turns his hearing aid off every time they go."

"No way. Who would go to the opera if he didn't like it?"

"A man who both loves his wife and knows how to work his hearing aid."

Unbelievable. "Does she know he does that?"

"I don't know. I never asked." He pulled off to the side of the road, put the car in neutral and set the parking brake. He unsnapped his seat belt then put his hands on her shoulders to turn her to face him. "Gina, sweet, I would very much like to be with you tonight, with nothing else between us." When she started to stammer, he put his finger up to her lips. "Shhhhhhh. Just us. No opera, no Jamesons, no niece, no chairmanship of the department. More than anything else, no Mike and Andi."

"But..." Maybe now she should tell him about Andi being pregnant. She looked him in the eyes. The flow of emotions she found in those gray depths rendered her speechless.

"No buts." He moved his finger to stroke under her chin, to bring her face close to his, then he kissed her. His lips were warm, soft and persuasive. "Come home with me."

Boy howdy! It got very hot in the car. She licked her lips, just before he captured her mouth again. His very clever tongue teased her mouth open, tempting hers to come out and play.

Lord love her, she did. She gave in to temptation, gave in to the desire she felt for this man and melted against him.

Well, she melted against him as well as she could, given that there was a gearshift and a parking brake between them. He pulled her closer. The brake jumped up and poked her in the ribs. She gave a grunt of pain against his mouth.

He broke the kiss immediately to give her some room. They chuckled, then he rested his forehead against hers. "Sorry," he whispered, his voice husky and low.

"I'm not." She kissed him, quick and acquiescent. "Let's go to your house."

He grinned like a pirate with a bag full of booty, sat back in his seat, released the parking brake and peeled out with a screech of the tires.

Ian must have broken a few laws along with all the speed records in *The Guinness Book of World Records* getting to his house. He pulled into the driveway of a large, old house and punched the button on the garage door opener. It groaned as it opened. Ian zoomed his car inside. Eating her up with his eyes, he said, "We're here. Are you sure?"

The look on his face, all hungry and male, made her quiver right down to the tips of her toes. Was she sure?

Ohhhh yeah. She was sure. "Yes."

His eyes crinkled when he smiled. "Come with me, then." Opening his car door, he got out, never taking his eyes off her. He hurried over to her side, opened her door, then held out his hand. When she put her hand in his, he pulled her to her feet and into his arms to kiss her just long enough to drive her crazy. Without another word, he took her hand to lead her into his house.

If she weren't so intent on the man with her,

she'd be checking out the house. Later. She'd indulge that curiosity later. Right now, all her awareness focused on Ian, the subtle, woodsy scent of his aftershave, the harsh sound of his breathing, the warmth of his hand holding hers. Each thing on its own was potent. Together, the three had enough punch to bring her to her knees.

Good thing she was made of stronger stuff. He nibbled her ear.

Well, maybe. Being made of stronger stuff was way over-rated.

Not even giving her a chance to take off her coat, Ian turned her into his arms, backed her against the kitchen counter, and kissed her again.

And again.

And again.

She clung to him and rode the wave. He pulled his mouth from hers and nuzzled her neck. At the same time, his hands worked her jacket off her shoulders. She returned the favor, using fingers that were suddenly stupid to work at his buttons. That done, she captured his face in her hands to kiss him long and hard.

He broke their embrace. "Let's go upstairs."

Beyond speech, she nodded. Then, in a thrilling display of masculine grace and romance, he swept her into his arms, carried her through his house, up the stairs to his room where he gently deposited her on his bed, tongues tangling all the while.

He toed off his shoes before joining her on the bed. She welcomed him back with hot kisses and open arms. He rolled her onto her back, his lips dusting over her mouth, her eyes, her cheeks, while his hands worked on getting rid of the rest of her clothes. Frustration nipped at her because he wasn't getting very far. She sat up and whipped her tangled blouse over her head. His eyes were on fire as he watched her, and she trembled under their heat. She

Doreen Alsen

raised weak, quivery fingers to undo the front clasp of her bra when his hand covered hers.

"Let me," he croaked with a voice that sounded like a rusty old spring.

She dropped her head back while he freed her breasts.

"Beautiful," he whispered like a saint witnessing a miracle. "You are so beautiful." Lowering her back down to the bed, he raised himself on one elbow. He reverently played with first one breast, then the other.

He stroked, he petted, he gently kneaded until her nipples were diamond hard. She cried out when he finally brought his mouth to her and suckled.

It felt good, so good, not just what he was doing, but how cherished he made her feel. His gentleness, his thoroughness both conspired to bring her to tears. Not slow on the uptake, he demonstrated his awareness of her. He stilled to ask, "Am I hurting you?"

"Oh, no," she sighed. "Please, more."

There was that pirate grin again, cocky and male. He pulled off his shirt before he started all over again, right from the very beginning. Gina moaned in frustration, to make him hurry. But those hands, that mouth of his, oh so slow and clever, were intent on taking their time and making her wet with wanting him.

She wrapped her arms around him to run her hands up and down his back. His body was a marvel and a surprise to her, much more muscular than she could have guessed from the look of him in his professor suit. She explored his back, then down to his butt, then around to cup and stroke the impressive bulge of his erection.

He sucked in a breath then moved against her hand, making her feel powerful. She undid his fly to get a better grip. Groaning his pleasure, he swelled and lengthened against her touch.

It wasn't enough for her, she wanted him naked. Reaching behind her, she pulled at his pants. He chuckled and lifted up so she could complete her mission. Once he was gloriously naked, she reached for him, but he moved out of range while he planted a kiss on her nose. "My turn," he smiled, as he proceeded to rid her of the rest of her clothes. He moved down her body, laved each new area he uncovered with scorching, open mouth kisses.

When he had laid her bare before him, he brought his mouth to her center and parted her with his tongue.

She cried out with the thrill of it, coming undone as he feasted on her. Once, twice, three times he brought her to the verge of climax, only to stop short and drive her crazy.

"Pleeeeeeease," she keened, lifting her hips to his mouth in supplication.

"Please, what?" the devil crooned, his breath hot against her.

The hell with pride, she would beg. "Please finish me."

He chuckled. "Patience, sweet. I haven't completed my research."

Research? *Research*? "Yes, you have. Please!"

"Ah, but that's where you're wrong. A good academic never comes to a conclusion without gathering all the facts." He kissed his way back up her body.

His erection was hot against her, hard enough to chisel granite. She parted her legs to make a place for him. He kneeled between them and over her. Wet with impatient moisture, he stroked her sweet spot with his penis to bring her to the brink one more time.

"Now, please, now," Gina moaned in supplication. She had never felt this needy and greedy.

Flashing that pirate grin, he suckled each nipple, then her mouth, on his way to reach behind her and liberate a condom from his nightstand. That accomplished, he sat back on his heels to sheathe himself. Finally, finally, *finally,* he parted her legs then slowly joined his body with hers.

Though he was careful, he was big. It took a while for her body to accept him. She felt full to bursting, her body, her heart, as they became one. He hilted, then shuddered, then began to move inside her.

Oh, *God,* the pleasure of it rose up, swamping her like a tidal wave. Screaming, she came in great, hot gushes that went on and on. He rode each one with ever-growing urgency, until; at last, he thrust hard and deep, jetting inside of her in long, shuddering, scalding bursts.

They took a long time coming back to themselves.

He moved off her and gathered her into his arms as though she were something precious. Nuzzling the top of her head, he cuddled her against his chest and stroked her back. "You okay?"

Gina sighed. "Oh, yeah." She felt more than fine. She felt alive and in love.

"Good." He was quiet a minute, then sighed. "I didn't ask. Can you stay with me?"

She tried to rise up on an elbow, but she didn't have the strength. "What?"

"Can you stay with me? Here. Tonight. All night." His voice held an endearing note of uncertainty.

"Yes. I have to work in the morning, but I can stay tonight."

"Good." He kissed the top of her head. She didn't even want to begin to imagine what her hair must look like.

She had questions, big ones, ones she feared to ask, but the time didn't feel right. There'd be time enough tomorrow to get things straight between them.

Doreen Alsen

Chapter Thirteen

Ian smiled while he kissed the tip of Gina's nose. He hadn't slept at all after making love with her. He'd held her close to his heart while she slept. He had been too revved, too jazzed, too amazed to sleep. Now, the first light of day started to peek through his bedroom windows. He felt loose-limbed and happy.

Incredible sex had a way of doing that to a man.

He couldn't decide if he wanted to let her sleep or to coax her awake so he could make love to her again. God knew, he was beyond ready for more of her loving, but she'd been so exhausted the night before. He didn't want to be selfish.

He shifted to increase the blood flow to his left arm. She mumbled and snuggled in closer. Dear Lord, she looked beautiful with her hair all rumpled, with her face ever so slightly flushed from both sleep and spent passion. Nuzzling her hair, he enjoyed the soft, floral scent of it. Then he kissed her, once, twice, three times. He stroked his hand down her back, soothing her soft, warm skin, smiling anew about his good luck.

Closing his eyes, feeling much like a well-fed cat, he finally dozed, and dreamed of Gina.

****

When Gina woke, she was alone. It took her a moment to get her bearings, but when she figured out whose bed she woke up in, her thoughts began to rumble around in her head like bumper cars. She

124

didn't know if Ian's not being there was a good thing, or not.

Lifting herself on her elbows, she took stock of Ian's bedroom. Big, masculine and furnished in dark blue, green and maroon, it stood as a testament to his profession, with floor to ceiling bookshelves on three of the four walls.

She suspected when she checked out the titles, none of them would be a language she could understand. She'd place bets on the fact there'd be no romances among them.

Just what she needed, another reminder of how totally out of her league Ian Ross was. She sighed as she sat up and pulled the sheet securely around her breasts.

She hadn't felt out of his league last night. Last night had been wonderful. Well, after the opera had been wonderful. She cringed all over again remembering how she had fallen asleep during *Tosca*.

He said it didn't matter, so maybe she should take him at his word. To do that, however, she had to find him first. Before she could track Ian down, she needed to find her clothes. Pulling the sheet out of the bed, she wrapped it around herself so she could go on a clothes-hunt. That accomplished, she located the bathroom attached to Ian's bedroom and did what she could to look as good as she could in the cold light of the morning. When she found Ian, she didn't want to look like something the cat dragged in. The results wouldn't win any Miss America pageants, but they would have to do.

She ventured out into the hallway, bracing herself to beard the lion in his den. In the end, like the children in *The Pied Piper of Hamlin*, all she had to do was follow the music.

She'd anticipated the musical soundtrack that accompanied Ian's life to be classical, opera no doubt, complete with sobbing strings and wailing sopranos. She found him in his kitchen, chopping some vegetables in time to Mick Jagger growling about some honky tonk woman.

How cool was that?

Gina grinned. How could she help it, standing in the doorway, watching Ian swivel his hips and do air guitar while he cooked breakfast? She cleared her throat.

Ian's hips came to an abrupt halt after he made one last swivel to face her. His face turned bright red. "Oh, good. You're up."

She smiled. "Looks like."

"Ah, well..." He returned his concentration to the chopping board. "I hope you like omelets."

"Love 'em." His sudden reserve gave her a hitch in her stomach. She'd fallen asleep on him last night. It wouldn't win her any points to have her stomach in such knots she couldn't eat the breakfast he diligently fixed.

The breakfast he was fixing for her. Well, hell. Hillary's husband had been president the last time *anyone* had cracked an egg on her behalf. "Smells good."

He hitched his shoulders up in response, but didn't turn to answer her. "Hope it tastes as good as it smells." His shoulder blades drew together, then he sighed. "Hope you're hungry."

"Famished."

Well, *that* made him look at her. He took his glasses off then swiveled his neck. A sly smile greeted her. "Oh, really."

Well, duh. Then, looking at the uncertainty in his eyes, she felt a rush of warmth. No *well, duh* about it. The man didn't know which end was up.

He put his glasses back on and turned to attend to the vegetables he was hacking at. He reminded her of a one man Ginsu knife commercial.

Frankly, it was all the more reason to fall in love with him. Her heart did a little two-step. "Can I help?"

Again, he turned to face her with that cute little smile. "Uh, no. I've got it under control." He motioned to the coffee maker with his knife. "There's coffee, if you want."

"I want. Thanks!" It smelled like glory, dark, warm and velvety. She poured some into a mug emblazoned with the logo of the local public radio station. Ian had thoughtfully left a carton of half and half on the counter next to the coffee maker. Gina poured a healthy dose of it into her coffee. Holding the steaming mug in both hands, she took a grateful sniff before taking her first sip. It was really strong, just the way she liked it. She closed her eyes. "Mm."

"It's good, then?"

Gina's eyes shot open to find Ian watching her with hunger in his gaze. Her mouth went dry, so she licked her lips.

He put the knife down, wiped his hands on his jeans, and walked over to her. He took the coffee cup away from her to set it on the table. Then, framing her face gently between his hands, he kissed her.

Boy, howdy, did he kiss her. They didn't come up for air until the smoke detector went off with a loud, obnoxious *beeeeeep*. Easing away, he laid his forehead against hers with a little laugh. "Do you know how to turn those bloody things off?"

Gina managed to shake her head. "I guess you could unplug it."

"Be right back." He grabbed a chair, pulled it under the offending alarm and stood on it while he tore the cover off to disembowel the batteries. Blissful silence ensued. The two of them sighed in unison.

The omelet pan still smoked like crazy. It was a wonder it hadn't caught on fire. Gina moved to the stove to rescue it, pulling it off the burner. She put it under the tap while she turned on the water full force. Sputtering, the pan smoked even more.

"Well," Ian said, straddling the chair under the smoke detector, "I had hoped to amaze you with my incredible culinary skills." He took his glasses off and wiped them on his shirttail. "Not much chance of that now."

He looked so woe-be-gone and miserable sitting there, barefoot, no glasses, hair all sticking up, chin unshaven, that she sighed. He had no idea what he did to her. "I distracted you."

He scrutinized a spot on his glasses, cleared his throat. He cleaned them then put them back on. "How about this? You give me a few minutes alone in here while I repair the damage to our breakfast."

She started to protest, but he held up a hand. "Please. Let me feed you."

Gina looked at her watch, decided she had enough time before her next shift, and nodded. "Okay. But can I make a few phone calls?" She needed to let Sandy know that she didn't need a ride to work.

"The phone's in the study. Down the hall to the right."

She lifted her eyebrows. "Only one?"

He grinned. "That's all I need."

She smiled back, then went in search of his study. It wasn't hard to find, a big comfortable room with a big desk and lots of books. A computer sat on the desk, next to a phone and an answering machine. She reached out to pick up the phone when it began to ring. She snatched her hand back, unsure of what to do.

She let it ring until the answering machine whirred. There was silence for a beat or two, then the caller's voice filled the room.

"Ian, darling, it's mum. I know you're there, so

pick up." A gusty sigh followed a pointed silence. "Fine, have it your way and pretend you're not at home. Anyway, I'm calling to let you know I've arranged my concert schedule so I can come visit you on the fourteenth of April for your thirtieth birthday. How could I miss my boy's big day? Anyway, I'll let you know my travel plans later."

Another loud beat of silence. "Have you heard from your father? I wouldn't be surprised if you hadn't. The entire town of London is abuzz with talk of his foolishness over his nymphet bride. I can't go anywhere without someone regaling me with stories of something ridiculous his ex-stripper wife has said. The woman is an absolute nightmare if even half of the stories are to be believed. The woman is always making some stupid, shallow comment, in an atrocious American, no doubt what they call a redneck accent, that just proves her lack of education and breeding. I shan't wonder if something..." The machine thanked her for her message before it clicked off.

Gina plopped herself down in Ian's desk chair and let out a slow stream of air. She'd never thought of Ian having parents.

The woman on the phone had sounded very daunting and forbidding. Cultured. Fussy.

Someone who didn't breathe the same air as a lowly waitress.

Gina didn't kid herself. If she were Ian's mother, she wouldn't like the thought of someone like Gina sleeping with her brilliant, wonderful son.

She did store the knowledge that Ian was going to turn thirty on the fourteenth of April. She'd have to do something with that. What, she didn't know, but something.

She reached for the phone and punched in Sandy's number. First things first. Sandy, breakfast, then Ian's birthday.

Sounded like a plan.

"Is everything okay?"

Gina hung up the phone and turned to find Ian waiting in the doorway, all barefoot, rumpled adorableness.

"I come bearing fresh coffee." He held the fragrant, steaming mug in front of him.

"Hmmmm." She took a step toward him, fresh arousal swimming in her body. What she really should do was tell him about his mother's phone call.

Yep. That's really what she should do. Later.

When she reached him, she took the mug out of his hand, smiled, then took a sip and put it aside. "That's really good coffee," she purred. She twined her arms around his neck while standing on tiptoes to kiss him. The man tasted like sin on a Saturday night. "How can I ever thank you?"

He returned her kiss, and his hands caressed her back down to her backside. "I can think of a couple of ways."

"Really?" She scooted her hands down to cup his amazing butt. "Like what?"

He backed her up against his desk then hoisted her onto it. He nuzzled her neck with a string of little kisses that made her weak as a newborn lamb. She whimpered.

"Like that, do you?" He smiled against her neck.

"Oh yeah. I do. I really do." If he didn't stop soon she was going to lose all power of speech.

His teeth gave her earlobe a gentle little nip. He chuckled when she jumped.

Aw, hell. She put her finger under his chin, diverting his mouth to hers.

Speech was way over-rated.

****

"Thanks for the ride. I really appreciate it."

As he drove her home, Ian cast a curious eye at Gina. He wanted to pull over to the side of the road and kiss her silly. Instead, he was taking her to work. "No problem." He swallowed. "Do you need me to pick you up?"

"What?" Gina blinked. "Oh, no. I don't get off until really late."

Ian narrowed his eyes. This didn't sound right to him. "How late is late?"

"I'm closing."

Ian did the math. "That's nearly a twelve hour shift! That should be illegal!"

Gina blushed an attractive shade of red as she looked away. Her skin nearly matched her hair. "It's not. I thank God for the hours." She shot him a glance. "I had an unexpected car expense, so I've been working double shifts to pay for it." She ran a hand through her curls. "That's why I passed out at the opera last night." She looked out the window.

No wonder she had fallen asleep. An overwhelming feeling of protectiveness gunned him down. She shouldn't have to work that hard. Someone should take care of her.

Like him, he thought. *Someone just like him.*

Hell, he had money to burn. "How much?"

She shrugged. "It's not a big deal. I've got it covered."

He wouldn't let her get off that easily. "Where did you take it?"

"I took it to Donnie's on State Street. Donnie is a good guy. Bobby would kill him if he hosed me." She seemed defensive.

"I'm not criticizing. I want to help." He put his hand out and rested it on the parking brake.

She covered his hand with hers. "I know. Thank you. But I've got it taken care of." She sucked in a big inhale, then let it out. "Only five more double shifts, and I've got it paid for."

Ian blinked. She shouldn't be nickel and dimeing her way through life. His knuckles turned white as his grip tightened on the parking brake. This incredible, amazing woman should not have to beg a mechanic named Donnie for her car.

He would just have to fix this. Calmer now that he had come to this conclusion, he took a deep breath.

There were many things that were simply beyond his control. But a car mechanic's bill? That problem he could take care of most handily.

Chapter Fourteen

"So girlfriend, you been holdin' out on me, or what?" Sandy plopped herself down onto a barstool next to Gina. The happy hour rush had petered out, dwindling to a sparse dinner crowd. Usually, that would worry Gina, what with the lack of tips and all. But today, the world was infused with a rosy, golden glow and ripe with birdsong.

Getting some could be good for a girl.

Gina grinned at Sandy.

Sandy studied her. "Yep. It is my considered opinion that you got lucky last night. What do you think, Spike?"

Spike frowned. "Since I wouldn't know lucky if it jumped up and bit me on my ass, I wouldn't begin to hazard a guess."

"Well, lucky and I have crossed paths a time or two, and I think I can say our good friend Gina got lucky with a certain French professor."

Still grinning because she couldn't quite help it, Gina groused, "Announce it to the whole bar, why dontcha?"

Sandy laughed. "Honey, the way you glow, I don't have to announce it. So," Sandy brought her voice way down. "I think it's a safe bet that the good professor knows his way around the boudoir."

Spike shook her head. "I can't believe you just asked her that."

"Oh, stop clutching your pearls and clucking your tongue. You know you want to know."

Spike sniffed, her nose in the air. "The thought never crossed my mind."

"Yeah, right." Sandy airily dismissed her. "So, spill, *chica*. Enquiring minds want to know."

"Hmmmmm." Gina tapped a finger against her lips. "The professor is, shall we say, thorough."

"Thorough." Someone at the end of the bar snickered. Sandy shushed him.

"Yes, thorough. And, hmmmmm, curious. Thorough and curious."

"Curious." Sandy nearly drooled.

"Yes." Gina tapped a pencil against her pursed lips. "He really likes to delve deep into the subject at hand and explore all his options."

"Man." Sandy started fanning herself.

Gina came down to earth a little bit. "I gotta tell you, Sandy, this is intense. I've never felt this way about anyone. It totally scares the crap out of me."

"Not even Mike?"

Gina sighed. "Mike who?"

"Oh, wow. What are you gonna do about it?"

"I *was* just going to ride the wave for as long as I can. But what if I want more?"

"What does he want?"

"Damned if I know." Gina scratched her ear.

"Does he feel the same way?"

"I don't know. I hope so. I can't stand the thought of sitting around wondering how he's feeling."

"So make the next move." Sandy stood up. "Don't wait for him."

"What? Tell him how I feel, just like that?"

"Why not?"

Gina sputtered. "I can't do that. What if he's still in love with Andi?"

"Did last night feel like he was in love with Andi?"

"No." She felt pretty sure that Andi Kelly was

nowhere in that bedroom last night. "I'm just not ready to make some sort of grand declaration."

"Do something else, then. Make dinner for him."

"Where? At my apartment?"

"No, at the soup kitchen." Sandy whomped her upside the back of her head with an order pad. "Of course at your apartment." She pulled her cell phone out of her apron pocket and held it out to Gina. "No time like the present. Call him right now."

****

Ian couldn't believe his good fortune. The very woman he'd been daydreaming about was on his telephone right that very minute. "Hello! Just who I've been thinking about."

"Oh, really?" Gina's sweet, sexy voice hummed down the line. "Only good things I hope."

"Only the best." A heavy handed knocking distracted him. He looked up to see Donald Unger standing in his office doorway.

Damn the bugger. "Excuse me." Ian clapped his hand over the receiver of the phone. He turned to face down Unger. "I'll only be a minute."

Unger's mouthed creased into that snakey smile. "Take your time." He stepped outside.

Ian didn't want to take any chances. He got up and closed the door, then settled back at his desk. He snuggled the phone back against his ear. "Sorry about that. Where were we?"

"Is this a bad time?"

Ian imagined she was frowning in that utterly charming way she had when she was unsure of herself. "Not at all. I'm glad you called, just so I can tell you how much I miss you."

"Oh my," she said in a breathless tone that made him feel like Tarzan. "Wow."

"Do you miss me?" he wheedled.

"Um, yeah, you could say that."

Now he felt happy. He had her absolutely

flustered. "So to what do I owe this incredible pleasure?"

"You're going to have to cut this out if you want me to remember why I called you."

He chuckled. "Go on then."

"Anyway," Gina's voice sang to him. "I was wondering if you wanted to come to dinner?"

"Dinner?"

"Yeah, dinner. You know, that meal you eat at night."

"Where do you want to go?"

Gina made a kind of *oomph* sound, much like someone had elbowed her in her ribs. "Uh, my apartment."

No woman had ever cooked him dinner before. Well, excluding when he was a boy and his nanny fixed his tea. That, to his way of thinking, didn't count.

"You mean you want to cook for me?"

"I kinda owe you for breakfast."

He wanted to bolt out of his desk chair and did a dance. She actually wanted to make him a meal.

Life was good.

"Couldja give me an answer here? I'm kinda really nervous about this."

Dear Lord, she was cute. "I'd love to. When?"

He could feel her hesitate. "Well, if you're free, how about tomorrow night?"

"Perfect." He grabbed a pencil to jot the time down on his desk blotter as he cradled the phone between his neck and his shoulder. He'd cancel whatever else he had planned to have dinner with Gina. "What time?"

"How does seven o'clock sound?"

"Great." He wrote it down, then underlined it twice. A heavy knocking interrupted his happy thoughts, and he grimaced. "Look, I've got to go, but I'll see you tomorrow night. I'm really looking forward to it."

"Great! See you then." She hung up.

Ian very carefully slipped the phone back into its cradle, then got up to let Unger in. "Donald, what can I do for you?"

Donald smiled, looking much like a crocodile on a manhunt. "It's what I can do for you, actually." He fully entered Ian's office then closed the door.

This couldn't be good. Donald Unger didn't do anybody favors. "Really?"

"I probably shouldn't be telling you this, but I thought you should have a head's up. I've decided to throw my hat in the ring for the chairmanship of the department."

"Okay." What a surprise. Only, not so much.

"I won't pretend that the committee isn't interested."

"Indeed." What did Unger expect of him here? "Why are you telling me this?"

"I just wanted to let you know." He shrugged. "I only wonder how things are coming along with this ultra secret project you're working on." He pulled a piece of string off his blazer lapel.

Ah. Unger was fishing. "My work is going well."

"I hope your lovely fiancée is not too much of a distraction."

Ian didn't know how he did it, but Unger managed to be more of a stupid git than usual. "My love life is none of your business."

"I didn't mean to offend you. I'm sure Gina is a lovely person and makes you very happy." He opened the office door. "I intend to do everything I have in my power to get the chair. I certainly deserve it, given all the years of service I've given to this department." He gave a curt little bow of his head. "Have a good day." The door thumped in his wake.

Ian carefully put the papers back on his desk. Bugger it all; Unger had just openly declared war.

But in the meantime, he had dinner tomorrow to look forward to. Because now that he was arse-over-kettle in love with Gina, he wouldn't to let her go. He'd find a way to get the chair *and* keep Gina.

Even though he couldn't afford to be distracted, he'd indulge himself in one very sexy, red-haired distraction.

****

With a sigh, Gina reached for her morning coffee and picked up the phone message Spike had scratched out for her.

She shook her head to clear it, held the note at arms' length, then squinted at it. The note said the same thing it had up close.

Donnie says your car is ready. You can pick it up any time. Everything's all set.

Well, that didn't make sense. She had a deal with Donnie. He'd hold the car until she could pay for it and not charge her any storage charges. He didn't take credit cards, and hers was maxed anyway. What did he mean by *everything's all set?*

Unless her fairy godmother had magically appeared out of nowhere armed with a transformed pumpkin, some mice on steroids, and an everlovin', freakin' pot of gold, there could be no way everything was *all set* with her car.

So, she ran by Donnie's the first thing the next morning. He was grinning as he held out her keys and the grease-stained invoice marked *paid*.

"No way." Gina stammered. "What's going on here?"

Donnie shrugged. "What I told you. This guy with a fancy accent came in and paid off the rest of your bill."

"You've got to be kidding!"

"He paid in cash. I don't kid about cash."

Gina looked around for a chair. "I need to sit down." Nothing looked promising, or safe, so she leaned against the doorway. "I can't believe this."

"Yeah, well, happy birthday to you. Here's your keys." He slapped the keys on the desk on top of an invoice marked *paid in full.* "Coming," he yelled back into the garage at the guys calling him. "Pleasure doing business with you." He smiled as he pulled a greasy rag out of his coveralls' back pocket. A huge crash from inside the garage had him wincing. "No, no, no, don't pull that out until you've..." His bellow faded as he disappeared into the garage.

She took her keys and picked up the invoice, staring at them like they held some kind of mysterious clues. Not that she needed any clues. She knew only one man with a fancy accent.

One of her major faults was that she had way too much pride. She didn't do well when people tried to help her. This felt a bit, well, icky. It felt a little too much like payment for services rendered.

As she went out to her car, unlocked it and slid behind the wheel, she fought the impulse to run right over to the college to confront him. No. He was coming to dinner. She would take the time to figure out how best to let him know that there was no possible way she wouldn't pay him back.

Every penny. Her pride would allow no less.

****

Gina had to make a quick trip to the grocery store on the way home from work since she didn't have anything in her apartment vaguely resembling the fixings for a real dinner. She wasn't going to wimp out and order take-out.

Oh, no. Not after Ian had paid for her clutch.

She begged Bobby for his marinara recipe. He made her sign a confidentiality form, claiming he'd sue her if she gave it to anyone else.

He'd do it, too.

Recipe in hand, she flew through the produce

section, grabbing peppers, tomatoes, lettuce, fresh parsley, basil, thyme, bay leaves and two kinds of onions. She segued into the pasta section after a fly-by in paper goods to get candles and napkins.

She spent a lot of time in the bakery. She shook her head at herself. Buying a loaf of Italian bread shouldn't be this hard a decision.

She really wanted everything to be perfect.

Glancing at her watch, she realized she was running way late, so she dashed to the check out and managed to find the slowest cashier.

On the ride home, she hit every single red light between the store and her apartment.

She found herself juggling grocery bags, her mail and her keys. Somehow, in the midst of all that juggling, the bottom fell out of one of the grocery bags, sending red and yellow peppers rolling in her hallway. She cursed when she broke a nail gathering them back up.

She managed to make it the rest of the way into her apartment without mishap, tossing her mail and keys on the coffee table while she dashed into her kitchen. She threw together the ingredients for her spaghetti sauce without bothering to take off her coat.

Picking up the mail, she rifled through it while she bopped into her bedroom to change her clothes. The bottom of her stomach dropped out when she found one of the envelopes contained a letter from her brother in prison.

She didn't want to deal with it, not then, so she absent-mindedly stuffed it in the first thing she laid her hands on, the latest hardcover by Suzanne Brockmann. Later. She'd cope with it all later.

Flopping on her bed, she lay flat on her back as she checked the clock. Twenty minutes to get gorgeous. She'd better get cracking.

She turned on the shower and let it run while

she rummaged in her closet for her favorite sweater, the red one with the Chinese characters embroidered in black on it.

It was in the laundry. Crap.

She ran out of hot water in the middle of rinsing the shampoo out of her hair. She soldiered on and shivered while she conditioned it. She had to if she wanted curls, not frizz.

As she put her make-up on, she prayed the rest of the evening would be perfect.

Her heart did a little jig in time to the ruckus the butterflies were making in her stomach.

****

The doorbell rang as she slipped a loaf of garlic bread in the oven. Lord knew she felt nervous about the conversation she planned to have.

She checked out her reflection in the shine on the tiny window over her kitchen sink, then bustled to open the door. Cooking dinner for a man was a fairly intimate thing, she thought. It certainly seemed to say she wanted more than a casual relationship. But it didn't seem quite enough to thank the man who had paid for her clutch. She felt *so* confused.

With a capital C.

She shook her hair back and opened her door. There stood Professor Gorgeous, looking all sexy and frazzled. He wore his standard professor togs, along with that crooked, shy smile she liked so much. In his hand, he clutched a cellophane-wrapped bouquet of irises, tulips and freesia. "Am I late?"

Her mouth curved with a broad smile. "Nope. Right on time." She stepped back from the door. "Come on in."

Ian handed her the flowers as he crossed the threshold. "These are for you." He grimaced, nodding his head slightly to one side. "Of course, these are for you." Then he squished them when he pulled her against him for a bone-melting kiss.

Her eyes crossed then uncrossed when he kissed her. The man sure knew how to lock lips. She cleared her throat and brought the flattened bouquet up to her nose. "Um, they're lovely. I love the smell of freesia."

Putting them aside, she looked back at him. His eyes held a warm glow that seemed meant just for her. She'd waited all her life for a man to look at her that way. Warmth flooded her from the top of her head to the tips of her toes. "Let me take your coat."

He was already slipping out of it and moving in for another kiss.

She put up a hand to stop him. "We have to talk."

He frowned. "This sounds serious."

She sighed. "It is." She fussed with his coat. "While I appreciate the incredibly generous gesture you made of paying off my garage bill with Donnie, I can't accept it."

"Ah. I'd rather wondered about that. Look, to me it was very simple. You were working too hard, I had a way to fix it."

"That was a lot of money." Her poor aching feet knew exactly how much that clutch cost.

"Not to me. I have a good salary along with a trust fund from a pair of grandparents who equated money with love. I wish you'd let me do this for you."

She swallowed, gathering her courage. "It feels a little bit like payment for services rendered, if you know what I mean."

"What? I don't see your... Oh, yes, I do see." He took his coat out of her hands and dropped it onto the floor. Then, he took her hands in his to kiss each one, first the backs then the palms. "That wasn't my intention. I'm sorry if I hurt your feelings."

Shoot, when he looked at her like that, her insides went all gooey. She almost forgot the point of the conversation. Almost. "I'm going to pay you back."

"There's no need."

"There's every need. I have to pay my own way."

He looked at her so hard she could see the wheels turning in his head. Finally, he said, "Okay, but on one condition. I insist you stop working these insane hours. I need you to be free to spend time with me." He dropped a kiss onto her forehead. "I quite desperately need to spend time with you and get to know you. Deal?"

Well, what could she say to that? Not a whole hell of a lot. "Deal."

"It smells wonderful in here. What are you making?"

"Nothing fancy. I stole Bobby's recipe for marinara sauce and stopped by the bakery for some bread." She picked his coat up off the floor to hang it on a hook beside the door. "Let me get you something to drink. I've got a bottle of single malt scotch that has your name on it." She grinned at him.

He grinned back. "What are you having?"

"I have a very nice Barolo that Bobby swears is the only thing to drink with Italian food."

"That sounds fantastic. I'll go with that if you don't mind."

"I'll go get it then. Why don't you make yourself comfortable? I'll be right back."

****

Ian didn't sit. Het wandered around Gina's living room, looking for clues to this woman who had his heart tied into knots. He really couldn't afford to take time away from his work this evening. Not only did he have a lecture to put the finishing touches on, he had three sets of papers to grade. If he were lucky, he had a package with absolutely vital proof of his research waiting for him at the office. The minute he had it, he could go public with his information.

But now, standing here, smelling the mouth-watering scents of tomatoes, garlic and basil, listening to Gina pop open that bottle of Barolo, he couldn't think of another place he'd rather be.

Unless it was with her, naked in bed, making amazing love to her.

Putting a leash on those hopeful thoughts, he took stock of her home. Paperback books lay everywhere. Piles and piles of paperbacks were stuffed into bookshelves, stacked in milk crates, Rubbermaid storage bins and leaning precariously against walls. There must be at least a thousand books in her tiny living room. He pulled one out of a bookshelf. A romance. He looked around again. Most of the books were romances.

How interesting. Never having read one in his life, he'd have to ask her about them.

"Dinner'll be ready in a few." Gina came back into the living room carrying two glasses of red wine and wearing a sweet smile. "You should sit and relax while I get it on the table."

"I'll help." He took a glass from her. He sipped and let the rich wine slide over his tongue, then hummed in appreciation. "Very nice."

That smile of hers quirked up a bit more. "Glad you like it." Their eyes caught, exchanging heat. She blushed then motioned with her head to the kitchen. "I've got to get back to the, uh, to the kitchen," she tripped over the words.

"I'm right behind you." He smiled while he motioned to the piles of books around her living room. "Read a bit, do you?"

She bit her lip. "It's sort of a passion of mine."

"Sort of a passion? I'd say it's a full-blown, knock-down, drag-out obsession, by the number of books you've got here. I know scholars who don't read as much as you do."

"I like to read." She left him behind as she stalked into the kitchen. "I hope you're hungry. I made a lot."

****

"I didn't really notice the last time I was here just exactly how many books you have." Ian stuck his fork into another mound of pasta and shoved it in his mouth. He pointed his now-empty fork toward his mouth. "This is really good," he managed around a mouthful.

"Thanks," Gina said as she pushed her own food around her plate. She wished he'd stop talking about her books. Not that she didn't yearn to talk about her books, she did. She just knew how most people thought romance readers were slightly less intelligent than the missing link. She did what any self-respecting coward would do.

She changed the subject. "Tell me about your research. I'd love to know about your big project."

Ian chased the pasta down with a healthy swallow of Barolo. "It's big, really big. In fact," he picked up a hunk of garlic bread, "I can't stay too long tonight, much as I'd like to. I'm waiting for some verification from France that should have arrived today." His shoulders drooped a bit. "I've also got a ton of papers to grade that I have to return to the students tomorrow." He sighed. "This fantastic meal and being with you are the high points of my day." A shy smile slid over his face. "Unless the verification for my work came in." He winced. "I'm sorry. I get carried away about my project." He chewed off a hunk of bread. "This is great."

She wouldn't let him get off so easy. After all, wouldn't he have shared it with Andi? "I'd really like to know about your research."

He swallowed his garlic bread, then picked up his napkin and dabbed at his mouth. His eyes were lively. "It's quite remarkable, really, how I fell into it. I was on holiday in France when I ran into this woman in the library at the convent of the Sisters of the Immaculate Mary in Tours. We got to talking about things, and it turned out..." He scratched his temple then took off his glasses. "That she was looking for letters from one of her ancestors, the Mother Abbess of the order who lived at the time that the nun I was looking for was there." Chuckling low, he put his glasses back on. "Was that last sentence in English?"

She smiled. "I knew what you meant."

"To make a long story short, I think I can prove that the love poetry of Jean-Louis Bauvet was really written by his sister, a nun of that order."

"A nun wrote love poems?"

"I think so, yes." He grinned his pirate grin. "Quite erotic love poems, actually. They are classified as some of Bauvet's greatest works. If I can prove his sister wrote them, and that he put his own name on them, it will be quite a coup."

She toasted him with her wine. "Here's to Bauvet's sister, the Sister."

He laughed, and toasted her back. "Amen." He took another swallow of Barolo. "But I'm still interested in all the books. Really. How many do you think you have?"

Gina knew exactly how many. "Oh, I don't know." She sighed. Might as well give it up. After all, he'd confided in her about his project. "About two thousand."

His eyebrows nearly shot off his head. "Two thousand! And I thought I had a lot of books."

Gina shrugged. "I know. But I can't bring myself to give any of them up."

"Nor should you, if they give you pleasure. I noticed they're mostly romances?"

She did her best to act nonchalant, but

defensiveness crept in. "I guess." Shrugging, she said, "Not all of them are. Mostly romance, though."

He smiled. "I don't think I've ever read a romance. Maybe you can recommend one and lend it to me."

Of all the things she had expected him to say, that wasn't it. She blinked. The man was a never-ending surprise. It was all she could do to keep herself from sighing. "Sure."

He laughed. "You look like I've just offered you a rattlesnake." He reached across the table to grab her hands. "Really. I'd love to borrow one, if you wouldn't mind."

She narrowed her eyes. "Why?"

"Because it's important to you, and I'd very much like to get to know everything about you." He kissed her hand.

Boy howdy, it made her tremble when he gazed at her with those eyes that looked like he could just eat her up. She had to be careful or else she was going to make a fool of herself and do something stupid, like drool all over his hand. "Do you want some dessert?" Her voice came out raspy and low, like someone had rubbed sandpaper over her vocal cords.

He kissed her hand again then let out a breath. "I'd love to, but I can't stay too long after that."

"I'd better go get it then. Do you want some coffee?" She stood and started gathering up dishes.

"Let me help you." He grabbed at things on the table, piling them up in his arms. Right that moment he tried to balance a plate, a serving bowl with pasta remains in it, both the wineglasses and a platter with half a loaf of garlic bread. He fumbled the platter, and the garlic bread went sliding down onto her kitchen floor followed quickly by the leftover pasta. "Oh, damn." He dropped to his knees, let go of the rest of the dishes, except for the platter, and tried to scoop up the pasta with the bread. He hung his head, and started to chuckle. "Damn. I look like an idiot."

Gina smiled. "Yeah, you do." She knelt to help him. "It's okay, you know."

He turned to face her. Suddenly it was the most important thing in the world that she kiss him. Dessert could wait.

So she did. Right there in the middle of the spaghetti mountain, garlic bread and the spilled red wine that would never come out of the carpet. She dropped the plates she held, then, grabbed him by his marinara-stained tie and pulled him in for a big kiss.

He let out a stunned *oomph*, before joining right in with enthusiasm. After he broke the kiss, he ran a finger down her face. "Is this how you treat all the men who destroy your kitchen?"

"There's a first time for everything." She licked her lips as she stood.

He stood with her. "Let me help you with the dishes."

"No." She shook her head. "I've got a better idea."

She pushed him with a not-so-gentle nudge back into a chair and straddled his lap. Taking his glasses off, she folded them and put them into his pocket. That done, she kissed him.

Ian didn't seem to have any complaints. He got into the spirit of things. He moved his hands underneath her shirt, praise all that was holy, undoing her bra, ridding her of the shirt. It didn't take him long. His hot mouth teased one nipple as his hand tickled the other one.

She threaded her fingers in his hair and moaned. He had a very clever mouth to go along with those magic fingers of his. Her hips made slow thrusts against his penis, which was springing to life between them.

She slipped her hands down between his legs, opened his pants to free him. He let out a long, slow hiss when her mouth touched him.

She stopped to look up at him. "Did I hurt you?"

"No," he breathed, then spread his fingers through her hair and nudged her back to her task at hand. She smiled. She gave a long, swirling lick around the head of his erection. He hissed when she lightly raked her teeth along the length of him.

He came in great scalding bursts. She hummed as she gave him one last lick.

"You're incredible." Ian purred as he looked at her from under heavy lids.

"I aim to please."

"So do I." He pulled her down to the floor and slid her little skirt up to her waist to slip her thong down. He gave each hip bone a gentle nip. "You are so beautiful."

He nuzzled her folds apart and feasted on her. There was no other word for it. She whimpered because the pleasure he brought her was so unexpected, so all-encompassing. It was as if her body was expressing her soul's most ardent wish. He palmed her buttocks in his big, warm hands and delved deeper. She felt the screams of pleasure leave her as she came, and came, and came.

She almost forgot to breathe. "Holy Moley."

"That about says it." He slid back up her body and cradled her to him.

"You ready for dessert?"

He barked out a laugh. "Didn't we just have it?"

"I've got Chocolate Decadence cake from Mario's Bakery in my kitchen waiting just for us."

"Sounds, uh, well, decadent." Ian Ross, word smith extraordinaire, seemed to be totally at a loss for words.

"You deserve it." She stretched up reached over

him for her bra but he stopped her.

"Leave it." He cupped her breasts and nuzzled his face in between them. "You are an amazing woman."

She sighed and held him there close to her, simply to enjoy the tenderness of the moment, such a rare and beautiful thing in her life. She wished she could bottle it so she could bring it out to savor whenever she needed an Ian fix.

He pulled away. "What time is it?"

"I don't have a clue." The magic fizzled out around her. She reached for her bra and put it on, then she got off of his lap.

He stopped adjusting his clothes to look at his watch. "Damn." He frowned. "It's late. Those bloody papers."

She pulled her shirt back on. "You've got to go."

"I wish I didn't." He adjusted his glasses. "After I help you clean up that mess."

"Oh, no." Gina shook her head. "Far be it from me to stand in the way of quest for knowledge."

He reached out a finger to lift her chin. "I'm helping." To that end, he gently kissed her mouth then waded into the pile of spaghetti and bread on the floor.

Between the two of them it didn't take long to clean up in spite of the fact they had to stop to make out a little bit every now and then. She loaded him up with a plate of Chocolate Decadence and marched him to her door, where they had to do a little more making out.

They stood for a moment in silence. He cleared his throat with a harumph. "What about a book?"

"What about it?"

"I want to borrow one. I've never read a romance." He smiled and gestured with his cake to the living room shelves. "One of your favorites."

"Um, sure." Only right now, she couldn't think of

one damn book that was her favorite. She went for easy and went to her room and grabbed the Brockmann hardcover. "Here."

"I'll guard it with my life. Thanks for dinner. I'll call you tomorrow. We can celebrate if my package has come in." He kissed her, then he left.

Much later, after she had taken a shower and watched a rerun of *Friends*, she remembered her brother's letter.

She'd stuck it in the book she'd given to Ian.

Ah, well. She'd already told him about her brother. Ian wasn't a snoop. He had never opened a letter that was addressed to someone else.

Chapter Fifteen

"So, his birthday is in a couple of weeks. What are you gonna get him?" Sandy was stacking cocktail napkins at the bar. Business had slowed, with only a couple of tables taken. As it happened, Mike and Andi were holed up in one of those tables, tucked away in a dark corner.

Once upon a time, Gina would have been miserable with jealousy that Andi was with Mike. Now she felt glad Andi was nowhere near Ian.

How about that?

"I have no idea. I don't even know if I *should* get Ian anything, since *he* didn't tell me about his birthday." Gina perched on a barstool and nibbled the end of her pen.

"Aw, c'mon, Gina. He's turning thirty, that's a big deal." Sandy plopped down on the stool next to Gina.

Spike wandered by, carrying a tub of ice. "I think you should throw him a surprise party."

Slapping her hand on the bar, Sandy laughed. "That's a great idea. You should throw him a surprise party."

Gina was appalled. "That's a cruddy idea. I can't throw him a surprise party."

"Why not? Aren't you supposed to be his hostess with the mostest?"

Gina blinked. She hadn't realized Sandy had brain damage as well as being too nosy for her own good. "Well, for one thing, I wouldn't know who to invite. And where would I have it? He's not an End Zone kind of guy."

Sandy shrugged. "So have it somewhere he'd go. Didn't I hear Mike moan and groan about having to go to Esmeralda's all the time with Andi? Have it there."

"You're insane, do you know that? This is absolutely the worst idea you've ever had."

"I think you should do it," Spike said as she walked by on her way back to the kitchen. "I know who you could get to help you."

"Who?" Gina got a real queasy feeling in her stomach.

Spike and Sandy exchanged a look then both motioned with their heads over to the booth where Mike was cuddled up with Andi.

"Oh, no," Gina said. "There's no way in hell I'd ask her help on something like this."

"I hate to say this, girlfriend, but she's not bad once you get to know her. She'd know who to invite. You don't need her help for the whole thing." Sandy tucked her pencil into her ponytail. "Just for the guest list."

"You are certifiable, you know that?" She glared first at Sandy, then at Spike. "Both of you."

"I think you should think about it." Sandy got off the barstool to see if her table needed anything.

"I have given the idea all the thought it deserves," Gina retorted to Sandy's back.

"What idea?"

The hair on the back of Gina's neck prickled. She knew that voice. Mike stood right behind her. She turned to look at him.

"Nothing." Gina fixed a smile on her face.

"Actually," Spike piped up. "Gina's thinking of throwing a surprise party for her boyfriend's birthday."

Mike's eyebrows shot to the top of his forehead.

"The Haiku Guy's your boyfriend now?"

"Mike." Andi put her hand on his arm. "Behave." She turned her baby blues to Gina. "I think it's a lovely idea. He's probably never had a birthday party in his life." She wrinkled her nose. "His family is unconventional, to say the least."

Gina remembered Ian's mother's phone message. Andi was probably being the queen of understatement. "Have you met them?" The question flew out of her mouth before Gina could stop it.

Andi nodded. "His mother. She's difficult." She looked at the ground, then back at Gina. She had a world of compassion in her eyes. "That's unkind of me to say. She's unhappy, so she takes it out on Ian. It's too bad he's an only child."

"Not for long." Sure she would regret this conversation, Gina couldn't stop herself. "His father just married a much younger woman, and she's pregnant."

"Oh, dear Lord." Andi slipped a hand down over her own still flat stomach. "Vivian is going to make Ian's life a living hell. This is Wife Number Six for his father. She goes a little crazy every time he remarries. This is going to send her straight over the edge." Andi put her hand on Gina's arm. "You have to give him a party. He's going to need all the support he can get."

Gina froze at Andi's touch. She bit the inside of her cheek to keep from pushing it off. "I wouldn't know who to invite."

Andi pulled her hand back, then looked at Gina. Her eyes were kind, but assessing. "The French Department would be a good place to start. If you want help, I'd be more than happy to do what I can. Just let me know." She looked at Mike, who was paying their bill at the bar. "Are you ready?"

"Yeah." He put his arm around his wife and

pulled her close. "For what it's worth, I think you should do the party thing. Sounds like the guy could use some cheering up." They left.

Gina glared at Spike. "I could kill you for this."

Spike didn't seem the least bit worried. "Take Andi up on her offer. Throw the poor guy a party." Spike went to the kitchen.

Gina leaned against the bar. How did she get into these things?

****

"So, how are the party plans going?"

Gina looked up from her check tally to see Dave smiling at her. On another man, she might have thought that smile made fun of her.

But this was Dave.

"I don't know." She pushed so hard against her pencil that the lead broke. "Damn." She tossed it onto the break station.

He sat down across from her. "I think it's good you and Andi are throwing Ian a party."

Gina would still rather stick rocks up her nose. However, Dave was Mike's best friend. He liked Andi. Well, she was starting to like Andi too. Something weird had gotten into the water in Addington. "I'm still not sure."

"You don't have a lot of time."

True. "I'm not sure I can pull it off."

"Of course you can. You're his hostess after all." Dave took her hands. He slipped easily into Assistant Principal mode. "This will be a good thing. Andi's not a bad person. She's part of your life now, if you want to continue to be Mike's friend."

"I do." Gina pulled her hands away from Dave's. He was the only other person besides Sandy and Spike who knew about her crush on Mike. "But it's not about Mike anymore."

Dave settled back against the banquette seat. "I see. Is Ian still in love with Andi?"

"I don't know. I really don't know." She gnawed her bottom lip. "We don't talk about Mike and Andi. It's sort of like a sacred pact between us."

"That's good. Here's another thing to throw into the mix. Andi's told me a little bit about Ian's family life. Even Mike agrees the guy could use a break and that you're good for him."

"Mike said that?"

"Yeah, he did. Further, we all think that it's a damn shame for a man to reach the age of thirty and never have had a birthday party." Dave's gentle smile held that hint of steel that made him such a good vice-principal. "This is a win-win situation, kiddo."

Gina said a quick prayer that he was right.

****

Donald Unger grumbled as he let himself into the French Department's main office. It irked him to be teaching an early morning class; it irked him further the class was French 101A. It irked him that the only time he could get into the office to copy his hand-outs was at the ungodly hour of six A.M.

Ian Ross, Jameson's fair-haired boy, was most likely at home, in his bed, curled around that curvy red-head. It was just another good reason to hate him.

As if he needed another reason.

He turned on the light and woke up the copier by sticking his key counter in it. While he waited for it to make his copies, he checked his mail. Yes! An envelope from the journal he'd just submitted his last article to lay inside. Something was finally going his way. He ripped the envelope open then unfolded the letter.

A rejection. Disappointment flooded him. The article happened to be ground-breaking, brilliant actually, if he did say so himself. They were fools to reject it. His fist clenched around the letter, crackling the paper.

Because it had become his habit these days, he checked Ian Ross' mailbox and saw a beat-up envelope sitting there. Feeling not one twinge of guilt, he took it out of the cubby and examined it. There was nothing particularly remarkable about it, no insignias from any French *université* or *bibliothèque*, only a return address from a small convent in Tours, written in a cramped, distinctly European hand. Sent by regular mail, it didn't look like anyone had signed for it when it arrived.

Hmmm. If an envelope arrives in the mailroom and no one signs for it, does it exist? "I think not," he chortled. If he slipped it into his pocket and walked out of the office with it, no one would be the wiser. If his hunch was correct, this innocent little envelope contained information on Ian Ross' big project. That meant Unger had to take it before Ross could get it.

Except stealing the United States Mail was a federal offense.

Well, okay, he wouldn't steal it. He'd just take it to his office for safekeeping until after he got the department chairmanship. Better yet, not his office but his home. It would be much safer there. He could say he found it in his mailbox buried under some things. He simply hadn't noticed the envelope was addressed to Ian.

It was all a terrible accident.

Whistling, Unger slipped the small packet into his pocket and grabbed up the handouts the copier had stopped spitting out.

Some days it paid to get up early.

****

"You don't have to have the party at Esmeralda's, you know. You can have it catered somewhere else." Andi tapped her short, French manicured nails on the cracked Formica of The End Zone's break station.

Gina looked across the table, straight into Andi Kelly's frustrated eyes. "Where do you suggest?"

Andi took her time, making a big, long, hairy deal of taking a sip of her herbal tea.

Gina clenched her jaw, impatience riding her hard. She wanted to hate Andi Kelly. It pissed her off Andi actually *was* nice. She couldn't help but like her. She cursed under her breath.

"Did you say something?" Andi put her cup down and stared at Gina. The intensity of her gaze made Gina squirm in her seat.

Andi was being really patient, which made Gina all the more bitchy.

Andi should, by rights, be ready to kill Gina by now. Gina had dumped on every suggestion Andi had made about Ian's party, whether Gina liked it or not. A couple of the suggestions had been pretty good.

But jealousy had welled up in Gina, because Andi knew way more about Ian than she did. Gina just couldn't find it in herself to be reasonable.

Gina really had to get over herself. Really. Sooner rather than later.

Like, right now. She took a deep breath. "Nothing. I'm sorry; I'm in a bad mood. I'm feeling totally out of my depth here, so I'm taking it out on you." There. Admitting that shouldn't have felt so good, but it did. Especially when she saw the look on Andi's face.

She looked, well, grateful. And relieved. Andi grimaced as she took another sip of herbal tea. "Yuck. It's gone cold." She pushed it away, then picked up her pen, tapping it on the legal pad in front of her. "So let's backtrack. What kind of feel do you want for this party?"

"Good food, good company, a good time had by all."

Andi shook her head. "If you're going to invite

his department, that ain't gonna happen."

Gina grinned. "You're sounding more like your dad every day."

Andi grinned right back at her. "My mother would be so happy. Seriously." Andi sat back against the booth and folded her arms across her chest. "You do know that you have to invite the department to this, in light of the whole quest for the chairmanship. You're going to be under a microscope, 'cause you're his hostess, so to speak. It's not going to be pretty." She leaned forward, resting her elbows on the table. "Donald and Mary Louise Unger are seriously twisted."

"I went to one department thing already. You're not telling me something I don't know." Gina bit her lip. "How do I keep that from happening? I mean it's the guy's birthday. Isn't there like some kind of academic cease fire clause for birthdays?"

Andi chuckled. "Like Christmas Eve in the trenches during World War I?"

"Yeah. Instead of *Silent Night*, they can sing *Kum-ba-yah*."

Laughing, Andi leaned forward. "Can you picture Ralph and Margaret Jameson roasting birthday wieners over a birthday campfire, singing *Kum-ba-yah* while Donald Unger accompanies them on the harmonica? Everyone will think they've fallen into another dimension."

Gina laughed, but the thought of odd people brought a more pressing problem to her mind. "His mother is coming into town for his birthday."

"I'm not surprised. Vivian is all about making big dramatic appearances. Let's do ourselves a favor and keep her out of the loop."

"Should I invite his father?"

Andi reached for the cup of cold tea, took a sip, suppressed a grimace then wiped her mouth with her napkin. The napkin came away from her mouth with a delicate smear of pale pink lipstick. "I don't see how you can avoid it."

"I was afraid of that." Gina put her elbows on the table and rested her forehead on her hands.

"It's very likely his father won't come. He's never visited Addington in the past."

Gina brightened and lifted her head. "That would be a good thing, yes?"

Andi shrugged. "I personally think Ian would have been a lot happier if his father had taken more of an interest in him." She picked up her pencil. "You still haven't answered my question. Where do you want to throw this clambake?"

"Oooooh, a clambake. Think I could get away with it?"

"In April? On the North Shore? Guess again, cupcake."

"Party pooper."

"It's a dirty job, but somebody's got to do it."

Andi picked up her legal pad and made a big show of studying it. "What do you think of having the party at Hope Monahan's new restaurant? The atmosphere will be nice, since she's also using the space as a gallery. We know the food will be amazing, and Ian's mother will applaud your superior taste."

Was that *superior taste* thing a joke? A put-down? Gina started to get defensive, wracking her decidedly *inferior* brain to come up with something to say.

"You know, I've never thanked you for getting me and Mike together." Andi put her hand on Gina's arm.

Hunh? "Come again?"

"I've never thanked you for helping get me and Mike together. If you hadn't dragged him to The End Zone last New Year's Eve, we'd still be trying to figure out how to talk to each other. I owe you more than you could ever know."

Well, put it that way... "You two belong together."

Somehow, saying the words out loud brought some closure for Gina. Mike and Andi did belong together. Gina was meant for greener pastures. Hopefully Ian.

All she had to do was win him the chairmanship and impress his mother.

Piece-a-cake.

****

"Emily, did I get an envelope from France yesterday?" Ian absent-mindedly rifled through his mail as he turned from the faculty mailboxes to face Emily Smithson, the department secretary. He'd checked his mail the night before. Nothing had been there, so he hoped against hope that somehow it had been mis-filed.

"No." Emily didn't even look away from her computer screen. This had to be due to the fact that he'd asked her the same question every day this week.

"How about this morning?"

"Not this morning either." Emily eyeballed Ian over her wire-rimmed bifocals.

"Are you sure?" Ian scratched his temple. How odd. He felt sure the envelope from the convent should have been there by now.

Heaving a sigh, Emily turned in her chair. She leaned forward and rested her arms on her desk's edge. "Professor Ross. I will check with the work study students who actually put the mail in the mailboxes, but I can pretty much say that to the best of my knowledge, you didn't get an envelope from France yesterday." She gestured to the mountains of paper, envelopes and books everywhere. "It's been a little busy around here lately. If you really think it should be here, you can check with Campus Mail."

She turned back to her computer screen.

"Well, yes, of course." He tried a smile, hoping it would win her cooperation. "I'm waiting for a rather important envelope. If you could keep an eye out for it, I'd appreciate it."

"Of course. Is that all you need right now?"

"Uh, yes." Summarily dismissed, Ian sidled out of the office into the hallway. Disappointed and impatient down to his toes, Ian wondered about what to do next. Time was running short. Soeur Helêne had been very clear in her answers to the many e-mails he had sent her. She had sent Ian a map along with a sample of Bauvet's sister's handwriting, one he could compare to his own copies of the Sister's handwritten poetry and get an expert to confirm it was the same handwriting.

Ralph Jameson trundled by him. "Ian." He stopped. "Got a minute?"

"Of course."

"The committee is close to making its final decision on the chair."

Ian had a bad feeling about this. "That's great."

Ralph looked down at the floor then back at Ian. "How's your project coming?"

"Just waiting for one key piece of evidence."

"That's good." Ralph shifted his briefcase to his other hand and looked at Ian intensely. "I hope it comes in soon."

"Any day now."

Ralph nodded. "Well, I'm off to the dean's office."

Ian watched his retreating back. That was a warning. He'd best get to his office and make a few phone calls to France.

Chapter Sixteen

Ian decided he wanted to take Gina out on a real date. A romantic evening would thrill her to her toes, make her a quivering puddle, and give her an idea of just how much she now meant to him.

That it was more than fantastic, curl-your-toes sex.

He sighed. First he had to finish grading the several mountains of term papers that were taking over his office. He looked away from his computer, took off his glasses then tossed them on his desk. Rubbing the bridge of his nose, he let his mind drift a minute.

He hadn't done so great in the date department with Gina, that was a fact. He wanted, no, he needed to come up with a perfect evening, one that her made her dreams come true.

Dinner? Dancing? Poetry? Flowers and champagne? Were all those things too predictable? Just the fact that he hadn't managed to hit it right so far really undermined his confidence.

The department party had been a bust. She'd fallen asleep at the opera, and she'd hated the movie.

The movie.

She'd mentioned her favorite movie was *Kate and Leopold*. He Googled it. As he read, a huge grin grew on his face. He had hit pay dirt. Ignoring the papers screaming for grading, he left his computer running and went to the video store.

****

"Sandy, I need to borrow your black BCBG stilettos." Gina cradled the phone between her chin and her shoulder while she waved her freshly polished, 'Passionate Pomegranate' colored nails in front of her. She'd used a pencil wedged between her teeth to punch in Sandy's number then spit the pencil out into her kitchen sink. Normally, she would have waited until her polish dried to make her call, but desperate times called for desperate measures.

A mystery date with her sweetie merited a bona-fide core meltdown, as far as she was concerned. Given the instructions to wear something really spectacular, well, that just compounded the panic quotient to an off the scale reading.

"What happened to *your* black evening sandals?" Sandy wanted to know.

"A heel snapped off when I tried them on with the dress."

"The dress as in *the* ultimate, man-killing, hootchie-mama, little black dress you spent a paycheck on at Macy's?"

"That's the one." Gina longed to shift the phone to her other shoulder, but couldn't because of the smudge factor.

"Amen." Sandy breathed, the word wreathed with all the reverence *the dress* deserved.

It was one hot dress Gina had to admit.

"And where is the good professor taking you, to deserve *the dress?*"

"I wish I knew." Her shoulder was cramping up. Polish be damned, she was moving the phone. With the deftness and gentleness of a neurosurgeon performing the most delicate surgery, Gina grabbed the phone in between the heels of both hands and slowly shifted it. In the process, she missed whatever pearls of wisdom Sandy was passing out.

"Come again?"

Sandy sighed. "I said, you two don't have such a great track record when it comes to dates. What if you get all dressed up and he takes you bowling?"

Gina hooted a laugh. "C'mon, Sandy. Can you see Ian bowling?"

"Good point."

"Besides, he told me to get dressed up."

"Maybe he's taking you to the opera again."

Gina shuddered. "I don't think so." But the thought had crossed her mind. "He'd be so excited about it that he wouldn't have been able to contain himself and keep the secret. Anyway, may I borrow your shoes, please, please, please, please, please, *please*?" That ought to butter her up.

"You already owe me big time for covering your shift the last time you went out with him."

Okay. Sandy wanted her to grovel she'd grovel. "I know and I'm *so* grateful! I'll cover two extra shifts for you, whenever you want, and you can borrow anything of mine you want." Gina used her best wheedle voice.

"And I suppose you want me to bring them over there?"

"Gosh, couldja? I'd really owe you. I'm standing here in my underwear." She smiled. She knew Sandy would come through.

"You're so lucky to have a friend like me, you know."

"I do know." Gina smiled at the phone receiver. "You're the best."

****

Gina's doorbell rang about a half an hour later. Gina was in her bathroom, leaning over the sink. Eyes wide open, she was painstakingly careful as she applied her mascara. Startled, she nearly poked herself in the eye.

She kept her eyes wide open as she went to open

the door, so she wouldn't smear black on her cheek and end up looking like a raccoon. It couldn't be Ian—it was too early. She hoped it was Sandy with her shoes.

She cursed as her big toe made contact with her coffee table. She hopped the rest of the way to the door. Wincing, she flung it open, prepared to greet Sandy and grab the shoes before Sandy had a chance to change her mind.

Sandy wasn't at the door. Gina greeted a delivery guy laden down with a mountain of red tulips. She stopped mid-hop. "Whoa."

"You Gina Francisco?" The delivery guy had to be about seventy years old if he was a day, with the voice of Satan in *The Exorcist*.

"Yeah. These are for me?" She thanked her lucky stars her bathrobe had remained firmly belted and that her modesty remained somewhat intact.

"No, they're for Kermit the Frog." Satan the Delivery Boy shook his head. "Who do you think they're for?"

Gina managed a weak smile. "Let me get my purse."

She signed for the flowers and tipped ol' Beelzebub. Weighted down by the tulips, she kicked the door shut.

Arranged in a cut crystal vase, the tulips were cheerfully gorgeous. They made her smile. She noticed the card when she put the tulips on her coffee table. Way beyond curious, way beyond hoping that the flowers were from Ian, she snatched the card from out of its nest of flowers.

Larger than a typical florist's card, and heavier, it rested in a vanilla-colored, finely-textured envelope. Her name decorated the front in a bold and decidedly masculine hand.

Ian's handwriting. Wow!

Almost afraid to open it, her hands were a bit

shaky and her fingers a bit clumsy. She slipped a finger under the edge then pulled the envelope open with a soft *thipppt*.

Her doorbell rang again. This time it had to be Sandy. She checked out her robe, just in case, as she went to open the door.

It *was* Sandy, bearing shoes. "You know, for anybody else I would have said... Holy crap! Where'd you get all those tulips?" She dropped the shoes and flew to the table.

Gina closed the door behind Sandy. "Ian." She sighed. "I think. I haven't read the card yet." She waved it in front of her face.

"Well, what are you waiting for? Crack that sucker open."

Gina's breath caught in her throat as she pulled the card out of the envelope. It was simple, no hearts or flowers, no cherubs or teddy bears. She opened it up and just about hit her jaw on the coffee table. Inside, in Ian's handwriting, was a poem. He'd signed and dated the card on the bottom right corner.

She read it once, twice, then a third time. He'd written her a poem.

Unexpected
I turned a corner
You were there
So beautiful,
Full of Life.
Unexpected.
My heart beat again
For the first time in
Forever.
Life began.
The man I could
Become because of
You.
Unexpected

Eeeeeeeeeeeeeeeee!

"What's it say?"

Gina clutched the card to her chest and looked at Sandy. "It's a poem."

Sandy whooped as she grabbed the card out of Gina's hands and read it. She sighed like the sappy romantic she was. "No one ever wrote a poem for me. This is kind of like when he used to send Andi poems when he dated her. Did he write it fresh, or did he recycle one of Andi's for you?"

Gina's brows mashed down as she grabbed the card back and stared at it. "I don't know. Way to burst my bubble, buddy."

Sandy plopped down on the sofa. "Sorry. I'm just lookin' out for you. Maybe you should find out."

"How am I supposed to do that, *Einstein*?"

"Read his book, *genius*. Don't cop a 'tude with me, sweet cheeks. I'm here to do you a favor. Do you want to borrow my shoes or not?"

Gina sighed. "I'm sorry. But what if he did just recycle one of Andi's old poems?"

Sandy shrugged. "Dunno, and I'm sorry I brought it up. But as I remember, you wanted a poem, and he sent you a poem." She motioned to the tulips with her head. "That's a truck load of tulips. The vase they're in is none too shabby. Looks like the good professor is trying to make a statement here."

Gina looked at the tulips, then at Sandy, all the while keeping the card pressed to her chest. "I think I'm going to hyperventilate. What if he does pull out all the stops tonight? What does it mean? What do I do?"

Sandy laughed. "Just enjoy it and have some fun. By the looks of those flowers," she nodded at them, "It's going to be one helluva ride."

****

Sandy stayed to help Gina with her hair. She

was still there when the doorbell rang, signaling Ian's arrival. At least, it should have signaled Ian's arrival. Gina's confusion-o-meter hit an all time high when she opened the door to find a chauffeur in full uniform on her doorstep. "Uh, hello?" she squeaked.

"Whoa, Nellie!" Sandy nearly crashed into Gina's back as she followed her to get a good look. "Willya look at that!"

Gina did. If she opened her eyes any wider, they'd pop out of her head and roll out her door.

There stood a chauffeur laden down with red tulips.

"Professor Ross has sent me to fetch you, ma'am," said the chauffeur. "He regrets he could not have come himself."

Sandy created quite a breeze by fanning herself. "Hootchie mama. Forget the professor." She nodded at the chauffeur. "Go for Gilligan, here."

"Where do you want me to put the flowers?" asked Gilligan.

Good question. "Put them inside, I guess." She opened the door wider and let him in.

"Professor Ross has a spectacular evening planned, so if you'll follow me..." The chauffeur offered his arm to Gina and nodded at Sandy. "If you'll excuse us..."

"Wait a sec, I need to get my jacket." Gina grabbed it from the top of the table by the door.

Gilligan smiled, grasped Gina's elbow and led her to the limo.

Gina grinned when she heard Sandy burst out of the apartment to follow. They weren't going make a clean get-a-way.

"Wouldja get a look at that," Sandy breathed as Gilligan opened the door to the limo. It looked like the entire thing was filled with red tulips. They were everywhere, springing out of every little nook and cranny.

Gina lost her breath. The whole thing was *so* beyond anything she had ever experienced.

She let the chauffeur tuck her into the back of the limousine. A little numb, she took in all the tulips crammed inside.

There must have been about a hundred cheerful, bright red flowers on fragile green stems. She reached out one finger to lightly trace a solitary, delicate bloom. Afraid to breathe, awed by the sheer extravagance of so many flowers, she picked one out of the side pocket of the door to brush it across her cheek. Low music filtered through the speakers, a pretty, restful piece played by strings. It was classical, and she couldn't put a name to it, but it sounded beautiful. It surprised her how fast she was getting to actually *like* that stuff, especially since she'd downloaded a couple of Ian's mother's solo cello CDs onto her iPod.

The ride didn't take long, just a few minutes really. More than a little intrigued when Gilligan opened the door, she found herself in front of Ian's house. Had she really gotten all dolled up just to stay in? She let him help her out of the limo and lead her up the walk.

Ian opened the door. He stood there with that shy, self-deprecating little smile Gina loved. He had one hand behind his back. "Good, you're here." He stepped out on his porch to take her hand, then presented a single red tulip to her. "For you."

"Ian." Gina shook her head as she accepted his flower. "All these flowers. I'm overwhelmed."

"Don't you like them?" He nodded at the chauffeur. "Thank you." Then he led her into his house then closed the door.

"I love them, they're beautiful. It's just that there're so many."

"I wanted to make a statement."

"Well, you did that." She glanced around his

house. "So, what are we up to tonight?"

"A little dinner, a little music, a little dancing. Let me take your coat." She slipped out of it with a little help from him. He tossed it onto the coat tree standing in his hallway and then he touched her hair and a tiny thrill moved through her. "You look absolutely beautiful tonight. I love your hair. I can't seem to stop touching it."

She shivered with delight. When was the last time anyone had told her that? "You told me to dress up," she stammered. "Where are we going?"

"Come on, I'll show you." He tugged on her hand to pull her along with him, but then stopped. "First, I need to get this out of the way. I've been dreaming of this moment all day." He turned her into his arms and kissed her.

His lips were firm and warm, but gentle, so gentle on hers. She opened up and let him into her life, her love, her heart. It was such a sweet kiss, such a perfect meeting of lips and hearts and minds, she nearly wept.

He murmured in pleasure as he broke the kiss, then pressed his lips to her forehead. "Dinner awaits."

He led her through his kitchen to his back patio. Not only were there more red tulips, there were white fairy lights strung up and twinkling everywhere and candles flickering in the balmy, mid-April evening. A table sat in the middle of everything, with a formal white tablecloth, pristine white china and napkins, along with gleaming sterling silver.

Realizing she held her breath, Gina let it out on a sigh. "This is amazing."

"Do you like it?"

"Oh, my God, yes!" She turned to look at him. "This must have taken you all day to set up."

He tilted his head slightly to the side, then

quickly back again. "It's all worth it, if you like it." He brought her hand to his lips to press a soft kiss into her palm. "Are you hungry?"

Yeah, she was, but not for food. The good professor looked absolutely yummy in that gray designer suit and silk tie. And the way he kept looking at her...

She melted in the glow and forgot the question. "What?"

He grinned, then kissed her palm again. "Come on." He led her to the table, pulled out her chair and kissed her. "Why don't you sit here, and I'll be right back."

Sitting seemed like a real good idea, since she was going a little weak in the knees and couldn't trust her legs to hold her body up. Dropping into the chair, she turned her face up. He cupped her cheek with exquisite gentleness, then leaned down to kiss her, long and languid, one more time.

"Be right back." He grinned then trotted off.

Gina put one hand on her lips and the other over her pounding heart. Oh dear, sweet, ever-lovin' Lord that man could kiss. Every cell in her body went on red alert.

True to his word, Ian wasn't gone long. He came back rolling a service cart laden with several shiny, silver-domed serving dishes. "Here we are." He flashed her that grin again. "Honesty demands I explain that I didn't cook any of this." He kissed her on the tip of her nose. "I threw myself on the mercy of my caterer. I hope you like what she came up with."

Curiosity piqued, Gina asked, "Where'd you go?"

He took her hand and lightly rubbed her knuckles with his thumb. "Hope Monahan, of course."

"Ooooh, I love Hope's food. How did you know?"

His eyes bubbled with mirth. "Remember that

ballet gala last year?"

Gina gave him a slow nod. Her most painful memory of that gala had to be her and Ian standing together, both their hearts swinging from their sleeves, watching Mike and Andi practically make love on the dance floor. "I remember."

"Well." He looked directly in her eyes. "I find that my most vivid memory of that night is a certain redhead rearranging the dishes on the buffet table, clucking over the presentation."

She thought no one had noticed! "You caught me. I'm so embarrassed."

"Don't be. I found it charming." He picked up one of the dishes, took the cover off and waved it under her nose. "I've got Hope's shrimp in puff pastry. She says it's your favorite."

Gina licked her lips. "It's everyone's favorite."

He picked one off the plate and held it expectantly in front of her. "Open wide."

She opened her mouth, and he put the flaky, buttery pastry in between her lips, his mouth open in a mirror image of hers. Closing her eyes, she savored the taste of the sweet, plump shrimp, spiced further by the taste of Ian's fingers. "Mm."

"It's good, eh?"

She opened her eyes to see him smiling at her. "Oh, yeah."

He picked up a crab-stuffed, mini-Portobello mushroom. "What about this?"

The man's eyes were practically on fire and made her feel very warm. Hot. Burning. She licked her lips before opening them. His gaze followed the motion of her tongue. Opening her mouth with a seductive little smack, she let him pop the mushroom in her mouth.

"It's good," she croaked, after she swallowed. Reaching out to the platter he held, she grabbed a piece of prosciutto-wrapped melon. "Your turn."

His smile turned absolutely wicked. He dutifully opened his mouth. His eyes glittered and danced with anticipation as he waited for her to make the next move.

She slipped the slice of cantaloupe into his mouth. His lips closed around her fingers, and his tongue coaxed the morsel out of her grasp. Some gentle suction, then his mouth oh-so-slowly, ever-so-reluctantly let go.

She watched him chew and swallow the fruit and warmed when he gave her a very wolfish, predatory smile. She invoked whatever saint was listening to give her strength.

Apparently, all the saints were out on a dinner break, because her strength failed her big time. No way she was going to be able to resist this man tonight.

Nor did she want to.

He leaned forward and touched his lips to hers. The contact was brief and lighter than air, leaving her needing more. Her soul groaned with need. As he retreated oh-so-slightly, she parted her lips and begged.

The next meeting of lips started slow and light, then grew exponentially as he coaxed her mouth open with his tongue. Not an invasion or an over-taking, just a subtle and skillful coercion into a deeper sharing of the heat that always lingered between them. Willingly going where he lead, Gina abandoned herself to the kiss.

She tasted the sweetness of melon. His body radiated heat, and he smelled amazing, all clean and woodsy. Somewhere along the way, he lost the tray he'd been holding and pulled her closer. His hands were hot and commanding, yet gentle in their insistent exploration.

She had never been so turned on in her life. She sank into his touch, his kiss, then twined her own hands around his neck, trying to bring him even closer.

Ian broke the kiss and leaned his forehead against hers. His breath puffed warm and sweet on her face. She could feel his smile more than see it.

"Let's dance," he murmured.

"Dance?" Feeling more than a little drugged by his touch, she leaned back to look at him. "You want to dance?"

He gave her a soft smile and sighed. "Yeah." He got up and offered her a hand. "Come dance with me."

She let him help her up. "You want to dance?" she repeated.

"Yeah." He repeated as he took her hand, brushed kisses along her knuckles, gave her a gentle tug. "Come with me."

What choice did she have? She followed her heart and went with him.

He lost his jacket as he led her further out onto his patio to a spot surrounded by tulips. Candles flickered and throbbing jazz filtered out of a hidden speaker. All of it was hot, but not nearly as scorching as the flames burning behind his gaze. Slightly off-kilter because of it, Gina stumbled.

Ian caught her. "Remember the first time we danced?"

Ohhh, yeah, she did. Smiling, she kicked off Sandy's shoes, ran her hands up his arms to clutch those amazing shoulders of his, and lifted herself to stand on his feet. "I think it went something like this." She raised her face in a mute request for a kiss.

He brought his head down and obliged her. Then, swaying gently to the music, he rubbed his hands low on her back and pulled her in tight against his body. "Hmmmm. I think you're right." He rested his cheek against the top of her head.

He cuddled her close as they kissed and swayed to the music. He felt so warm. He made her feel so safe, so cherished, she melted against him.

His lips moved against her hair. Tightening her arms around his neck, she gave herself over to the amazing sensation of being loved by this man.

Lips met and clung, tongues played hide and seek as the two of them moved in time to the music. He found the zipper of her dress and slipped it down. The air was cool against her back, but his hands were warm as he explored her bare skin. Nimble fingers managed to undo the clasp of her bra while they meandered around her back.

The dress slithered down Gina's body and pooled at her feet. Ian lifted her into his arms, never breaking their kiss.

Gina worked at his tie, pulled it off and flung it aside. She went to work on the buttons of his shirt, anxious to be skin to skin with him. A few of the buttons popped off and pinged against the floor.

Ian carried her through his living room. Somehow, she lost her bra on the way to the staircase. They made it to the top of the stairs, and he let her slide down his body. Devilish, bringing his hands around to cup her bottom, he knelt before her and pressed open-mouthed kisses on her breasts, her belly. He stripped her of her tiny black lace thong panties and flung them over the banister. After peeling her silky, smoky black, thigh-high stockings slowly down her legs one at a time, he kissed his way back up to where she was already embarrassingly wet for him. She twisted her fingers in his silky hair as he parted her center to taste her with his tongue. Whimpering, helpless, against the magic he worked with his clever mouth, she purred. When she hovered right at the brink, when she didn't think she could take anymore, the devil stopped and flashed her a sexy smile.

Ian stood and scooped her quivering body into his arms. "Let's take this to the bedroom."

She gasped as he lifted her. Ian caught that gasp with a kiss, then nearly bounced them off the hallway wall. Laughing and awkward, he trundled her off to his bed.

He made it, and dropped both of them down. They bounced, and she made a lunge, got him onto his back and straddled him. "Gotcha!" she said, feeling a grin spread across her face.

"Help." His devil's voice was a sexy whisper, hoarse with need as he grinned back at her. Those wicked eyes were filled with the knowledge and promise of every naughty fantasy she had ever had, and maybe a few she hadn't.

Looked like tonight might be her lucky night.

She went to work on the clothes he still had on, her fingers clumsy in their haste. It didn't help that he busied himself by teasing her nipples into tight peaks.

Finally, she managed to get his trousers undone and *off*. He stopped her hand when she tried to caress him through his silk boxers. "Not yet," the devil, *her* devil, hissed. Sitting up to look at her, his eyes clouded with passion and need. "I want this to last." He shook his head while he used his other hand up to cup one of her bare breasts. "You are so beautiful."

She shivered, but pressed herself deeper into his hand and wrapped her arms around his neck. Kissing him deeply, she gave herself to him, heart and soul.

Chapter Seventeen

Though he hadn't had a drop to drink, Ian felt woozily drunk, just from the joy of having Gina warm and willing in his arms. He'd planned, he'd imagined, he'd dreamed, and not a single plan or dream came close to the reality of how amazing the very naked Gina Francisco felt in his arms.

He pretty much figured he had died and gone to heaven. No dream had ever felt this good.

If he didn't lose himself inside her incredible body within the next five minutes, he might quite literally die. Expire right there on the spot. Ripping his mouth away from hers and grinning his best piratical grin, he flipped her over and on to her back.

He reclaimed her mouth with a fervor that made them both hum with pleasure. She parted her thighs, so he snugged his erection close against the wet warmth of her as he kissed her.

Her body felt so soft against his. She had on the most amazing perfume, something spicy and exotic. That scent combined with her own perfume, hot and moist just for him, Gina nearly drove him stark raving mad.

Once more, he broke their kiss, this time to reach across her and dive into the nightstand for a condom. The drawer didn't cooperate, so he had to yank really hard on it. It pulled out of the nightstand and crashed to the floor, along with the reading lamp and a pile of books.

He didn't care. He only cared about getting that

condom *on*. She watched him, and it filled him with power. Her smile held all the wisdom of Eve. Her eyes were heavy-lidded with desire for him. No longer Clark Kent, he'd morphed into Superman and was going to get the girl.

Warm and soft in his arms, she smelled of roses and woman. She tasted like all his dreams come true. Desire rode him hard. Unable to wait any longer, he joined his body with hers in one long, slow, excruciating slide.

She gasped, a cute, sexy, little sound that he caught with his mouth. Using his tongue to match the rhythm of his lower body, he began to move.

Oh, dear Lord, she felt tight and hot around him, her inner muscles squeezing him, goading him on. It was sweet, so sweet. Her hips churned beneath him as he plunged into her again and again. He grew impossibly hard inside her, ready to burst. He slowed his thrusts to torture them both.

Shifting so he could reach between their bodies, he found her sweet spot and rubbed it. "I want you to come for me," he whispered into her ear, smiling when she moaned. Then, keening *Oh, my Gaaaawwwwd*, she arched against him and detonated into a million pieces.

After that, all bets were off. He moved hard and fast into her, sliding his hands to cup her bottom and hold it steady for his thrusts. Her orgasm went on and on and *on*, milking his shaft mercilessly, bringing him to flashpoint.

Unable to hold on for a second longer, Ian surrendered to his body's demands and came in long, hot, pulsing waves.

****

"How are you feeling?" Ian asked, after he had found the strength to lift himself off her and snuggle her close to his chest.

Gina sighed and stretched like a sleepy kitten.

Doreen Alsen

"Amazing," she purred. Her hand snaked down his body to trace lazy designs on his abs.

Her blatant female appreciation of his body felt so good that Ian thanked his Maker for the genes he'd inherited along with his fitness routine. He kissed the top of her head, then smiled against her wild red curls. "Good."

She yawned. "I can't believe you sent me all those tulips. And the food from Hope's and all those lights and candles."

"Did you like it, then?"

"Oh, yeah. It was sooo romantic. Almost like that scene from *Kate and Leopold* when Hugh Jackman fixes that dinner for Meg Ryan on the roof of her building. I love that movie."

He could feel her smile against his chest. He matched it with one of his own. "I know."

She raised her head to look at him. "How so?"

"Well, I wanted this to be special for you. Since I hadn't had too much luck in predicting what you'd like, I watched that movie, hoping to find a clue there."

She sat up. "No way!" Her eyes had popped open.

"Shouldn't I have?" He pulled her back down against him. "You mentioned you liked it. I wanted to find out more about what you like."

"I guess I just never gave it much thought." Her brows squished and met in the middle of her forehead.

"Well I did." He kissed her. "Give it that much thought, that is. Pleasing you is very important to me."

Stunned, Gina said, "Wow."

"Did you get the part about the flowers?" His tone sounded a bit anxious now, like he was suddenly nervous.

"I got the tulips, they're beautiful. I've never

180

seen so many in one place at one time."

"But did you get what they mean? The language of flowers and all that."

"Leopold didn't send Kate tulips."

Ian kissed her. "Never mind. I'm glad you liked them."

Gina kissed him back and clung to him, so much in love, she felt almost like a cliché.

There were several times during the night that they almost made it downstairs to eat some of the dinner Hope Monahan had made. The first time, they got waylaid by Ian's inability to go more than two steps without kissing her breasts. The second time, they had to go back to bed because of Gina's fascination with Ian's body, which she just *had* to play with, kiss and tease. The third time, they never made it off the bed, because Ian had to return Gina's favor. He loved her with his mouth, with his tongue until he had her practically howling with pleasure.

On the horizon, the sun peeked at them when they finally fell into a deep, sated sleep.

****

"Ian, wake up! I think someone's downstairs!"

Ian's eyes jostled open, his vision blurry due to lack of sleep and Gina's urgent shaking. Blinking a couple of times, he ran his tongue around his teeth and slapped around on the nightstand for his glasses. Memory came back pretty quickly. The glasses weren't there. He'd lost them somewhere between the patio and the bedroom. Damn.

"There it is again! Hear that?" Gina sat bolt upright and clutched the sheet to her chest. "It sounds like it's coming from downstairs."

There was a definite thumping and scraping, much like the sound his front door made when the lock got tricky. If someone was breaking in, he wasn't being subtle about it. "I'd better check this out." Kicking the tangled sheets from his legs, he got off the bed and grabbed his robe from the closet. "Wait here," he told Gina.

"No way," Gina said. "I'm coming with you."

"Gina," he said, helplessly watching as she wrapped the sheet around her like a toga. "It might be..." He shook his head as he noticed the determination glinting in her eyes. "All right, then, come along. But stay behind me."

"Think we need a weapon?" She scoped out the room. Without waiting for an answer, she picked up the lamp off his floor and tested its weight while she pulled it out of the wall.

Ian had to smile. There she stood, her red hair wild, her skin flushed with sleep and whisker burn, her tiny frame swathed in his navy blue Egyptian cotton sheets, armed with a lamp, ready to do business with whomever they met down in his living room. His darling, little warrior. "Let's go, Xena. Time to beard the lion trying to get into my den."

She muttered something he couldn't quite make out, about beards and lions, but he didn't bother to stop and ask her about it, because there *was* someone trying to open his front door. Truly concerned now, he took off towards the sound.

He bounded down the stairs just as the door flung open to reveal his mother. "Bloody hell."

"Ian, darling," Vivian Morgan Ross Tremayne chirped as she stepped across his threshold into his house. "I've come for a visit."

He went to her to give her a hug, but remembered he was totally naked under the robe. He dodged her arms while managing to kiss her cheek. "Mother. What a surprise." The door remained open, and the morning air held an April chill. He moved behind her to close it, noticed the mountain of luggage and sighed. Looked like Mum planned a long visit. "What brings you here?" What the hell? He'd deal with her bags later. The door swung closed with a heavy thump, like an oversized question mark at the end of a sentence.

Vivian didn't answer. Even travel-mussed she still looked elegant and formidable. Not one of her champagne-blond hairs were out of place. Her classic Dior travel ensemble didn't have a single wrinkle. And her frosty blue eyes were taking in the clothes on his stairs.

It wasn't pretty.

There were clothes scattered everywhere, most of them obviously female, obviously lingerie. Ian stifled a groan.

"Ian?" The voice from the top of the stairs might have been soft, but it exploded into the living room like a thunderclap.

Vivian looked up the stairs at Gina, then back to Ian. Both perfectly plucked brows were arched with unspoken disapproval. "Aren't you going to introduce me to your friend?"

He cleared his throat and reached for his glasses, remembering too late he wasn't wearing them. His hand continued up to his hair, which he raked his fingers through. "Of course. Mother, this is Gina Francisco." He winced when he heard Gina's strangled *eep* of alarm. "Gina, this is my mother, Vivian Tremayne."

Gina struggled down the stairs, obviously attempting to preserve her modesty, clutching a lamp and a queen-sized sheet to her bosom. The sheet happened to be way too long, making it almost impossible for her to walk as well as hold on to the lamp and banister at the same time. She bobbled a bit on the bottom step, but kept her dignity pretty well, Ian noted with pride.

Not every woman could look so splendidly regal wrapped in a sheet and armed with a reading lamp.

"Mrs. Tremayne," Gina let go of the banister and extended her hand. "I'm pleased to meet you."

Vivian looked at the hand as if it were a Gila monster and shook it gingerly. "*Ross* Tremayne," she corrected. "Vivian *Ross* Tremayne."

"I'm sorry, Mrs. Ross Tremayne." Gina turned mortified eyes up to Ian. "I'd better go, uh," she nodded her head back up the stairs, "you know."

He did. He most certainly did know. He was quite painfully aware of the fact that she had no clothes on under that cotton sheet. "Of course. Take all the time you need." He caught her grateful smile before he turned his attention to his mother, who shot daggers with her eyes at the love of his life. "Why don't you sit down out here, Mother. I'll go to the kitchen to make you a cup of tea. You must be exhausted after your flight."

Vivian looked at him while giving an injured sniff. "I don't want to be a bother."

"You're never a bother." She was *always* a bother. She *lived* to bother him. It never stopped with her. He watched Gina grab her thong panties off the newel post and skedaddle up the stairs. She tripped with a couple loud thumps at the top while trying to retrieve those wispy thigh high stockings he had peeled off her luscious legs last night.

Best not to think of last night. Mother. His mother. He had to make tea for his mother. "I'm going to the kitchen to make you some tea."

"I'll go with you." Vivian didn't give him a chance to argue, and followed. He sighed and accepted his fate, then groaned when he saw the state of the kitchen and the back patio and garden.

Not to mention the kitchen was bloody cold from the patio door being open all night. He tugged his robe around him.

The fairy lights were still on, but the candles had guttered out, leaving hardened, vanilla-scented wax puddles all over. The bucket of ice had beaded with water droplets, but he knew that the ice had long melted, that the unopened bottle of champagne in the bucket was now tepid at best. The plate of goodies he had been feeding Gina lay on the floor right where he had put it, right next to where Gina's sexy little black dress lay in a tiny heap. He looked back at his mother, with a thought to stutter out some sort of explanation.

She bent down to pick up his tie and a couple of buttons that had fallen to the floor after Gina had attacked his shirt. She held them out to him, along with his tie. "You ought to be more careful where you put your things," she told him.

Well, bloody hell. He felt a spurt of anger at both her presence and her attitude. He damn well didn't owe his mother any explanations or justifications about his personal life. He snatched the things out of her hands. "I'll take these upstairs. I'm sure you can find the kettle."

Her mouth flopped open, but Ian ignored her. Deliberately, he slowly gathered Gina's dress from off the floor and left the kitchen, picking up other articles of clothing as he went.

****

Gina sat in the middle of Ian's bed, on the verge of tears, wondering what the hell she should do. She heard the door open, but didn't look up. She didn't quite know what she to say to Ian.

"Hey." Ian's voice sounded soft and kind. He sat beside her, put whatever he carried down next to him, then lifted her face with one finger so she had to look at him.

She parted her lips to babble out an apology, but he kissed her before she had a chance. It was a sweet kiss, a comforting kiss, but by no means was it chaste. She felt quite breathless when it was over. He smiled. "Good morning."

"Is it?" She swiped at the moisture welling in her eyes. "A good morning, that is?"

"One of the best."

"Right." Like she could believe that. "Your mother just let herself into your house and caught us in…"

He kissed her again. "It's one of the best mornings I've ever had because I got to wake up with you next to me."

Well, that made her feel all warm and squirmy inside, and left her at a loss for words. She looked around to avoid saying anything, then noticed he had brought up her clothes. Twin waves of relief and gratitude washed over her. She snatched the clothes up and leapt off the bed. "Thanks for bringing these up. I'll just get dressed and get going."

"You're not going to leave me here to face her alone, are you?" He frowned. "You can at least stay for a cup of tea."

No, she was quite sure she couldn't. She needed to get out of here fast. "I think it's better if I go. I've got stuff to do today, and I need to get to it." She didn't look at him as she wiggled back into her clothes.

"Gina, don't go." He took her hand and made her stop and look at him, at his face. What she saw there nearly broke her heart. "I know this is embarrassing, but it'll be okay, I promise."

Gina shook her head. Nothing would make this okay. He hadn't seen the *You Jezebel* look his mother had flung her way. "Please. Not now." She shook her head. "It's really not the best time to sit down and meet your mom. Let's give her some space."

He shook his head, clearly disagreeing. He ran a hand over her hair, his touch so light it could have been a sigh then he kissed her cheek. "All right. Give me a chance to get some clothes on, and I'll take you home."

Ugh. Gina had forgotten about the limo. "That's okay. Just let me call a cab."

"But…"

"Don't worry about it. I'll be fine." Fully dressed now, except for Sandy's shoes, she felt a bit more in control.

Ian stood there giving her a look she couldn't decipher. "Very well, then. There's a phone and phone book in my study." He turned his back on her to rummage through his closet.

It was best for her to go home, she decided as she quietly opened the door and slipped from the bedroom.

****

After she called the cab, Gina hid in Ian's study until she heard him go downstairs and into the kitchen. She still had to retrieve Sandy's shoes from the patio. The possibility of dying of embarrassment by crossing paths with Ian's mother held less danger than the possibility of Sandy murdering her if she returned without the shoes. The lesser of two evils, and all that jazz. Plastering a brave smile on her cowardly face, she marched herself to the kitchen.

Ian puttered at the kitchen counter while his mother hovered over a cup of tea, enumerating Ian's father's current misdeeds. She stopped abruptly when she caught sight of Gina. Ian turned at the lapse of sound, but smiled when he saw her. It was a tight, controlled smile, not one of the sweet smiles Gina had gotten used to.

"I'm sorry," she said. "Don't let me interrupt you. I'm just going through here to get my shoes."

"I already retrieved them for you." He picked them up and brought them to her. "Did you get hold of a cab?" He kissed her on the top of her head.

A kind of strangled noise peeped from the peanut gallery.

Gina took her shoes. "Yeah. It'll be here in a coupla minutes."

"Are you sure you can't stay for some tea?" Ian's

mother's silky tone left no doubt that she wanted Gina to disappear off the face of the earth.

"Thanks, but yeah, I'm sure." If there was one thing she was sure of, it was that she'd been born a coward. She plonked down in a chair to put her shoes on.

Ian smiled and took her shoes from her, then crouched. One at a time, with tender care, he pressed a little kiss to each foot as he slipped it on her feet. "There you go, Cinderella."

She heard the brittle sound of a china teacup meeting a saucer with considerable force. They both looked over to where Vivian sat, very pale in her chair, ferociously studying where her cup and saucer met the wood surface.

Ian unrolled himself from his crouch and kissed Gina again. "Mother, may I refresh your tea?"

"No, thank you." Vivian's voice sounded sharp enough to cut glass.

Gina leapt up. "That's my cab. I've got to go."

Ian followed her. "I'll walk you out."

"There's no need to. I'll be…"

"There is every need," he interrupted.

"Fine." She looked at Ian's mother. "It was nice meeting you, Mrs. Ross Tremayne."

"Call her Vivian," Ian offered.

Vivian looked snake bit. "Yes, please do. It was nice meeting you." She turned her attention back to her tea, dismissing Gina.

Ian didn't talk as he walked Gina out to the cab. They got there, he opened the door for her, but before she could escape into the car, he grabbed her up into his arms and kissed the living daylights out of her. "This isn't the end of the world, you know. It's embarrassing, yes, but it's not a big deal. My mother will come around."

Gina felt dubious. "I've got to go. Thank you for an amazing evening."

His smile warmed. "No. Thank *you*." He kissed her again. "You'd better go while I can still let you."

She slipped into the cab. He closed the door behind her, then opened the front door and handed the cabdriver a wad of bills. "Keep the change. Just make sure you get the lady home safely."

The cabbie took the huge fistful of money. "Thanks, Mister."

Ian closed the door, then tapped twice on the car's roof and stepped back.

Gina put her hand up to the window and watched him grow smaller as the cab took her away.

****

There were days when it just plain paid big time to get out of bed, Donald Unger thought as he checked his e-mail. He'd been working overtime to track down Ross's French connection, and he'd finally found it.

Okay, so the nun in question thought she'd spoken to Ian Ross via e-mail. She barely even questioned why Ian had a new hotmail account.

Ian Ross didn't have a new hotmail account. Donald Unger did, though. Little by little, he had put together the bits and pieces of Ross's work.

Unger sat back in his chair and put his hands behind his head. He had to hand it to that bastard Ross. As theories went, this one was a doozy. Without the hard evidence to back it up, no one would believe him.

With it all together, it would cement Ross' place as a superstar in French criticism. And at the tender age of thirty no less.

But he would go nowhere without the contents of the envelope Unger held on to for safekeeping.

As long as Ian Ross taught anywhere else but Barrett University, that was fine with Donald Unger. The man was a flash in the pan. No good would come of his being the chair of the French

Department.

Unger would be damned to hell and back before he would work for that upstart.

And all he had to do was hold up the confirmation of Ross' research until after the search committee named himself as chair. It was like shooting fish in a barrel.

He smiled, leaning forward as he shut down his computer. It shaped up to be a great day.

Chapter Eighteen

T-minus two hours until B-day, a.k.a. the birthday party upon which all Gina's hopes and dreams for impressing Ian's mother and the entire French Department depended.

Once she realized this would be the litmus test of her being able to plan and execute department functions, she nearly had a crow.

Gina was, no question about it, a mess.

"So how are you getting Ian here?" Sandy plopped a bowl of guacamole next to a huge basket full of tortilla chips.

Gina moved a stack of napkins from one spot on the buffet table to another. It had to be the fifth time she had done that, not that she was counting. At that particular moment, getting all the details right for Ian's birthday party was more important than finding a cure for cancer.

She also needed, very desperately, to make Ian's mother like her. It had been an extremely difficult week.

She had done absolutely everything she could to make Vivian happy, even to tracking down some of her out of print, solo cello recordings and listening to them. The music was beautiful. She tried to tell her this, but Vivian had shot her down. No matter what she tried to talk to her about, Vivian remained cold. Gina had yet to figure out how someone who could make such lovely music could be so mean at heart.

One thing was certain. Absolutely no way she

was going to give Vivian Ross a reason to complain. Everything was going to be perfect.

****

Vivian felt not one single pang of remorse as she shut the door to Ian's study behind her. Knowing her son's habits, she sat in his desk chair and surveyed his desktop.

While some might call going through her son's things snooping, she called it protecting him from himself. Right now, he very much needed protecting from that little red-headed floozy he fancied himself in love with.

She sniffed as she opened the top drawer of the desk. There was no way she would let her son repeat his father's mistakes. She was disappointed to only find a neat row of red pens, paper clips and postage stamps. Further rifling of drawers also yielded nothing good. She really didn't know whether to be relieved or not.

Vivian Ross Tremayne did not subscribe to the notion of no news is good news. Her first ex-husband had disabused her of that notion when he had slept with scores of younger women and she'd never suspected because she hadn't been able to see past the stars in her eyes.

It had been an eye-opener in more ways than one when she had come home from a concert tour and walked into her bedroom and found Arthur in bed with the maid, in a position that would have shocked the authors of the *Kama Sutra.*

She sat back in Ian's desk chair and shook her head. Andrea had been perfect for Ian. It made her want to spit nails at the unfairness of it. Andrea had up and married that lout Mike Kelly then left Ian ripe for the picking. She might as well have put him in a box with a bow and handed him over to that waitress, who, apart from a pair of very obvious assets, was the absolute *wrong* woman for Ian.

It was intolerable from beginning to end. Ian constantly touched the twit's hair, those scandalous red curls she did nothing to contain. When he thought she wasn't looking, Ian would squeeze the girl's derrière.

She shuddered. Someone had to save her boy from himself. She would look after him as she'd always done.

She used a nail file to jimmy open a locked drawer on the bottom right hand corner of the desk. Sighing as she poked through the piles of zip drives, CD's and floppy discs, she began to despair about finding something useful. When she moved a trashy hardcover novel to see underneath it, an envelope fell out of the book. Curious, she picked it up.

Hmmm. Addressed to Gina and unopened. Her heart did a little happy dance as she slid a letter opener under the flap.

As she read it, a smile blossomed on her face. The little tramp had a brother in prison. Even though the letter was in Ian's possession, she doubted he even knew about it. He could be remarkably dense about some things.

At any rate, here was the ammunition she needed to get rid of Gina Francisco once and for all. It would not be good for her baby's career to have his wife's brother in prison.

Wife, ugh, she shuddered at the thought. Her boy was ambitious. He would be at the top of his profession; it was just a matter of time. But he wouldn't get there with that red haired albatross around his neck.

She would use this information to rectify this situation. She just had to be careful to use it at exactly the right time.

Vivian would save Ian from himself, by whatever means necessary. It was her sacred duty as his mother.

****

Ian considered himself the luckiest of men to have escaped a fuss on his birthday. He'd managed to talk his mother into going out with him and Gina for a quiet dinner at Hope Monahan's brand new restaurant. No fuss, no mess. Gina didn't even *know* it was his birthday, so he felt sure he could just lean back and enjoy the evening.

Well, enjoy it as much as he enjoyed any evening that included his mother glowering at his ladylove.

That had to change sooner rather than later. Gina was in his life, hopefully for a long time to come.

Like forever.

He sighed as he maneuvered his car through the rain soaked streets of Addington. He hated his birthday, hated it with a passion. It was always just one more thing for his parents to fight about, especially after their divorce. His birthday had been less about him and more about them trying to outdo each other with trips and gifts.

Never, ever a simple party with other children.

Now he shuddered at the thought of a party. He preferred to spend his birthday quietly and alone, emphasis on *alone*.

No, he felt glad there'd be no fuss on his birthday. He neatly slid his car into a space in front of Hope Monahan's restaurant, aptly named All About Hope.

Vivian sniffed. "Doesn't look like much, does it?"

Ian shook his head. "Mother, the restaurant looks charming." It did, with neat cedar shingles, a warm glow shining from every window. A trellis, which would be covered in roses come June, marked the entrance to the gardens, through which ran a well-marked flagstone path. Ian got out of the car, moved around to open the door for his mother and helped her out. "Hope Monahan is a genius with food. I'm sure you're going to love it." If God existed, and if He was merciful.

In the end, all he could really hope for was that she'd just be quiet and keep her jaundiced opinions to herself. He watched her get out of the car and sniff distastefully at the air.

Fat chance.

****

"They're here?"

Gina bit her lip and cast a sideways glance over to Andi and Mike. "Looks like. Guess it's magic time."

Andi shook her head. "Don't be so worried. Everything is lovely." She gave Gina a quick hug. "This is a good thing."

"I sure hope so." She looked around the room. A sea of men in tweed jackets with suede patches on the elbows and women dressed in clothes that would never go out of style, mainly because they'd never been *in* style to begin with, filled the room. Without a doubt, this was not her usual crowd. Picking up a glass and pinging on it, Gina caught most everyone's attention. "Quiet, folks! Ian's on his way." She gave them all a big grin and knew pure terror.

The door snicked open. In walked Ian and his mother while the room exploded into loud shouts of "Surprise!" Gina flung her arms around a suddenly stiff-as-a-board Ian, as she gave him the best birthday hug she could manage. Then she looked up at his face, ready to kiss him.

If looks could kill, she'd be not just six feet under, she'd be seven. She looked again. Nope. Better make it ten feet under.

Stunned, Gina stood back to let Ralph Jameson and his wife bring Ian and his mother into the room. Ian's eyes met hers, though, over the tops of the Jamesons' heads. He made it real clear what he felt. He was not a happy man.

195

But he was a game man. As the Jamesons led him into the room he smiled, shook hands, accepting any and all manner of birthday greetings. Someone, Andi maybe, shoved a glass of champagne into his hands, and he took one big gulp, then another and drained that sucker.

Nope. Not happy at all. She wished the floor would open up so she could disappear.

"Hey, kid. Buy you a drink?" Mike appeared in front of her, holding two beer bottles by their necks. He held out one to her while toasting her with the other.

"Oh, yeah." She took the bottle, toasted him back then took a big swig. They stood there together for a moment, watching the crowd.

Mike swallowed his beer. "Who's the lady in the flowery tent thing?"

"Huh?"

"Over there, talking to the prince of poetry." He pointed his longneck at Ian.

Gina laughed. "That's Margaret Jameson, Ian's boss's wife. That's not a tent. It's a caftan."

"Coulda fooled me. Did it come with sunglasses so the rest of us don't hurt our eyes?"

Gina laughed. "It's designer and made out of pure silk. Probably cost more than I make all year."

"Designer tents. Who knew?"

Gina slapped his arm. "You're so bad."

"Yup." Mike squinted. "Uh oh. Incoming."

Gina followed Mike's line of sight and saw Donald Unger huffing his way toward her. "Don't go."

Mike had already started to leave. "Sorry, I think I hear my wife calling me."

"Chicken."

"Damn straight!" Mike disappeared into the crowd.

Gina sighed and braced herself to deal with

Ian's least favorite colleague. Truth to tell, Donald Unger made her feel uneasy, like she was a mouse, and he was some big, bad ol' cat.

Unger touched her arm. "Lovely party, Gina. I do think you managed to surprise Ian."

"Thanks, but I can't take all the credit. I had help." She resisted the urge to rub off where he touched her.

"Well, everything is top notch. Just like Ian's research. That's a stunning project he's got going."

Every nerve that Gina possessed jumped up and tingled in alarm. She took a drink from her beer. "We don't talk much about his work."

That earned her a smarmy smile from the Donster. "Of course. I imagine you have much better ways of spending your time." The rat bastard looked at her chest and licked his lips.

Yuck. The man had a lot of nerve. She ought to poke him in the eyes with one of those bamboo fruit skewers.

She looked around for a polite way to disentangle herself, but it didn't look like she could get away any time in, oh, say like the next millennium. She sighed inwardly, smiled at Unger, opening her mouth to say something, *anything*.

A loud crash, followed swiftly by an unholy screech stopped her. Both she and Unger jumped and looked for the source of the noise.

"You bastard! What are you doing here?" Vivian stood proud and pale in the middle of the room, a veritable Valkyrie ready to do battle.

In the doorway stood the object of her wrath, an older gentleman who looked remarkably like Ian. A very pregnant woman with blond hair and dark roots stood next to him, her eyes wide, her chin high. The man had his arm wrapped tight around her waist, as if he were afraid to let her go. "I'm here to help celebrate my son's thirtieth birthday," answered the man. "Where is the boy?"

"Father." Ian broke out of the crowd. "What a surprise."

Boy howdy, did Ian look shocked. And pissed. Mostly pissed, actually. His jaw was set so hard it could crack walnuts. His eyes were chips of ice behind his glasses. He didn't even look at Gina as he passed by her on the way to greet his father. Her heart swooped, dove, then fell to the ground with a splat. This did not bode well.

Very cool fingers came from behind her to take her hand. Gina cast a glance over her shoulder to see Andi smiling a wan smile at her. Gina squeezed Andi's fingers back. It felt good to have moral support.

Even from Andi. Especially from Andi.

The man stepped toward Ian and extended his hand. "Ian, m'boy, you look well. Happy Birthday."

****

Ian looked at his father's extended hand and blinked, unable to think of anything to say. He focused on his father's face, which looked, as usual, guarded and cool. What in the name of all that was holy could Ian say?

Especially in light of the fact that Vivian wailed a rather effective imitation of a banshee. Ian hid a wince.

His father raised his eyebrows. "Good lord, Ian, is that your mother? No one told me she was going to be here."

That accusatory tone frosting his father's voice never failed to raise Ian's hackles. "I assure you, sir, had I known you were going to grace us with your presence, I would have made other arrangements for Mother."

Vivian stormed up in a cloud of Patou's Joy. "Arthur, how dare you show up here with her!" Vivian's head made a violent nod in the direction of

Ian's father's companion. The poor girl's eyes grew moist, but she kept her chin high.

Arthur tightened his grip around her waist. "Courtney is my wife and Ian's stepmother. She has as much right to be here as you do."

Ian choked at the words *stepmother*. Damn it, the girl looked several years younger than himself. But he didn't have the luxury of recovery time, as his mother was about to have a hemorrhage over the whole thing.

"Stepmother? You bring that underage tart here and dare call her Ian's stepmother?" Vivian had turned a lovely shade of red. Her breathing became labored. "Nothing makes you happier than undermining my position in my own son's life."

Oh, yeah. Mum was about to explode. Just what Ian needed.

"Vivian, really, do calm down." Arthur slipped into his I'm-the-most-superior-human-being-in-the-universe persona. "Stop shrieking like a fishwife and display some tact. In fact, I think you should apologize to Courtney."

"Oh, you do, do you?" Vivian tossed her head back and bared her fangs. The battle was on. "When hell freezes over."

Arthur sighed. It was the sound of suffering. "I can see you're in one of your moods." He launched an extremely pointed look at Ian. "I thought it time you met Courtney. After all," he patted Courtney's very big tummy, "she's carrying your baby brother or sister in there."

Courtney kept her eyes glued on Ian. She looked as red as the proverbial beet. "It's so nice to finally meet you."

She looked impossibly young and eager with her overdone make-up, bad dye job and flashy designer clothes covering her very pregnant belly. Ian felt sorry for her, plain and simple. "It's nice to meet you."

Her gratitude was obvious and painful. Hell, the whole situation felt painful. His father's forced *bonhomie*, his mother's rampant hostility, Courtney's pregnancy, this whole sordid domestic drama being played out in front of every single one of his colleagues... Ian was getting the biggest headache of his life. He wanted to say something to diffuse the tension, but words escaped him. He took his glasses off to pinch the bridge of his nose between his thumb and forefinger.

He felt a small hand give him a pat on the back. He looked. Sure enough, Gina stood next to him. She touched him with a motion that was most likely meant to be reassuring. Her eyes were clouded with emotions—worry, chagrin, remorse. Whatever. She apparently was the architect of this disaster; she *should* worry about what might happen next.

****

"Hi!" Gina thrust her hand out at Arthur. "I'm Gina Francisco, we e-mailed a few times about the party..."

A sharp gasp punctuated that statement. "You!" Vivian stood there, pale as a cadaver, shaking with violent emotion, pointing a bloodless finger at Gina. "You're responsible for this?"

Gina swallowed. Ruh-roh. Though she quivered in Sandy's designer stilettos, she straightened her spine to face Ian's mother. "If by that you mean, did I invite Ian's father and his wife to Ian's thirtieth birthday party, then yes." She nodded her head once, then turned her attention to Arthur and Courtney. "Why don't you come with me? We'll get you something to drink."

"That would be lovely." Arthur's face sported a grim smile. He gave Courtney a loving squeeze on her shoulder. "Why don't you go on ahead? I'll catch up to you after I've had a few words with Ian."

Courtney went on tippy-toe and kissed Arthur on the cheek. "Okay, Pooh Bear."

"Oh, please." Vivian's tone dripped with disdain.

Ian sighed. The sound ripped a small chunk off of Gina's heart. She wanted to look at him but didn't dare. She forced herself to focus on what she did best—getting food and drink for people. Tugging a little on Courtney's arm, she put on her game face. "Come with me, Courtney. You're going to love the shrimp in puff pastry."

Chapter Nineteen

"And, oh my God, look at my roots! Look!" Courtney fluffed her mostly blond hair to present exhibit A to her gathered audience. "I haven't been able to do 'em for eight months now."

Gina looked at Mike and rolled her eyes. He grinned and gave Andi's neck a gentle squeeze. Courtney had been regaling them to pregnancy horror stories for the better part of the last hour. Gina had whisked her out of Vivian's line of fire and set her up at a table with Mike and Andi. Upon learning that Andi was pregnant also, Courtney had begun a long litany of pregnancy woes, everything from swollen ankles and sore nipples to hormones and hemorrhoids.

After Ian's father's arrival, the party had taken on a bizarre feel. Ralph Jameson and his wife had descended upon Ian's father and had introduced him around to the French Department folks. Right now Ralph and Arthur were in a heated conversation on the pros and cons of the Euro versus the Pound Sterling. Ian danced attendance on his mother, trying to interest her in chatting with some of the other guests, but it didn't look like he was having very much success. Gina, by default, had taken custody of Courtney.

It didn't take long to figure out Courtney wasn't the brightest crayon in the box.

She was nice enough, sure, but Gina had heard enough of the trials and tribulations of pregnancy, and, by the looks of her, so had Andi. Whoever said pregnant women glowed had never slapped eyes on Andi Kelly. She appeared pale, sported dark circles the size of Cleveland under her eyes, and she had, due to horrendous morning sickness, actually lost significant weight she couldn't afford to lose. Poor Andi.

Courtney leaned forward as far as her amazingly huge belly would let her and patted Andi's hands, which were ripping up a napkin on top of the table. "What are you doing about the irritable bowel syndrome?"

Mike choked. "Wouldja look at the time?" He sprang to his feet and clasped Andi's shoulders. "Better get you home, spud."

Gina chuckled in spite of the fact her buds were deserting her. Only Mike Kelly could get away with calling the woman who looked like Grace Kelly reincarnated, spud. "You sure you have to go, Mike?"

Mike yawned a very large, very fake, jaw-popping yawn. "Oh, yeah." He dragged Andi out of her chair. "Got a real early day tomorrow."

"You're leaving?" Ian's voice sounded clipped and controlled from behind Gina.

She turned to face him. He looked especially grim. "Hey, Ian." She wanted to touch him, but didn't dare.

"I've got to take Mother home, she's not feeling well." He took his glasses off and shined them on his tie. "I wanted to say thank you and good night. No one's quite ever done anything like this for me before."

"Aw, Ian, sweetie," Courtney lumbered to her feet. "We didn't even get a chance to talk."

"Yes, well, regrettable as that is," Ian put his glasses back on, "I have to take Mother home. Perhaps another time."

Courtney narrowed her eyes. "Your daddy and

me flew all the way in from London to see you." Along with Courtney's dark roots starting to show, her Tennessee ones were beginning to make their presence known. "He'll be real disappointed if you don't spend some time with him."

Ian pursed his lips, something Gina knew he only did when he was seriously pissed. "I'll be in touch."

Gina desperately wanted him to touch her, kiss her good-bye, anything, Ian just turned and walked away, over to where Vivian waited. In the flick of an eye, they were gone.

Ian hadn't even spared her backwards glance.

****

Alone with his mother in the car, Ian's emotions churned in an extremely unhealthy stew. Most of it came from the woman in the passenger seat, spewing venom about Gina with reckless abandon.

He couldn't take it anymore. "Mother, if you say one more word about Gina, I will pull the car over, push you out and leave you on the side of the road."

"Don't be silly, Ian. I'm your mother, you wouldn't do that to me." She waved a hand. "At least not over that stupid cow of a girl. What was she thinking, inviting your father like that?"

"She probably thought it would be a nice thing to have my family there to help celebrate my birthday." He gave a mirthless little chuff. "How could she possibly realize how toxic a situation that would be?"

"Toxic? Now really, Ian, aren't you being overly dramatic?"

"No, I don't think so. You and Arthur need to be experienced to be believed."

"That's rather rude, Ian. I only have your best interests at heart."

Something snapped inside him, like a snarling dog finally free of his tether. "*You* were the rude one.

You have done nothing but belittle Gina time and time again. And that's not to mention the way you've talked up Andrea every time you could."

She sniffed. "I like Andrea. This Gina is far beneath you. Her brother is in prison, for pity's sake."

Ian felt side swiped. "How do you know that?"

"I found a letter he wrote to her in a book I ran across in your study."

"That was in a locked drawer in my desk. You had no business being in there."

"How else can I protect you?"

Unbelievable! Absolutely unbelievable. "I don't need your protection."

"Of course you do. Every boy needs his mother to look out for him."

"Oh please." Ian was done. She was out of his life as of now. "What I need is for you to go the hell away and leave me alone."

"You don't mean that."

"I absolutely *do* mean that!" He gripped the steering wheel tighter. "As of right now. We're going to my house, and you're going to pack your bags, and I'm going to put you on the first plane back to London."

Tears welled in her eyes. He'd been there, done that. No more. "Please, spare me the waterworks."

"Ian, how can you be so cruel?" she mewled. "I'm your mother."

"I'm well aware of that. What do you expect me to do? You violated my privacy, you opened mail not addressed to you, you insulted the woman I'm in love with. I'm done until you can behave better."

"I shan't apologize to that tramp."

"Very well. That's your decision. But listen to me, Mother. You're not welcome in my life until you accept Gina and respect my privacy."

****

205

"Ian, wonderful party the other night. Margaret wants me to thank Gina for inviting us." Ralph Jameson huffed as he trundled down the French Department hall, trying to catch up with Ian.

Ian turned and put on his best manners. No need reminding anyone that the party had been a bloodbath. "Thank you for coming."

"Eh, no problem, that. We always love a good party." Jameson's face turned serious. "I wanted to ask you something. Have you gotten final confirmation from your source about your research?"

Ian rubbed his chin. Come to think about it, no he hadn't. He'd had so many distractions lately. It made him ashamed to have lost sight of his career. "I'm still waiting for some information. I should have it soon."

"Will you have it by this afternoon?"

"This afternoon?" He calculated the time difference to France. Any faxes or e-mails would have already come. "No. Why?"

"I am sorry to hear that." Jameson shook his head. "We begin final deliberations tomorrow."

"So soon." Ian fought against a huge bubble of panic forming inside him.

Jameson sighed. "It's no secret you're my first choice, but I'll have a difficult time selling it to the committee without this extra little boost from your project. Donald Unger has a lot of years of service under his belt. That's hard to beat."

"I see," Ian managed to say.

"I'll do what I can, of course." Ralph looked at his watch. "There'd be no problem convincing them about you if you had your project set to publish." Jameson patted him on the arm and left him standing in the hall.

Right-bloody-oh. Ian didn't think he would ever feel better again, at least not in this century. He rubbed an unsteady hand over his churning stomach. His life had taken a distinct plunge into hell.

He'd thought that losing Andrea to Mike Kelly had to be the worst thing that could ever have happened to him. Boy, had he been wrong. Losing that chairmanship would be so much worse. That position meant so much more than a job.

He made it to his office, unlocked the door and sat down at his desk.

As much as he hated to admit it, he needed to show his father he was a success. His father had been disappointed he'd gone into academia instead of medicine. Arthur Ross, power surgeon that he was, thought academia to be a small step up from music, which had been the field his mother wanted him to go into.

It didn't matter to her that he hated playing the viola and really wasn't musical. It didn't matter to either of his parents that he loved French and was happy being a teacher.

They both loved titles. Being the chair of the Barrett French Department would have satisfied them on some level.

And now, he might fail at that. Damn, his career was going down the loo in a big hurry. Ian should have been paying more attention.

Especially to his research.

This Bauvet discovery would be the cherry on the top. They couldn't ignore his achievements if he scored that coup. Unfortunately, he had no idea where the information he should have by now actually was.

He'd been so distracted. What had happened?

Gina. He'd been paying too much attention to wooing Gina.

He looked at the shelf where his journals had been before Unger had nicked them. It *had* to be Donald Unger. No one else had a reason to do such a ridiculous thing.

He should have told Ralph about it when it happened. Again, there was that distraction.

Okay. A plan. He needed a plan. Of the most urgent importance was to find out how Unger had undermined his research, as he suspected he had. If Unger had indeed derailed his work, he would find out. He needed all his mental and emotional energy for that. No distractions. No letting his mother dump her emotional garbage on him any more. No more of his father showing up with nubile stepmothers.

As much as he didn't want to, he had to cool things off with Gina for a while. She was a distraction, a delicious one at that, but one he could ill afford at this juncture. He had to tell her, of course. He'd been avoiding her, which was unforgivable. He needed to apologize as well as explain.

Filled with new resolve, he put his glasses back on and marched down the hall to his office to make the phone call he should have made a week ago.

****

"Hey, Gina, slow night?" Dave sidled up to the bar.

Gina sat there, working on a crossword puzzle. She sighed as she slid her gaze up to look at Dave.

The man was a major honey, gorgeous inside and out. If Gina had half a brain, she would fall in love with him. He had an amazing body. His face looked so handsome, it made angels weep. He had a steady job he loved; he didn't kick kittens and puppies. He probably spent the bulk of his spare time helping little old ladies across the street.

He didn't get bent out of shape when you did something nice for him like, oh, say, celebrate his birthday... Unlike some people she could mention.

She tapped her pen on her crossword puzzle. "Hey, Dave. What's a four letter word for urban blight? Starts with an *s*."

He sat on a bar stool next to her. "Got to think about it." Smiling at Spike, he waved her over. "Hey, Spike. How's it going?"

Spike put a napkin down in front of him. "Hey, Dave. What can I get for you?"

"A Sam Adams sounds pretty good right now." He drummed his fingers on the bar then rolled his shoulders. "It's been a bitch of a day."

"Oh, yeah? Well, tell ol' Doc Spike all about it." Leaning in on the bar, Spike preened a little as she spoke. Gina rolled her eyes. The entire wait staff at The End Zone knew Spike had a bit of a crush on Dave. Never mind she was a little too young for him. Never mind she wasn't at all the type of woman he usually went for, Spike carried an Olympic-sized torch for Dave Mason.

Dave shook his head. "Not worth reliving." He reached out to tweak Spike's pierced nose. "Bobby making onion rings tonight?"

Spike's face turned bright red. It really clashed with the flamingo pink hair. "I think so. I'll go check." Off she went.

Gina took her turn to shake her head.

Dave looked at her. "What's wrong with you?"

Gina sighed. Exasperation with Dave warred with loyalty to Spike. Loyalty won. "Nothing. This crossword is really frustrating."

"Smog." He tapped the crossword puzzle with his index finger, grinning at Gina's blank look. "Your four letter word for urban blight." Dave turned on his bar stool around and looked around the dead End Zone. "So. How'd the big birthday bash go?"

Oh, goody. Gina's favorite topic—how she'd screwed up with Ian. Maybe giving up Spike would be better. She glanced at Spike, who looked so earnest and eager as she hustled down the bar with Dave's beer. Nope, couldn't do it. "You obviously haven't talked to Mike yet. The birthday bash managed to be a big bust, thank you very much."

Dave lifted his eyebrows in question. "What happened? You and Andi had everything planned down to the last cupcake crumb."

"Yeah, well, I didn't take into account that Ian hates birthday parties. Then, I went and invited his father, who brought his very pregnant, very young wife, who just happens to be a retired stripper, which sent Ian's mother through the ceiling. Good times, I tell ya, good times." She rolled her eyes when Dave chuckled. "His mother and father made a huge scene, right in front of all of Ian's colleagues." She conjured up a ghost of a smile. "Ian won't return my calls, probably doesn't ever want to see me again, and you know what?"

"What?" Dave actually seemed a little bit pissed.

"I don't blame him. I engineered a perfectly horrible situation and put him right in the middle of it."

"Ian Ross is a big boy. It's not your fault his relationship with his parents is crappy." Dave picked up the bottle Spike had left on the bar and took a swig. "Man, that's good." He set it back on the bar. "I see this with kids all the time. The parents have a bad relationship, and the kids blame themselves. Drives me crazy. Big newsflash, Gina. Ian's parents are responsible for their bad relationship. Ian can't fix them. Neither can you."

"I don't want to fix anything."

Dave skewed her with a very pointed look.

Gina puffed out a breath. "Okay, maybe I *did*, but I should have known that throwing them all into a social situation where everyone Ian works with could watch the freak show was really boneheaded."

"How could you have known that they wouldn't behave?"

"I just should have known. I've spent enough

time with Vivian to know she's a drama queen and a major manipulator. That woman can pull strings like nobody's business." Gina reached up to pull her ponytail tighter. "She hates me. She's been looking for just the right thing to make Ian break it off with me. I handed it to her on a silver platter."

"So there *was* something to break off?"

"Yeah, there was." Admitting it brought tears to her eyes. She blinked them away. "We had nothing in common except for getting our hearts tromped on, but we were having a good time. I thought it had potential to turn into something special, but obviously I thought wrong."

Dave took another pull off his beer. "Maybe not. He might surprise you."

"The only thing that would surprise me at this point is if Ian marched right through those front doors now with a song in his heart, a twinkle in his eyes and proclamations of undying love dripping from his lips."

Dave chuckled, leaned up against the bar, prepared to take another swig of his beer. The sound of the front door opening obviously caught his attention because he swiveled his head to take a look, then whistled. "Don't look now, baby, but prepare yourself to be surprised."

Gina turned in her seat and saw one adorably rumpled French professor coming through the door. He wore his professor uniform, a blue oxford button down shirt tucked into a pair of khakis, loose tie, and a slightly wrinkled jacket. His hair looked like he had combed it with a garden rake.

He looked preoccupied, but then again, the only time he didn't look a little befuddled was in bed. Sandy nearly ran him down with a tray full of beers and he hardly noticed.

Gina sighed. She turned her head to see Dave staring at her. "What?"

"Want me to beat him up for you?"

She snorted. "Not yet. Maybe later. I want to hear what he has to say first."

Dave winked. "You sure about that? I think he should have his ass kicked just for not returning your phone calls."

"Tempting as that offer is, I still think I want to hear him out. Then you can kick his ass if I don't like what he has to say."

"Sounds like a plan." Dave turned in his seat and faced the bar. He fished a peanut out of the bowl next to him, threw it up in the air and caught it in his mouth. "Go get 'im, tiger."

Gina's knees were a little wobbly as she slid off the bar stool and waited for Ian to make his way to her. A veritable squadron of butterflies had taken up residence in her stomach. For one brief, panic-filled second she thought she might lose her lunch, dinner and tomorrow's breakfast.

Wouldn't that have been special, barfing all over Ian's Clark desert boots as he told her he loved her eternally? Or not.

Oh, God.

"Gina. I'm glad to catch up with you here. I've been trying to call you, but I went straight to voice mail." He inclined his head slightly to one side, like he usually did when he was embarrassed. It was cute.

No, it was not the least bit cute, her inner-diva reprimanded her. You've been trying to call him all week. He should be embarrassed.

"Hi, Ian. What's up?" There. That sounded breezy, nonchalant and to the point.

"I'd, uh, like to talk with you, if you've got the time. When do you get off?"

Gina looked around at the deader than a doornail bar. "I'm on until closing."

"Oh." Ian's brows squashed together into a fuzzy

V over his nose.

Sandy pulled up and dumped her tray on the waitress station. "If you want to leave, it's okay with me. It's really slow. I can handle the floor alone." She gave Ian a dirty look.

Gina pursed her lips. It was dead and not likely to get busy. They didn't need two waitresses working the floor. Sandy could handle it alone, no sweat. But did Gina really want to hear what Ian had to say?

She shouldn't, but of course, she did.

He started to put his hand on her arm, then pulled it back and stuffed it in his pants pocket, as if he reconsidered the gesture. Not a good sign, to Gina's way of thinking. "I'll have to ask Bobby."

"I can wait." Ian glanced around the bar as if he just figured out where he was. "Or I could meet you someplace later, like Esmeralda's."

Esmeralda's? Where they could run into Mike and Andi? Where all the wait staff spoke French like they were born to it? Where the music was so tastefully understated so as not to cover up any loud contributions to the conversation she might make? No, thank you. An idea struck her. "How 'bout this? You go wait for me at that Mickey D's down the road, you know the one, while I go ask Bobby about punching out early. I shouldn't be more than a half an hour or so."

Ian looked at her with speculation running rampant through his gaze. "If that's what you want to do, then that's what we'll do." He smiled a queasy little smile. "If you're not there in an hour, I'll assume you can't get the time off." He shrugged his shirt cuffs out of his jacket arms. "But if this doesn't work, we'll have to come up with another time. It's very important."

Woo-freakin'-hoo. Gina watched him turn and leave the bar. Either way, this meant progress. If they were over and done with, she could laugh and get on with her life. She could be glad she had dodged a bullet and found out his true colors before she gave her heart to him.

Who was she fooling? She had given him her heart many times over already, more the fool she.

Sandy nudged her. "What are you waiting for? Go talk to Bobby."

Gina's feet felt like lead blocks as she turned toward the kitchen.

Chapter Twenty

Well, this certainly felt familiar, Ian thought as
he sat with a cup of coffee at a table in Mc Donald's
and let the sense of déjà vu settle over him.

Now, as then, he felt like he would quite
literally choke on trepidation. He had so much more
at stake this time, now that he knew Gina and knew
how wonderful a woman she really was. She
certainly deserved better than a man who might
very soon be unemployed, who was saddled with
family obligations too twisted to untangle. He would
have to make her understand, and do it so he didn't
hurt her too badly in the process. He was good with
words, wasn't he? He was a poet, for God's sake.

Of course, he would have to tap a merry dance to
get her to forgive him for not returning her calls all
week. *Merde*! It hadn't been very well done of him.
He was beyond sorry about that. He reached into his
pocket and touched her brother's letter. He certainly
had a lot to apologize for.

He took a sip of his coffee then cursed as it
burned his tongue. No wonder the damned stuff
came with a warning label.

A haggard woman, with three very young, very
rambunctious children, sat at the table next to him.
On her hip she toted a screaming baby, while trying
to get the three older children to listen to her over
the racket the baby made, as well as the commotion
they themselves were causing.

It appeared to be of no use. The kids tore into

their food, ripping open Happy Meal packages with gleeful abandon. Ignoring the food, they proceeded to argue about who got what toy. A wrestling match over a miniature fire truck was destined to end badly, as all three boys grabbed, lunged and tugged on the hapless toy. The three were a wiggly tangle of elbows, fists and pulled hair. The poor woman hollered, "You boys cut it out before you spill something!"

The woman was a prophet. No sooner had the words left her mouth when an elbow sent one of the sodas flying through the air to land smack dab in Ian's lap.

A split second of stunned silence ensued. Even the baby stopped wailing. Then the woman picked up a wad of napkins and recited profuse apologies while she frantically tried to mop up the spill. All four children recommenced with their caterwauling. The baby screamed as the three boys pushed each other amidst hurled accusations of, "You did it!" "Did not!" "Did too!"

Ian stood and took a napkin of his own to swab down the damage. The napkin didn't do much but leave little white specks of paper on his drenched pants and shirt. "It's all right," he muttered, wanting nothing more than to get to the bathroom to repair his appearance as best he could.

"Need some help here?" Of course Gina would pick that moment to arrive and witness him in all his dripping glory.

A sodden, shredded napkin in one hand, Ian looked up at Gina's face. She looked pretty amused by his distress. "Uh, no thanks. I've got it under control." He picked up another napkin. "If you'll excuse me, I'll head off to the men's room."

"Why don't I grab us another table?" Gina folded her arms under her breasts, plumping them up just the way he liked. He mentally kicked himself. Those were just the type of thoughts that he had to avoid if he wanted to get his career back.

A kid in a McDonald's uniform with a mop and a bucket arrived on the scene. Ian had to stop short or else walk right into that bucket of steamy, soapy water. "I'll be right back."

He took his time in the men's room, but really, there was nothing he could do to alleviate the fact that it looked to all and sundry like he had wet himself. Short of taking off his pants and holding them under the hand dryer, he was doomed to have this conversation with Gina while wearing wet pants.

Bloody everlasting hell.

****

Gina stabbed at the fruit and yogurt parfait she had ordered and smashed the granola topping into it. She didn't feel hungry, didn't want to eat, but her hands needed something to do. Her stomach felt so jumpy there was no way she was going to keep anything else down. She'd chosen a seat close to the front door but within sight of the men's room so Ian could see her once he'd cleaned himself up.

That poor woman and her demon spawn children had packed up and left after their mishap with Ian, leaving the McDonald's a much safer place. Gina sighed while she stabbed at her parfait some more. The spoon got stuck and broke in two when she tried to get it out. She sighed again.

"Well, that was exciting." Ian had somehow made it from the bathroom to her table without Gina noticing.

"I bought you some fresh coffee." She motioned to it as he sat down across from her. "The other cup got pretty cold in all the excitement."

Ian nodded and reached for the cup. "Thank you." He looked down at the table as he toyed with the cup's lid.

Gina cleared her throat and ignored how tight it felt. "So. What'd you want to talk about?"

Ian looked at her with eyes clouded by trouble. Her heart would have gone out to him if not for the fact that she felt pretty sure he was going to break it before their little *tête-à-tête* was done.

"How have you been? I've been meaning to call and it's been a really busy..."

"Good." She cut him off before he could pawn some flimsy excuse on her. "Me, too. Busy."

He took a sip of coffee and winced. "I got some really bad news today from Ralph."

"What happened?" By the look on his face she could tell he meant it when he said the news was really bad.

He blew out a harsh breath. "The search committee for the chairmanship is meeting tomorrow to decide who should get the job. The proof of my Bauvet suspicions hasn't come, and without it, it doesn't look good for me getting the chair, not with Donald Unger's years of service." He fisted his hand around the coffee cup. "I think he found a way to sabotage me."

"Oh, Ian." Boom. In spite of her best intentions, she felt sorry for him, at once mad on his behalf. "What are you going to do?"

"That's the sixty-four thousand dollar question, isn't it?" He glanced down at his very wet shirt, pulled it away from his chest, then gave up. "I don't know. I absolutely do not know. I guess all that's left to do is prove that Donald Unger sabotaged me and confront him, if I even can." He looked less than thrilled with that idea. "I may even be out of a job. Once Unger is chair, what's to stop him from putting every stumbling block he can in my way? He'll make sure I don't advance at the university, put me on all the worst committees and dismiss my research. I wouldn't put it past him to manipulate my evaluations to make it look like I'm a bad teacher. I probably should get my CV ready so I can look for another job."

She had no idea what to say to him. "I'm really sorry, Ian."

Ian kept his eyes glued to the tabletop, but didn't say anything. Just when the silence started to wrap itself around her last nerve, he cleared his throat. "I never really thanked you for the birthday party."

"Please don't." The words tripped over themselves as they flew out of her mouth. "I'm really sorry about all that, too."

"It was a lovely gesture." His tone sounded achingly polite and formal. "You have nothing to apologize for."

Well, that was the truth, but she didn't want to kick him when he was down. Besides, maybe he wasn't going to break her heart. Maybe she was just over-reacting and imagining things. "Andi and I had no idea you would hate a party."

"I know." He took another sip of his coffee. "We'd never talked about birthdays. I'm embarrassed to say I don't even know when yours is." He narrowed his eyes. "How did you find out about mine?"

"I overheard the message your mother left you on your answering machine the morning after that first time at your house."

"Ahh." Ian gave her a smile. It didn't quite make it to his eyes. "I should have figured that out."

"It was a bad idea all around." Gina's foot itched to kick Ian, just to get him to drop all that damn stiff upper lippiness. He seemed so far away from her. She couldn't figure out what he was thinking. She'd rather he got mad, enough to put it out on the table.

Mad she could do. Obscenely polite drove her crazy.

"No, it was a perfectly lovely idea. Anyone with

a normal upbringing would have been ecstatic beyond belief to have his family and friends around him on his thirtieth birthday." He gifted her with another smile, that small, self-deprecating, shy, sweet smile. This time it looked so heartbreakingly sad, instead of the polite one she hated. "I have to ask. Whatever possessed you to invite *him*, especially knowing what Vivian is like?"

Gina knew very well who *him* was and shrugged. "It seemed like a good idea at the time."

How could you have possibly thought it would be a good idea to have my mother and my father in the same room at the same time?" His tone implied that a child of two would have known better.

"Look, I'm sorry, okay? Believe me, I'll never make the same mistake again."

Taking a deep breath, he shook his head again. "I'm the one who should apologize. My mother is a nightmare. She's treated you awfully. I've told her as much. She needs some serious help, though God knows I'll never get her to admit it. I think she's bi-polar." He looked her in the eyes, straight and sincere. He reached into his pocket then pulled out an envelope and handed it to her. "She found this and opened it when she was rifling through my desk. It's unforgivable, I know, but I hope you can accept my apology on her behalf."

She took the envelope out of his hand, recognizing it. "I imagine she was delighted to find out I'm related to a convicted felon. Must make her feel real good about hating me."

"I'm so sorry. I sent her away. But, I don't want to talk about my mother anymore."

Well, that was okay with Gina. She didn't want to talk about Vivian either. She folded the letter in half and stuffed it into her pocket. "What *do* you want to talk about?"

"I have to get my career back on track. This

thing with the chairmanship and my job... I have to fix it. I've got to show Unger up for the sodding bastard he is."

"Of course you do." Ian was a good teacher and a brilliant man. He deserved that chairmanship. She scratched her thumb against the jagged edge of the broken spoon sticking out of her yogurt.

"I've got to do it alone. It's the only way I know how to be. I should have known better than to get so distracted." The words rushed out of him, then he shook his head, and turned it to the side while he swallowed hard. "I just should have known better." He looked back at her, his eyes again distant, cool and polite. "I think it's best that we cool it for awhile. Take a little break while I get things sorted out."

Even though she knew it was coming, the *I should have known better* got her hackles up. "Oh, really?" Well, boy howdy, that stiff upper lip thing came back, just to piss her off. Pissed off felt a whole lot better than pathetic.

"Just for a while. Until I get things worked out with Unger."

What about your mother?"

Ian blinked. "My mother? I've already apologized for her. I've practically kicked her out of my life."

Like Vivian would let that happen. Man, Gina felt frustrated. "She doesn't like me. She'll never accept me. She turned what could have been a lovely evening into a circus freak show."

"I've apologized for that."

"You shouldn't have to apologize for her. She's a big girl. She can apologize on her own."

Ian quite obviously clenched his teeth. "I've told her she has to apologize to you before I let her back in my life. The best I can do right now is apologize for her, make her go away and hope that it's enough for you."

She knew she should keep her mouth shut, but she couldn't. She felt so very mad on his behalf. His parents sucked. "I'm sorry, you deserve better from both of them. Who knew they couldn't get along for even five minutes, especially at their only son's birthday in front of all his work colleagues?"

He leaned in on the table and glanced around, then back at Gina. "You should have known."

"How could I have known? You never told me how bad it could be!"

"You've spent more than five minutes in my mother's company. You've heard her talk about Arthur. Anyone with half a brain would have figured out that the two of them in the same room at the same time would be disastrous!"

Half a brain? Gina felt all the breath leave her body. "I may not be a rocket scientist, or a chorus teacher, or a damned French professor, but I'm not stupid. I resent your implying that I am."

"I didn't say you were stupid. I only said that..."

"I heard what you said." The space he'd mentioned was starting to sound pretty good. She gathered her dignity about her and stood. "You want to be alone, fine. Knock yourself out. You can be sure I won't be bothering you any more."

"Gina, please." He stood as well and reached for her arm.

She pulled it away, out of his reach. "Don't touch me. I may only have *half a brain*, but I sure as hell deserve better than this."

"Look, it's only for a little while. As soon as I nail Unger's hide to a wall..."

"Oh, no. It's not for a little while. Just stay away from me for good. I don't need you or your mother."

"My mother has nothing to do with this, why don't you understand that?" He stabbed his fingers through his hair.

"I only have half a brain, remember?" She shook her head. "You're a total fool if you think your mother has nothing to do with this. She treated me like crap, and you let her do it."

"I didn't! I spoke to her numerous times about you." Again that hand went through his hair. "I had it out with her and packed her off back to England. She's simply not an issue anymore."

"You don't really believe that, do you? Of course she's an issue. She'll always be an issue." She tossed the half of the plastic spoon back on the table. It slid across and fell off. "I can't do this any more. For years, I waited for whatever crumbs Mike tossed my way, always hoping for more, that I'd *be* more, that I'd be all he'd ever need. I'm not going to do that with you."

"I'm not Mike Kelly, damn it."

"No." She shook her head agreeing with him. "You're not. You're worse. At least Mike never led me on."

His face went absolutely blank, suddenly wiped clean of all emotion. "Again. You're quite right. I'm nothing like Mike bloody Kelly. How could I ever even hope to compare to such a paragon?" He looked at his watch. "I think I'd better go now, rather than inflict myself upon you any longer."

She was going to pop a blood vessel. Bam! Right there and then. How dare he play the injured party?

She opened her mouth to tell him so, but he had already turned his back on her to leave. She felt the urge to pick up the melted yogurt parfait and throw it at him, but she didn't. Unfortunately, she had a whole McDonald's full of people looking at her, waiting for her next move.

She hated to disappoint them. She left via the opposite door. Head held high, she didn't crumble until she got in her car and tried to jab the key in the ignition. Frustrated it wouldn't go in, she banged her head against the steering wheel, giving in to the hot tears she hadn't even known she'd been holding back.

But it was over, that was for sure. Ian was right, it was all for the best. But it still caused more than a pang of regret. Like the chump she was, she had fallen in love with him. And like everything else in her life, she'd deal with it alone.

Chapter Twenty-One

"Ian," Donald Unger swiveled in his office chair to greet Ian as he knocked on Unger's office door. "What brings you to my door?"

"You know damn well what brings me here." Ian pushed into the office and shut the door behind him. He neither wanted, nor needed, an audience for what he wanted to say.

Unger smiled as he folded his hands over his stomach. "I'm afraid I don't. You'll have to enlighten me."

Ian took a deep breath to help him keep cool. It was difficult task, when he really wanted to rip Unger's face off with his bare hands. "You sabotaged my research. I don't know how, but I know you did. Why else were you sneaking around my office?"

Unger's eyebrows nearly jumped off his face. "Did I? I'm sure I don't know what research you're talking about."

"Cut the bull. You know very well what I'm talking about. You intercepted a letter with proof that Jean-Louis de Bauvet's sister wrote all his poetry."

Unger's smile grew, and his eyes sparkled. "What an idea! The man who could prove that would be quite the scholar."

Ian curled his hands into fists, then relaxed them to avoid the temptation to plow those fists into Unger's smarmy, self-congratulatory gut. "Is that so? I've got a call in to a certain convent in France. As soon as Soeur Helêne returns my call, I'll prove you're a liar and a thief."

Unger leaned back in the chair, flexed his arms and linked his fingers behind his neck. "Going to be hard to do that now that the good Sister is cloistered."

"Cloistered." This was the first he'd heard of it.

"That's right. Out of sight, out of touch, totally unavailable to the world." Unger grinned. "What some people won't do for a little bit of peace and quiet."

Ian shook his head. "Doesn't matter. It only means it'll take me longer to prove you stole my mail to delay me from going public with my findings. But mark my words. I will prove it."

"You're welcome to try. No one will believe it's anything other than sour grapes and professional jealousy."

Ian's fingers itched to choke the bastard, to wrap themselves around his neck and squeeze. "Don't flatter yourself. You must have been in the right place at the right time. I was just too busy to notice. Shame on me. But mark me well. I'm not too busy now. I will do everything humanly possible to show the world what a sham you are and claim back my work."

Unger burst out laughing. The braying sound grated on Ian's last nerve. "You're welcome to try, but I'm afraid you have no leg to stand on."

"You're a bloody thief. I intend to prove it."

"Ian. Dear boy. Face it. You've lost both the research coup and the department chairmanship. You might as well go find a job teaching high school French somewhere in the boondocks where the students have bad skin and worse accents." Unger snapped his fingers. "Here's an idea. Why don't you go tend bar at the place where your fiancée works, because you're washed up in academia. That's something I can promise you."

"Washed up? Hardly." Ian had to get out of Unger's office before he seriously hurt the man. "But if I were you, I'd watch my back. I will find a way to take you down." He moved to the door and wrenched it open.

"You're welcome to try. Face facts, Ross. It's all over except for the fat lady singing."

"We'll see." Ian left then took off down the hall to his own office. His palms itched to break something. He wished he could call Gina and have her talk him down, but after the way they had left things, he knew his call wouldn't be welcome. Things were done between them. They didn't even have to pretend to be engaged anymore, since he had probably lost the chairmanship.

His office phone rang as he let himself in. He wanted to ignore it, since he was in no mood to be civil to anybody, but it might be from the good Sister in France. Getting back his research was his top, his *only* priority. He flung himself into his office chair as he grabbed for the phone. "Ross."

"Ian, m' boy." His father's voice rang loud and clear over the line. "Glad I finally reached you."

Ian gritted his teeth. "Arthur. I'm quite busy at the moment."

"I won't keep you long then. Courtney and I have an early flight out of Logan tomorrow, and we'd like to see you before we go."

Not bloody likely. "I'm afraid I have another engagement tonight. Perhaps the next time you're in town."

A sigh rushed across the phone line. "We're not likely to be in town again any time soon, Ian. Let me phrase it another way. We came all this way just for your birthday. For myself, I don't care. I'm quite used to your rude behavior. But I must insist you do better by Courtney." He made a husky harrumph into the phone. "We have a matter of great importance to discuss with you."

Ian resisted the urge to pull the phone out of the wall and throw it across the room. Maintenance had read him the riot act the last time he had done that. Instead, he looked at his watch and accepted his fate. "I can't possibly meet you before five."

"Six o'clock, then, at the bar in the Addington Hotel."

Ian rubbed his forehead. However much he didn't want to deal with his father, the conflict looked inevitable. He might as well get it over with sooner, rather than later. He pulled open a desk drawer and rummaged in it with one hand, searching for the bottle of aspirin he kept stashed inside. "Fine."

"Splendid. We'll see you then. And Ian?"

He stopped before he shoved the aspirin down his throat. "What?"

"I mean it when I say I'll tolerate no disrespect toward my wife. You will treat her with courtesy."

"When have I not?" Weariness weighed like a concrete yoke around Ian's shoulders.

"Just getting my cards on the table, boy. See you at six, then." The connection clicked off.

Ian set the receiver back very slowly, very deliberately. How desperate he suddenly felt to see Gina, to hold her, to kiss her. He shook his head. He couldn't let himself go down that road right now. He had to get rid of his bad baggage so he had something better to offer her, something other than a failed academic with a family from hell. She deserved so much better.

****

Ian chalked up the pang of jealousy that stabbed him when he saw his father with Courtney to lack of sleep, rather than to lack of Gina, even though he knew he was lying to himself. Rather, he concentrated on putting one foot in front of the other as he approached their table, much like a foot soldier might do on his way to a battle he's sure he won't win. Left, right, left, right.

Arthur saw him coming and rose to greet him. Courtney sat there looking impossibly young and sweet, wearing her brown-blond hair up in a ponytail and a soft pink sweater covering her very pregnant stomach. His father looked the way he always looked—dapper, distinguished, every seam in place, every button polished. But something seemed different this time about Arthur, something Ian didn't think he had ever seen. It was so new, so blindingly strange, Ian hadn't the faintest clue what to name it.

"Ian, so glad you could make it." Arthur held his hand out for Ian to shake. "You remember Courtney."

Like he could forget? Ian, being a paragon of politeness, shook his father's hand then smiled at his father's wife. "Of course. How are you?"

Courtney smoothed a hand down the massive bulge of her sweater. "Great, thanks," she chirped. "A bit on the huge side, but great otherwise."

"You look lovely." The pleasantries done, he sat, folded his hands on the table and waited for Arthur to get to the point.

"Let me get the waitress over here to get you a drink. Still drinking single malt scotch?" Arthur searched the room for a server.

"Yes, please."

Silence reigned while they waited for the waitress. The background noises—silverware clinking against china, muted conversations buzzing, strains of Mozart filtering through it all—lingered, but didn't make any difference to the quiet that hovered over their table like an unwelcome, and uncomfortable, guest.

"Addington is such a pretty town. I can see why you like it here." Courtney looked as desperate as Ian felt.

"Uh, yes, yes it is." He took off his glasses and cleaned them with one of the napkins. "I'm very happy here."

Arthur harrumphed. "Wasting your life here is more like it. I heard about the opportunity from..."

"I'm very happy here at Barrett University." Ian hoped that would stall his father's tirade about how he was throwing away his career by teaching at Barrett. Though, since he had, for all intents and purposes, lost the chairmanship, maybe his father had a point. But Ian would die before he conceded that. "My career is just fine, thank you."

"You could be the British ambassador to France. Instead you're teaching silly schoolgirls how to conjugate irregular verbs. All you have to do is say the word, and I could make a single phone call, and you'd be working in Paris."

Ian suspected his father was more concerned with impressing people with his ability to use the phone than he was with Ian's career. "I'm happy conjugating verbs. I'm good at it."

The waitress came, at long last, to take Ian's drink order. She smiled, big and toothy, and Ian thought she looked familiar. "What can I get you?"

Arthur, of course, stepped up to the plate to place the order. "Ian, here, will have a Glenlivet on the rocks, and I'll have a refill." He looked at Courtney with soft eyes. "Another ginger ale, sweet?"

She shook her head and smiled at the waitress. "No thanks, I'm fine."

The waitress nodded, her own smile firmly in place. She looked at Ian and tapped her pencil on her pad. "Scotch, huh? I thought champagne was your drink."

Ka-ching. The bartender from Andi and Mike's

wedding. Amber. Gina hated her. Amazing how she could remember him and what he drank that night. Of course, that would mean she clearly remembered who he'd been drinking with. He really didn't want her to bring up Gina in front of his father. "Well, nothing like variety."

"Hmm, guess so. Gina's here tonight you know."

"Oh, really?" *Bloody hell.*

Amber motioned with her head. "Yeah, over in the taproom with Mike, Andi and Dave. I'll go get those drinks and come back to get your order."

Dave? Ian's ears started buzzing. "Dave? Dave Mason?"

"Yep. I'll be right back with your drinks." Off she went.

Gina here with Dave Mason. With Mike and Andi. Like a double date. It didn't bear thinking about.

"I actually have something I need to speak with you about other than your lack of a career." Arthur's voice cut through the buzzing in Ian's ears. It was his paternal, no nonsense voice, filled to the brim with discipline while being totally devoid of any affection. It was the voice Ian was most used to.

Shifting in his seat, surreptitiously trying to get a bead on the taproom, Ian tried to focus on his father at the same time. "I'm all ears."

"As you know, Courtney and I are expecting a child. As you are my only family, I suppose there are certain expectations, or so Courtney informs me."

Dear Lord, his father was going to ask him to have something to do with the child. "I don't know…"

"Just hear me out, boy, let me say this. I realize we are not close. We're not likely to ever be close. I acknowledge I bear some responsibility for that, as does your mother. But you bear some of the responsibility, too."

Doreen Alsen

"You got me down here to scold me about my lack of filial devotion? I'm not going to sit around and listen to this."

"Yes, you damn well are going to sit around and listen to this. It's been a long time coming. You have always known where I was and how to find me. If you had wanted a relationship with me, you could have had one."

Ian longed desperately for that scotch his father had ordered. He had a couple of choices. He could argue with his father and cite chapter and verse about how he hadn't been welcomed by his father's women. He could tell a story or two about one of the ex-Mrs. Arthur Rosses who had been ready, willing and eager to take his virginity, though he'd only been fourteen at the time. He could spin a yarn about the time he had found his mother passed out on her bed, a victim of too many sleeping pills. He'd only been eight at the time. Fortunately, one of the maids knew what to do.

But what would be the point? He did what he always did. "Yes, sir. I'm sorry. You were the best father you knew how to be. Is there a point to this?"

Arthur stared at him for a long moment, then up-ended the dregs of his drink down his throat. "All right, then, to the point we go. You are going to have a little half-brother or sister. Normally, you, as my first born, would be my heir. However, since we are not close, and you shall inherit a good deal of my money via my divorce settlement with your mother, I find it necessary to leave you with a token, and leave the rest of my money to provide for my new family with Courtney."

Ian felt a bit light headed. For a sickening, stomach-churning minute there, he had thought the old man was going to ask him to be the baby's godfather. He definitely should have known better. It was much better knowing he was only talking about money. "Okay."

Arthur raised an eyebrow. "Okay? Just like that?"

Ian chuffed a breath out his nose and felt a faint smile lift his lips. "Just like that. I neither need, nor want your money. I've got enough of my own."

Amber trundled up to the table with their drinks. "Are you ready to order?"

"Thank you, not yet." Ian accepted his scotch. He sucked it down a big sip.

"Well, let me know when you're ready then." Off she went.

Arthur started to say something, but Courtney put her hand on his arm. "You're being very generous about this," she said to Ian. "Thank you."

"Don't thank me. If anything, I should be thanking you. This conversation has only served to prove to me for once and for all how insignificant I am to Arthur's life."

"What are you talking about?" Arthur put his drink down and sputtered. "I came here for your damn birthday party, didn't I?"

"You used the birthday party as an excuse to come here and disinherit me. My whole life I've been nothing to you but an inconvenience or a trained seal brought out to entertain your friends or reflect glory on you." He drained his glass. "I'm done. Keep your money; keep your damned new happy family. I wish you well."

He stood and along with nearly up-ending his chair, he almost knocked a passerby in the face. Startled, he attempted an apology, only to find the very pale face of Andi Nelson Kelly staring back at him. Reaching out a hand to steady her, he croaked. "Andi."

Her husband inserted himself into the mix. "Ian. Watch out for my wife's nose. I like where it is on her face."

"Mike. Hello." He'd called Ian by his name. Well, it was better than Haiku Guy. Ian felt his composure flow out his toes. "What brings you here?"

Andi took control of the situation. "Arthur. Hello. Courtney. How are you feeling?"

"Great, thanks." Courtney nudged Arthur. "Honey, this is Andi Kelly and her husband, Mike. You met them the other night."

Arthur chuckled as he stood. "I'm not in my dotage yet, sweet. Of course I remember." He extended his hand, all gracious charm. "Good to see you again."

And once more, Ian became a footnote in his father's life. Bloody hell. He had to get out of here.

"You remember my friends Gina and Dave? You also met them the other night." Andi may have been talking to his father, but Ian knew the words were for him. That was the last coherent thought he had, for Gina stood right in front of him, more beautiful than a woman had a right to look.

She also had bloody Dave Mason's hand on her elbow, like he was staking claim. The sight rankled enough to burn through Ian. He wanted to pound his chest, grab her and whisk her away by swinging from chandelier to chandelier, out of the restaurant, out into the night.

"Of course I remember Gina. She was gracious enough to invite me to my son's party." Arthur took every advantage to play the poor martyred father, only invited into his son's life by the kindness of strangers.

"It was my pleasure." Gina looked so tiny next to Dave, and in that moment, Ian felt clearly all that was lost to him. Gina had been the best thing he had ever known, and he had pushed her away with both hands.

"Gina." He stuffed his hands in his pockets. "Good to see you."

Gina flicked him a look but didn't linger over it. "Ian. Good to see you."

He couldn't help himself. "What brings you here tonight?"

Gina looked at Andi, who took it upon herself to answer. "We're here celebrating. Dave got promoted! He's now the principal of Addington High School."

Ian finally made himself look at Dave, who glowered and hovered over Gina. "Congratulations. I didn't know you had applied for the job."

Dave grinned. "Lots you don't know about me, *old chap.*" He winced and looked at Gina. "Ow."

"I think we need to go," Gina said to Andi. Without dropping a beat, she nodded to Arthur and Courtney. "Nice to see you again." Without looking at Ian, she grabbed Dave's hand and pulled him along with her. "Let's go."

Ian barely heard Mike and Andi make polite good-byes while he watched Gina drag Dave Mason out of the dining room. No doubt about it, he thought. His life sucked.

A cold, pale hand dragged him out of his self-pity. He looked down to see Andi. "I'll see you at Tuesday's board meeting, right?"

He smiled at her, he had to. After all was said and done, she *was* a good friend. "Right. See you Tuesday." Then he sat back down in his seat, for he didn't think his legs would hold him up anymore.

He knew he wanted to get out of there, but he thought he'd just sit there for a while after that, just to make sure Gina and Dave were gone before he went out to the parking lot.

"You're a fool to let that girl get away."

Ian looked at his father. "I suppose you're going to describe in detail, again, how foolish I am."

Arthur laughed, for once. "No, I think it's pretty obvious you know just what you're letting get away." He looked away, thought for a moment then looked back at Ian. "I think I'm safe in saying that the problem between you and that girl is your mother."

"Please. The last thing I need from you right now is to run down Vivian. She is what she is. I'm a grown man. I know how to deal with her. I've a lifetime of experience dealing with her."

"Vivian has failed at everything except playing the cello and having a child. She has driven away every man who ever loved her, except you. I am ashamed to say that I think I could have saved you if I had put my foot down. I didn't because I had to focus on my own career. That is my shame." Arthur put his hand over the one that Courtney had put on his arm. "You're a man now. You can make your own choices. Don't let a bitter woman make them for you."

"She doesn't."

"Doesn't she? I was at that party, Ian. I saw how she treated Gina."

"Leave it alone. Gina is out of my life, and it has nothing to do with Vivian." Ian looked up and met his father, stony gaze for stony gaze. "I've screwed up quite royally. You should be happy. All your pronouncements about me have turned out to be true."

Arthur shook his head. "I never wanted you to be unhappy. I only wanted..."

"Can you fix this?" Courtney rested her chin in her hands as she interrupted his father.

Ian looked back at her. "I honestly don't know. Just two hours ago I thought it was better that it was over."

Courtney smiled. "Now after seeing her with another man you're not so sure."

"Something like that."

"You men are so predictable. You don't know what you want until it's out of your reach."

Arthur bristled. "Surely that doesn't include me,

sweet."

Courtney laughed. "You're the worst one of them all, dumpling." She looked at Ian again. "Nothing he said to you tonight came out the way he meant it. We both want you to be a part of this child's life." She patted her stomach. "On your terms. You and your father, you have so much pride and not a whole lot of people smarts."

"Courtney, you told me you'd keep out of this."

"I lied. And you've made such a mess out of the whole thing, I have to step in. My family, we're love rich and money poor. This child I'm carrying will never want for love, and thanks to you, anything else. The only thing he'll need is a big brother."

Big brother to an infant? His skin crawled. "I don't know if I can do that."

"That's honest. I respect that. I hope one day you can see your way clear to be family to my little baby." She patted her stomach again. "Can I say one more thing?"

"Why not?" His night had already gone to hell in a hand basket anyway.

"Don't let Gina get away."

Ian felt the warmth of his father's gaze. "I agree, Ian. Whatever it takes, go after that girl and keep her."

"She doesn't want me. She never wanted me."

"Bullshit." Courtney obviously wasn't one to mince words.

"Succinct, but perfect my dear." Arthur stroked an indulgent hand over his wife's hair. "You'd be wise to do as my wife says, Ian. She's never wrong."

Chapter Twenty-Two

Gina was done for the day and ready to go home. She sat at the bar in The End Zone, staring at her shift drink, feeling just the teensiest bit sorry for herself. It had been one week since Ian had broken up with her. Who knew she'd miss a man so much?

Taking a sip from her glass of chardonnay, she shook her head and mentally chided herself. She wasn't supposed to miss him. Their relationship, or arrangement, rather, was supposed to have been fun, easy and light. Natural born screw up that she was, Gina had gone and fallen in love with the creep.

"Hey, Gina, what's up?" Mike came behind her and squeezed her shoulders, then sat on the bar stool next to her.

"Mike. Hi." She looked around for Andi, rather than reflect on the fact that Mike had touched her and she hadn't swooned, hadn't even been fazed. She didn't know whether to thank Ian for helping her get Mike out of her system or to murder him. "You on your own tonight?"

Mike nodded. "Andi's got a ballet board meeting tonight." He shuddered. "I personally don't understand the appeal, but she goes for it in a big way, so there you go. Hey, Spike."

"Mike. The usual?"

"Yeah, thanks." He popped a pretzel into his mouth from the bowl Spike had left in front of him, then slid Gina a glance. "Haiku Guy's probably going to be there."

"No doubt. He *is* on the board." She pushed the glass of wine away from her. It didn't taste good and soured her stomach. Or, just maybe that happened because Mike mentioned Ian. "That's a terrible nickname."

"Andi hates it, too." He shrugged. "What can I say? I don't want to kill him anymore, that's progress to my way of thinking. Although, after what he did to you, maybe killing him would be a good idea."

"Oh, don't on my account. It's not worth it."

"Aw, come on. Dave and I would love the chance to take him apart, especially after seeing how upset you were the other night."

"I wasn't upset. I was just surprised." That was her story and she was sticking to it.

"You were practically shaking."

"I was cold."

"You were upset, just admit it. Seeing him bothered you."

Gina sighed. "Maybe just a little. Now will you get off my back? I don't want to talk about it."

Spike arrived with Mike's Heineken. "Thanks."

"No sweat. You gonna eat?" Spike reached beneath the bar to wash some glasses.

"Maybe. Bobby make onion rings?"

"Yep. Just for you."

"Spike, you old sweet talker, you. How about a burger and some onion rings?"

"Comin' up." She motioned with her head toward Gina. "See what you can do to cheer this one up. She's been mopey all week." She went to the kitchen to place the order.

Gina stuck her tongue out at Spike's back. "Don't listen to her. I'm fine."

"I can see that." Mike sipped his beer. "You might remember that Andi and I hit a real rough patch right around Christmas. I really thought it was over."

"You were miserable." Gina remembered that time vividly. She had spent her days wondering if she should take a shot at comforting him and helping him get over Andi or helping him get back together with her. She chose helping him get back together with her.

"I *was* miserable. I gave her that ultimatum about getting her stuff with Deke worked out. I meant it. I didn't know if she'd put us first and confront him. It was hard for her, but she did it." He swallowed some more beer. "Now you, you've got a different choice. Once he's got this thing with his job worked out, you should be good to go."

"That's not all it is, Mike. His mother hates me."

"His mother hates everybody."

"True that." She shook her head. "I don't know. He might not ever get his job thing worked out, in which case, I can't see him sticking around here." Sighing, she met Mike's eyes in the mirror behind the bar. "It is a very big deal to have your life's work stolen. I don't know if he can come back from it."

"I agree, so *you've* got to give him a reason to stay." Mike's cell phone chirped. He dug it out of his pocket and looked at the display. "It's Andi. Hey, Spud..." His brow knit and the blood drained out of his face. "Where? Be right there."

His eyes were grim when he looked at Gina. "That was Ian. He had to take Andi to the hospital. I've got to get there right away." He slipped off the barstool, a little unsteady on his feet, and patted his pockets for his keys. "Damn! I don't have my car. Dave dropped me off. Andi's supposed to meet me here."

Gina didn't hesitate. "Come on, I'll drive you."

****

Ian didn't know the last time he'd been this scared. One minute, he'd been walking Andrea to her car, listening to her harangue him about the mess he'd made about Gina, the next minute, she was gasping in pain, clutching her middle, unable to stand, let alone walk. He'd scooped her up, stuffed her into his car and took off for the emergency room, hell bent for leather.

He couldn't be certain, since they'd kicked him out of the little room they'd stuck her in, but he thought he heard one of the nurses say Andi was having a miscarriage. His stomach had clutched at the thought. In between calling him all kinds of a fool, she had been waxing rhapsodic over having Mike's baby, even though she was constantly sick. Now, thinking back on it, he had been happy for her. There were no hard feelings at all, where only a couple of months ago, he might have felt like blowing his brains out over the whole thing.

She had asked him what in the long run would be worth losing Gina. Were his parents ever going to be impressed with his choice of career? No, not really. Did Gina make him happy? Yes, definitely. Did the next forty-odd years look good without her in his life? No. Then it looked downright stupid to her to cut Gina *out* of it.

Andi was about to get to the good part of the haranguing when she got ill. He hoped like hell that her reading him the riot act hadn't precipitated the whole thing.

Scraping his hand through his hair, he glanced again at the Emergency Room doors as they opened with a gush of fresh air and sheer panic. Mike Kelly had arrived.

"Where is she?" Mike was already surveying the waiting area with terror in his eyes.

"Back there." Ian pointed to a curtained area. "I think they're going to move her soon." He blinked. What was Gina doing here with Mike?

Gina came up to Ian, all the while watching

Mike hustle over to Andi. "He's scared to death." She looked directly at Ian. "What happened?"

Ian cleared his throat. She looked so beautiful—her hair all disheveled, her eyes bright. He found it hard to breathe. "I think she's losing the baby."

"Oh, God. What makes you think that?" She tried to look around him, obviously trying to see what was going on.

"I overheard the nurses saying something about a miscarriage."

"Then you could have heard wrong."

"Well, uh, yes, of course." He had the sudden, overwhelming urge to pick her up and carry her off someplace where he could have her all to himself. He'd really missed her.

"They both really want that baby. It's been hard, with her being so sick all the time." She hugged herself and rubbed her hands up and down her arms. "Everything'd better be all right."

"Do you want to sit over there and wait?" He motioned with his head to the waiting room.

"I don't know, I think I'd better go."

A burst of activity from the curtained area caught their attention. Andi was being wheeled off to another area. She was crying and clutching Mike's hand for all she was worth. Mike walked alongside the gurney, all his attention lasered on Andi. "It's okay, Spud. Shhhh now."

Gina stopped a nurse who had been with Andi. "Is Mrs. Kelly going to be all right?"

The nurse stopped and sighed. "Are you family? I can't tell you anything unless you're family."

Gina sputtered and tried to finesse an answer out of the nurse, but Ian didn't need to hear confirmation from anyone. He could tell Andi had lost the baby. Only that could cause that horrible look of heartbreak he had seen on her face. He had to get out of here. Putting his hand on Gina's elbow, he got her attention. "Do you want to go somewhere and get a coffee?"

Gina looked at him as if he had grown another head. "I don't think so. I want to wait around for a bit, and see if they need a ride home." She bit her lip. "I drove Mike here because Andi was supposed to pick him up."

Mike. Of course. "I see." Bollocks to that. She was going to talk to him come hell or high water. "We can just sit here, then. I really want to talk to you."

"Okay, I guess." Gina looked away, toward where Mike and Andi had disappeared. "The waiting room's over there."

He reached out to touch a stray lock of her hair.

She flinched but didn't look at him.

"Gina, I've missed you."

She shook her head. "Please don't touch me. It only makes it harder."

He had no choice but to take his hand away. "It doesn't have to be." He shoved his hand into his pocket. "I'll get things back on track at work, then be able to be with you again."

"Ian, a relationship isn't like a spigot you can turn on and off." Her eyes sparked and her voice held a note of asperity. "And it's not fair to me."

"But don't you see?" Ian felt a bit desperate. "How can I be with you when I don't have anything to offer? Any way to take care of you?"

She smiled sadly. "Don't you see that for once in my life I need to come first? Not put away while you take care of more important things?"

"I *am* putting you first. I'm insuring a future for us. Once I publish my project, I can write my own ticket at any university in the world."

"I know how to work hard and how to get by. We don't need money and prestige to be together."

"You shouldn't have to work hard." He ran his

fingers through his hair then straightened his glasses. "I want you to have the best of everything. I wish you could see how much this Bauvet project means to me. To *us*!"

"I do know that. I'm sorry it all got derailed. But whether you publish it or not shouldn't have to do with our relationship. I just want to be loved." She sighed. "I love you whether you become the god of French poetry or not." She looked around again. "I can't do this anymore. I'm going to find a ladies' room." She swiped at her left eye and turned her gaze to him. "Good bye, Ian." She left him standing alone in the middle of the emergency room.

Feeling moist-eyed himself, he left before anybody could see how truly pitiful he really was.

****

Days later, Ian still felt like an idiot, but at least he had come up with a plan to do something about it. Did he want his career back? Yes. Did he want to fix his relationship with Gina? Hell, yes.

So, he thought as he tromped down the French Department hallway to Ralph Jameson's office, first things first. Once he got his career back, once he had something to offer Gina, he'd do whatever it took to get her back, grovel, beg, borrow or steal. Whatever.

But first, he had to prove Unger a liar and a thief. He hoped the ammunition he had would be enough. Right now, his briefcase was filled with every piece of documentation that proved his ownership of the Bauvet discovery. It wasn't everything; he hoped it would be enough to convince Ralph

Stopping outside Jameson's door, he paused, patted down his tie and adjusted his blazer, then knocked.

At Jameson's harrumphed acknowledgement of his presence, he opened the door, as prepared as he'd ever be.

244

Jameson sat at his desk, glaring at his computer screen. His distrust of computers was legendary at Barrett University, spoken of with amusement by the younger faculty, and with commiseration by the old timers. "Ian." One of Jameson's eyebrows raised. "What can I do for you?"

"I'm sorry to interrupt, but it's something quite serious, actually." Ian took a step in.

"Really? Come in, then. Have a seat." Jameson waved a pudgy hand at the empty chair next to his desk. Crushing his brows together, he hit a key on his computer before he turned his full attention to Ian. "I can't tell you the number of documents I've lost because I forgot to save them before turning my attention to an interruption." He shook his head. "Damned machines."

Ian didn't need his Ph.D. to figure out Jameson meant his computer. He felt a flicker of hope, the first real hope he'd felt since he'd heard Soeur Helêne was newly cloistered. Sitting in the offered chair, he shifted his briefcase onto his lap and popped it open. "This is very difficult for me. Donald Unger stole items from my office. I know it, and I should have told you sooner." Ian held up a hand so Ralph couldn't say anything. "I also think, but can't prove, he stole mail from my mailbox. That's the reason I couldn't submit my research before the final interviews. Donald Unger stole it."

Ian could see by Jameson's raised eyebrows that he'd shocked him, and the man was resistant to accept the truth right away. Very well. He'd expected that. With a mental sigh, he braced himself for a long fight.

Jameson reached for the coffee cup stationed on his desk next to his recalcitrant computer. He took a long and deliberate sip, obviously stalling for time while he thought about what to say. Still cradling the cup, he looked at Ian. "Do you have any proof?"

Well, he hadn't totally dismissed Ian's claims. This was a good sign. "Some. I found him in my office, and soon after, several journals with my articles in them went missing from my book shelves. When I tried to get copies of the journals from the library, they were checked out by a graduate student in France who worked for Donald last semester. With regard to my mail, I'm still trying to piece it all together. Much of it lies with a nun in France who is cloistered."

"I see." Jameson set the cup back on the desk. "These are very serious charges. Tampering with the mail is a federal offense."

"Believe me, I know that. I don't have a choice. This is my life's work. I can't let Donald Unger steal it, not without a fight at least."

"No, of course not. It would be irresponsible to let an action of that sort stand unchallenged." Jameson stood and started to pace. "Not to mention the embarrassment to the department if your accusations are true."

Trust Jameson to think of the department first. "They *are* true."

Jameson scratched his head. "I'll have to take this to the dean and see how he wants to proceed. Gather up the bulk of your proof and bring it to me. I imagine the dean will want to see it." He looked right at Ian. "We're just about to announce that Donald is my replacement. This couldn't come at a worse time. I wish you'd told me sooner."

"I'm sorry. You can imagine how difficult it was to bring this to your door. I didn't want to be accused of sour grapes." Ian hoped that would suffice as an apology. "What's going to happen?"

"Usually we look at the evidence. If we decide you have a case, we'll bring you in to present it. Of course, if we decide you don't have a case, Donald can bring proceedings against you. Defamation of character and all that."

Impatience thrummed through Ian. He wanted this over and done with. He wanted Unger's lying hide nailed to a wall. He wanted his career back, his life back. The life that included Gina.

"Your professional lives will be under scrutiny, so I hope for your sake there are no skeletons in your closet. No lies, no unprofessional conduct."

Ian quickly thought of the lie he'd been living since he had Gina agree to be his false fiancée and hostess. On the surface of it, it *was* minor. On the other hand, this could seriously hurt his case and keep him from reclaiming his work. After all, if he lied about one thing in order to get the chairmanship, he could very well lie about something else. A huge ball of regret and frustration lodged in his belly. "Of course," he said through a clenched jaw. "I'd expect nothing less."

"Very well, then." Ralph looked at his watch then shook his head. "I've got to run to a curriculum committee meeting. Bring me your materials as soon as you can. If you still want to, we'll get this ball rolling." He got up from his chair and picked a file folder off his desk. "While I have to be absolutely impartial, I can tell you this one time that I hope you can prove your claims. I hope you have the fortitude to go the distance."

He had the fortitude, and hell yes, he wanted to get that ball rolling, no matter what the cost. He wouldn't let Donald Unger win without putting up a big fight.

****

Ian was in the main office gathering his mail when Emily Smithson, the department secretary, called him over to her desk. "Dr. Ross, may I have a word with you?"

He nodded. "Of course."

When he reached her desk, she stood. "We can

Doreen Alsen

talk over here." She led him over to the copy machine. "I remember the other day when you asked me about an envelope you were expecting."

"Yes, I've been waiting for it for quite a while." A frisson of hope fluttered in his chest.

She frowned. "I'm afraid I was too short with you when you asked me about it. At any rate, I questioned all the work study students just to make sure."

"And?"

She frowned. "It took a while, but I found one who did remember putting a large envelope from France into your mailbox around the time you were looking for it."

His heart started beating hard in his chest. "That's fantastic."

"She's sure she put it into your mailbox. She's sure that it had one of the flaps left over from the green receipts stuck on the envelope when you have to sign for something. I've got a call into the mailroom." She smiled. "I'm hopeful we can locate this envelope for you."

Ian wanted to kiss her. "Outstanding!"

"It's a long shot. I'm sorry it's too late to give to the search committee." She frowned. "Trust me, I will get the name of who tampered with the mail."

"I have a few ideas."

She snorted. "I bet you do. I have an idea of my own. I imagine it matches yours. I'm bringing the copier people in to give me a log of when key holders were copying. It may place certain people in the office at the time the envelope went missing. We may have just enough circumstantial evidence to get a warrant." She laughed. "I think I'm watching too much *Law and Order*."

"I'm definitely going…"

She held up a hand to stop him. "Let me do it. It'll stick much better if an impartial party proves this."

He did kiss her, then, right on her tight, stern mouth. "Thank you. You have no idea what this means to me."

"Don't thank me yet." She went back to her desk. "You should go and let me get to it. I'll call you if I find out anything."

She didn't have to tell him twice.

****

Donald Unger looked out into the lecture hall and cursed the faces assembled before him. French 101A was a joke. None of the students could tell a noun from a verb, never mind ever have a chance in hell at getting a conjugation right. Ah, no matter. As soon as he was officially chair, he could make sure he never taught freshmen ever again.

That would be sweet, as those freshmen would say. Ah well, until then... "So you see, you always need *être* or *avoir* for *passé composé*. Let me put the following sentences on the board, and you can convert them from the present tense to the past, using *passé composé*. After that, we'll talk about the future tense."

As he turned to write on the whiteboard, he heard the door open and a shiver ran down his back. Talk about tense. Unable to quell his curiosity, he looked behind him.

What the hell? Ian Ross and Emily Smithson had come in and were sitting down in the back of the room.

The door opened again. This time, Ralph Jameson and two members of the Addington police force came in. Jameson stood in the back. A sinking feeling settled in Unger's stomach as the cops marched down the center aisle, their attention riveted on him.

"Professor Unger, we need you to come with us," one of the cops told him. "Please come quietly so you don't cause a scene."

"I'm not going anywhere with you until I know what this is about."

The taller of the cops pulled out his handcuffs. "We can do this the easy way or the hard way."

The students whispered like mad, pulling their cell phones out, taking pictures and texting like fiends. His own phone buzzed like an angry hornet trapped in his pocket. He gathered his dignity about him and grasped for some straws. "You are disrupting my class. Please explain yourselves and then leave."

One of the cops said, "Tampering with the U. S. Mail is a federal offense."

"I did no such thing!"

"Unfortunately for you, the search warrant we got for your office and your house helped us find the evidence."

Unger sucked in an outraged breath. "You went into my house and through my things?"

The other cop pulled his handcuffs out. With an easy flip, he turned Unger and slapped the cuffs on his wrists. "Donald Unger, you have the right to remain silent..."

Only the fact that the cops were holding him up as they dragged him out of the classroom kept him on his feet.

The last thing he saw was Ian Ross's satisfied smile.

****

"Thank you," Ian said to Emily Smithson. "You can't believe what this means to me."

Emily's lips pulled tight. "Nobody messes with the mail on my watch. I'm very sorry it happened to you. We can only hope he hasn't destroyed what was in the envelope he stole." She shook her head. "I know it contained your life's work." She turned and went to her office, her sensible heels clapping on the marble floor.

Ian sat back down in the now-empty lecture hall. He had won. Unger had gotten his just desserts. Ian was free to publish his findings and really move up the academic food chain.

He'd have everything he'd ever wanted, right?

Well, no. He wanted more. He wanted Gina.

She'd said she was done being second best. He supposed it was his fault he made her feel that way. He felt lower than dirt because of it. But he had to get his career in order so he could take care of her.

He wanted to make sure she never had to work another shift at The End Zone, unless she wanted to. He wanted her to go to college, like she dreamed of. He wanted to make a family with her, to create what the two of them had never had.

She was pretty cross with him, and with good reason. He had to convince her he could be the man she wanted him to be.

Life's work be damned. It all felt hollow without Gina. He had done everything backwards. He needed her by his side. She'd been right all along.

Time to fix that. He'd grovel, beg, do whatever it took to get her back, to get her to believe in him again.

He slammed a hand down on the back of the seat. No time like the present. It was time he took a trip to The End Zone and got his ladylove back.

Chapter Twenty-Three

Ian couldn't remember being more nervous in his life. He'd stopped at home, changed his clothes five times, slipped his paternal grandmother's antique diamond ring into the breast pocket of his blazer and made his way to The End Zone. He figured she was there, working, since she hadn't answered her phone. Dreading the fact he would have an audience when he groveled at her feet, he should have eaten a mountain of Tums before setting off to court Gina.

He pulled into The End Zone's parking lot, cut the engine and sat back in his seat. Without a backwards glance, he got out of his car and took a step toward what he hoped was his future.

It was a pretty, late-April day, warmer than usual for New England. The sun was bright and the sky a clear, brilliant blue. He took it as a good omen. The parking lot was pretty deserted. He thanked his lucky stars for that. The fewer people witnessing this, the better. Not that he didn't feel comfortable with the whole world knowing he adored Gina, not at all.

He just didn't need the whole world witnessing his humiliation if Gina didn't feel the same way. His heart in his mouth, he walked across the parking lot and pushed open The End Zone's front door.

It took Ian's eyes a minute to adjust to the artificial light inside the bar. He blinked a few times to clear away the spots while he tried to find Gina.

It didn't look like she was here. Dave Mason, however, sat at the bar, a cell phone plastered against his ear. He didn't look happy.

Spike was wiping down the bar. She looked up and spotted him. No hiding now. He nodded at her. Spike sniffed and turned her back to him. Well, he should have expected the cold shoulder from Gina's friends. Hopefully, it wouldn't last long. Perching on a stool, he tried to break the ice. "Hey, Spike. Is Gina here?"

"No." Spike didn't bother to turn around.

Undaunted, Ian muddled ahead. After all, faint heart ne'er won fair lady. "Is she working today?"

She pulled a wine glass out of the overhead rack. "Dunno."

Well, this wasn't working out the way he planned it. Then again, when had anything in his relationship with Gina gone according to plan?

Never, that's when.

Dave snapped his phone shut and leaned against the bar. "Spike! You have any friends who play softball?"

Spike gave Ian a parting glare and moved over to Dave. "No Mike?"

"Yeah. Andi's supposed to be taking it easy and Mike doesn't think he should leave her alone right now. She's really taking the miscarriage hard." Dave shook his head. "Puts us in a bind, though. We need one more player or we forfeit the game."

"Wish I could help." Spike grimaced. "My friends aren't the softball type." She gave the bar a quick swipe. "Let me see if Bobby's got your order ready." She went to the kitchen.

Dave tapped his phone on the bar and finally looked at Ian. "Ross. What are you doing here?"

Ian could feel the hostility dripping off Dave. "Looking for Gina. Do you know where she is?"

"Why should I tell you?"

To hell with pride. "Because I adore her, and I'm going to grovel abjectly until she takes me back."

"Oh, really?" Dave shifted and braced his right elbow on the bar. "This ought to be good."

"I know I made so many mistakes with her, but I want the chance to make it up to her." He pushed his glasses back up his nose. "I'm quite desperate, actually. I'll do anything to get her back."

Dave nodded. Out of the blue he asked, "Would you play softball?"

"I beg your pardon?"

"Here's the deal. Today is the season opener for the restaurant softball league. The End Zone is supposed to be playing Zack's Grille. But if we can't field a complete team, we have to forfeit. Believe me, it's not an option."

"What does that have to do with me?"

"Mike can't play today, and you're going to replace him."

"Come again?"

Dave slapped Ian on the back. "It's the perfect solution. We don't forfeit to Zack's, and you can use the opportunity to grovel to Gina." Dave smiled. "It's a win-win situation."

He highly doubted that. "Now might be a good time to mention that I don't have the foggiest idea of how to play softball."

"Don't worry. We'll stick you in the outfield so you don't have to worry about having to catch anything fast. And batting?" He snapped his fingers. "Piece-a-cake."

"How will this help me with Gina?"

"Didn't I mention Gina's on the team? She hates to lose. She especially hates to lose to Zack's. She and one of Zack's bartenders, Amber, have a huge rivalry. If we forfeit the game because you won't play..." Dave shook his head sadly. "You can kiss any second chance with Gina good-bye."

Ian knew he was being played, but Dave didn't give him a choice. "One way or another *you're* going to regret this. Wouldn't it be better to forfeit rather than lose outright?"

"No." Dave was emphatic. "C'mon, you're playing. We'll get you an End Zone team shirt at the field." Dave dragged him off the bar stool and propelled him toward the door. "You'll be a pro in no time."

Ian didn't know who would regret this more—him or Dave. He suspected it would be him.

****

Sandy nudged Gina in her side and motioned with her head. "Get a look at ol' Amber over there. Is she dressed for a softball game or a beauty pageant?"

Gina looked where Sandy indicated. Amber was seriously dressed for attention. Clad in pale pink, clingy, sweat pants with Zack's written across the butt in hot pink glitter, and a pink hoodie that was at least one size too small, Amber looked like she was aiming to score more than one kind of home run. Her hair was pulled back into a pony tail, just like every other female's, but it was curled to perfection and pulled jauntily through the back of her pink Zack's cap. "Man, she bugs the crap outta me."

"I think she does it on purpose so the guys will be thinking with their other head when she pitches. That wiggle routine she does oughta be illegal."

"I'm not worried about that. The guys on our team are immune. They know she's a barracuda." Gina chuffed out a breath. "Besides, can you imagine Mike Kelly even looking like that at anyone but Andi?"

"Yeah." Sandy frowned. "Speaking of whom. Think Mike is going to play today?"

"God, I hope so." Gina stuck her hands in her pockets and rocked back on her heels. "I really want to wipe the field with Amber."

Sandy laughed then turned when she heard a car door slam. "Good. Dave and Mike are here now." She whistled. "Uh oh. That's not Mike."

Gina turned and looked. Hell *yeah*, that wasn't Mike. That was Ian. What was he doing here? It couldn't be to play softball. Ian couldn't tell a softball from a cantaloupe, and that was on a good day.

She watched Dave hand him an End Zone tee shirt and ball cap. Ian looked at the things and heaved a sigh. Dave clapped him on the back and jogged over to Gina.

"Hey!"

"What is Ian doing here?" Gina hated that her voice shook all over the place.

Dave expression turned sheepish. "Uh, playing softball?"

"He doesn't know how to play softball. Where's Mike?"

"Can't make it. Look." Dave took her hands. "We need one more player so we don't forfeit the game. We'll stick Ian in the outfield where he can do the least amount of damage. Okay?" He squeezed her hands. "I know this is hard for you, but we've got no choice. Do you want to lose to Amber?"

"Hmmmpf." Gina grabbed her hands back and crossed her arms over her chest. Looking past Dave, she saw Ian had taken off his tweed jacket and was pulling the End Zone tee shirt over his head. His glasses got caught on the neckline and got all twisted on his face as his head popped through. The shirt was a tad on the small side and Ian had to wrestle it down. As he straightened his glasses, he noticed her looking at him, and gave her a hesitant, embarrassed smile.

Gina looked away. "Whatever."

Dave reached out and gave her shoulder a friendly squeeze. "It'll be okay."

She tossed her head back and nodded. "It always

is."

Reaching up, she adjusted her hair under her cap. Her hands trembled slightly, annoying her further. She didn't want to have *any* reaction to Ian Ross. She jumped up and down a little and shook her arms and hands out to get rid of the feelings dogging her.

****

Tee shirt too small, hat too big, dress shoes too slippery for the muddy field's grass, Ian couldn't remember the last time he'd felt quite this out of his element. Oh, wait. Yes, he bloody well could. The hockey game. His love for Gina Francisco always seemed to hand him his most admirable moments on a platter.

He hoped Gina didn't think he looked as ridiculous as he felt. He glanced her way and was struck dumb at the sight of her and her breasts jumping up and down. The woman *really* had a superlative chest.

She obviously noticed him ogling her, because she stopped jumping and stood frozen still. Absolutely sure she was going to bolt and give him no chance to talk to her, he jogged over, his shoes making squishy sounds in the mud. "Gina!"

She didn't run, but she wanted to, he could tell by the stiffness in her shoulders and the jerky movement her legs made. "Hey, Ian."

"I guess you're surprised to see me here." He huffed a little as he caught his breath. Damn, he felt as useful as a fish with hands.

"To say the least." She looked up at the sky. "Do you even know how to play softball?"

"Sure." He tried out his cockiest grin. "You take the bat, someone throws the ball at you, and you hit it."

"Hm." She squinted at him. "I guess you're all set then." She started to walk away.

He grabbed her arm and tried not to wince when she flinched. "Can we go somewhere after this and talk?"

She pulled her arm out of his grasp. "We don't have anything to talk about."

"Yes, we do."

She shook her head. "No, we don't. Let's just leave things as they are. It's better for everyone that way." She stepped further away from him.

"It's not better for me." He might as well get the whole thing out at once. "I'm bloody miserable without you. I want you to forgive me and then..." He sighed. "I want you to marry me."

She went about as pale as a full moon on a black night. "Damn you." Closing her eyes, she took a deep breath then opened her eyes and avoided his gaze. "Please, Ian, just go away."

"Just give me a minute. Just... just... hear me out, please." He didn't mind his voice trembled like a leaf in a hurricane.

She shook her head. "I can't do this anymore." She ran away, her feet making splooshy sounds as she went.

Well, he thought, that hadn't gone very well. His ego already bruised beyond recognition, he should give up and quit the field. He couldn't. He would get her to listen to him and believe him if it was the last thing he did.

****

"So, what did he say?" Sandy didn't waste any time pouncing on Gina the minute she got within speaking distance.

Gina shook her head. "Nothing I want to listen to." Much.

Sandy wouldn't have any of it. "C'mon." She tilted her head out toward the field and chuckled. "That boy ain't here to play softball."

That was for sure. Ian struggled to put a softball

glove on the wrong hand.

"Someone should put him out of his misery." Sandy gave her a hip check and walked away.

"Someone should just shoot *me*," Gina muttered.

The day was perfect. There was a slight breeze, the sky was bright blue, the sun high and warm as the teams took the field. The competition between The End Zone and Zack's Grille was fierce and keen. It didn't take long for Zack's team to smell fresh blood. Amber wore a smirk so annoying, Gina itched to rub it off her face.

Zack's team was doing a pretty good job at knocking the ball in Ian's direction. Everyone ran like crazy to catch the ball before it got to him. Nevertheless, they couldn't stop Zack's from racking up a few runs before getting their turn up at bat.

Gina wheezed a little as she loped to the End Zone bench. "This is all your fault," she hissed at Dave as she passed him. She noticed, with quite a bit of satisfaction that Dave huffed and puffed just as much she did.

"Would you rather have forfeited?" Dave collapsed on the bench.

Gina dropped down beside him. "No." She blew up at her bangs and sent them fluttering. "But, *Ian*? You couldn't have found someone else?"

"No, I couldn't." He wrapped his arm around her shoulders. "Seems to me, a guy puts himself into a situation where he comes off as a fool or worse, all just to talk to a woman, well, that woman's got to mean a lot to him." He stood up as he pulled the bill of her ball cap down over her eyes. "Don't be stupid." He walked off.

Scowling, she pushed the bill of her cap back to where it belonged. Her stomach did a little hitch as she caught a glimpse of Ian, all muddy and confused. He looked pretty cute which made her little heart do an annoying pitter pat. Damn, damn and double damn. She supposed she *would* have to talk to him at some point. It was only polite.

Ian approached the bench, worrying the leather softball glove with his hands. His cap was still on his head, but his glasses were askew. Giving her the sweetest, shyest of smiles, he indicated the space on the bench that Dave had just vacated. "Is that seat taken?"

She swallowed. She was a sucker for that smile. "Uh, no. It's all yours."

"If I sit here, are you going to run away?"

Since her mama hadn't raised any cowards, she sighed. "No."

He sat. "The game seems to be going well." He sounded very hopeful.

"Could be worse." Man, she could feel her heart pounding in her ears.

"What happens now?" He rubbed his hands together. "Is it our turn to have a whack at the ball?"

"You could say that."

"It looks a bit like cricket, actually."

A small flare of hope flickered in her. "Do you play cricket?" Maybe he was better at sports than she gave him credit for.

His smile turned sheepish. "No. Arthur wanted me to, *ergo*, Vivian wouldn't let me."

Poof, that flare of hope went out. "Oh." Maybe he wouldn't get a turn at bat. Maybe they could get someone to bat for him.

"I'm looking forward to trying, actually. I always wanted to play cricket."

"Hm." She turned her attention to the game, or at least she *tried* to turn her attention to the game. It proved very difficult when every cell in her body jumped for joy at being close to Ian.

"You know, I'm not going to give up until you forgive me and agree to marry me." Ian's tone sounded blandly conversational, like he was ordering some lemon to go with his tea.

Starting to feel like a fly stuck in a spider's web, Gina shook her head. "Ian, I told you. I can't talk about this now."

"I'm not giving up."

A distraction. What she needed was a good distraction. Otherwise, she'd never survive the next inning.

Amber was pitching. Good. She hated Amber, from the top of her streaky blond hair to the soles of her pink softball cleats. Amber hate was always good for a distraction. Who the hell had pink softball cleats?

Sandy was up at bat. Good. Sandy had been on the state's all-star softball team in high school. Amber lobbed the ball. Sandy swung and connected with it, making a very satisfying *thwack*, sending it far into the outfield. She made it to second base before the ball did.

Dave was up next. Gina felt confident he'd bring Sandy home. He hit it, a low grounder which slipped through the short stop's legs. The short stop scrambled, getting to the ball in time to stop Sandy at third and Dave at second.

The End Zone crew ticked down the ranks and through sheer determination brought the score even. Gina's turn came up. After two foul balls, she sent the ball deep into left field. She made it to first base and danced on the bag, just enough to get Amber's goat.

Ian's turn was next. She shouldn't have celebrated. It looked so obvious he'd never held a bat in his life. It could have been anything from a machete to a golf club, judging by the way he swung it.

Like a predator scenting a kill, Amber licked her lips. That big butt of hers did an extra wiggle as she wound up for the throw. It was a picture perfect pitch. Ian swung at it, missing it by a mile. The force of his attempt nearly spun him around.

Smiling a gloating grin, Amber looked at Gina.

Gina glared back, wanting to wipe that damn smile off Amber's face.

Amber threw the ball at Ian again and, *surprise!* He missed it.

Zack's outfield stopped paying attention. They tossed jokes around at Ian's expense. Gina's temper perked up, along with a healthy dose of guilt. She was the reason Ian was here, making a total fool of himself. She clenched her fingers into a fist as her indignation began to burn.

Clearly ready to add insult to injury, Amber wound up with a couple of extra swivels of her hips then let the ball loose. Since Ian hadn't yet met a pitch he wouldn't swing at, he let 'er rip.

No one seemed more shocked when he actually hit the ball than Ian did. Rooted to the spot, mouth agape, he stared as the ball flew through the air.

Screams of "Run! Run!" flew through the air. Someone came from the bench and pushed Ian in the direction of first base. Gina high-tailed it to second, checked to see where the ball was, and took off for third. Caught by surprise, Zack's outfield scrambled to get their hands on the ball. The first base coach pushed Ian in the direction of second base.

By that time, Zack's right fielder got his act together and threw the ball to Amber who had come off the pitcher's mound, ready to catch and deliver it to the second baseman. She rocketed the ball right after she caught it. The second baseman jogged backwards two steps to catch it in time to get Ian out. Instead, with a mighty *clonk*, the ball connected with Ian's head.

Ian crumpled to the ground like a sack of cement.

Gina didn't even think. She switched direction

and ran to him, pushing Amber away when she got there. "Ian!"

His glasses were broken. He already had the makings of a major goose egg on his forehead. He had lost his cap when he ran hell bent for leather toward second base, and his too small End Zone tee was twisted and dirt streaked. The tail of his blue oxford shirt had slid out of his pants in the front.

He looked like hell.

She knelt beside him, picked up his head and cradled it in her lap. "C'mon, sweetie, open your eyes." Her voice cracked with panic.

He groaned, and his eyes fluttered open. Suddenly, hell had never looked so good. "Hey, baby," she crooned.

Gina helped him as he tried to sit up. He struggled to focus his eyes while he patted his face for his glasses. She held the two pieces in front of his face for him. "There you go."

He blinked. "Did we win?"

Okay, he was just so damn adorable. How could she stay mad at him?

"He okay?" Dave crouched next to them, his brow furrowed. "We should take him to the emergency room."

"No! No, I'm okay." Ian pulled away from Gina to try to stand, but unable to find his pins, he slumped back down against her.

She kissed his cheek. "I think maybe you better let us take you, slugger."

He pulled away again, but didn't try to stand again. He looked pretty dizzy. "Only if you promise you'll marry me."

"Oh, Ian." Now, she felt a little dizzy herself.

He took her hands and planted a kiss on first one palm then the other. "I love you. I miss you. I'm miserable without you. Please marry me." He wiggled around so he could get his hand in his front pants pocket, winced and pulled out a ring box. He held it out for her.

"Oh my God." She couldn't breathe.

He took her hands again and pressed the ring box into them. "Open it."

She did.

The box held the most beautiful diamond ring she had ever seen. It caught the warm spring sun and flashed all over the softball field. She didn't know what to say, even if she could think straight.

"Say something." Ian looked a little desperate.

"Um, Wow?" She felt a tingle of tears in her eyes. "I want to believe this." Sniffing, she swiped at the tears threatening to flow. "I want to believe this is real."

"Please believe it." He brought his finger under her chin, and lifted her face up to kiss her. "I won the day with Unger and got my work back, but none of it made me happier than just being in the same room with you."

Can I trust this? Oh, she wanted to believe him. With every fiber of her being, she wanted it.

"I promise I will do everything in my power to make you the happiest woman on earth." He cleared his throat. "I nearly lost the best thing to ever happen to me. Please. I don't mind begging. Marry me." He kissed her again. "Make a family with me."

She looked from that bright beautiful ring to him, all disheveled, dirty, his sweet, sweet smile both hopeful and wary. Suddenly the answer shone as clear as the sky. "Yes," she whispered. "Yes, I'll marry you."

He let out a relieved breath, leaned in and kissed her, then moaned when his banged up face bumped hers. It didn't matter.

Gina knew she was what Ian wanted, which was good, because he was what she wanted too. "Let's get you to the emergency room."

Epilogue

Ian Ross stood in the front of the church and watched the love of his life walk down the aisle toward him. She was the most alive, beautiful, magnificent woman in the world, from the top of her bright, coppery curls to the bottom of her three-inch stiletto heeled shoes.

Adorable in her simple white gown, she smiled that special smile he knew was just for him. The closer she got, the more he could feel the waves of love emanating from her. Of all the things he loved about her, and there were many, he loved her generous heart and capacity to love. She made him feel things he never thought he'd feel.

She took his breath away.

Then she stood there with him, surrounded by the scent of the lilies of the valley she carried. He took one of her trembling hands and pressed a kiss into her palm. "Ready to do this?" he whispered.

"You bet!" Her grin grew wider and warmer. Her eyes sparkled with delight.

A word about the author...

Doreen has wanted to be a writer all her life but took a brief detour into being an opera singer and conductor. She realized that maybe she should spend more time writing when creating the back stories for her operatic characters was more fun than actually singing. Plus, her romance-lovin' heart couldn't take all the dead bodies littering the stage at the end of the performance. She is still an active conductor and is regularly found waving her arms around in front of singers.

Thank you for purchasing
this Wild Rose Press publication.
For other wonderful stories of romance,
please visit our on-line bookstore at
www.thewildrosepress.com.

For questions or more information
contact us at
info@thewildrosepress.com.

The Wild Rose Press
www.TheWildRosePress.com